HE WAS SUCH A COMFORT
TO HER

That a young girl should be left to deal with everything on her own was insupportable.

Kneeling as he was, with Philadelphia's hands still clasped in his, Mr. Atherton looked up at her from this somewhat unusual angle. She had a most delightful figure, the curves of which were plain to see as he gazed up at her, and her face, seen close to, was really an extraordinarily pretty one. And she certainly had the most enchanting hair.

Mr. Atherton rose at last to his feet. For one second the two of them were so close that his face almost brushed against hers. The contact startlingly excited him so that the thought shot through his mind and stayed there: I want this girl, she is different, she is like no one I have ever met, I want her, and I am going to have her.

Miss Philadelphia Smith

Paula Allardyce

GOLDEN APPLE PUBLISHERS

MISS PHILADELPHIA SMITH

A Golden Apple Publication / published by arrangement with
Coward, McCann & Geoghegan, Inc.

Golden Apple edition / January 1984

Golden Apple is a trademark of Golden Apple Publishers

ISBN 0-553-19756-8

Published simultaneously in the United States and Canada

PRINTED IN THE UNITED STATES OF AMERICA

Chapter 1

"Dearest Diary," wrote Philadelphia, hunched up on the small, high stool by her dressing table:

I have been unable to write in you for the past four days as poor mama has been having one of her bad turns; she has been unable to take more than a little cordial and soup. Naturally, I have sat up with her at night and, as you will understand, I am a trifle fatigued and been in no mind to write—indeed, little has happened worth the mentioning. I lead, I sometimes think, a very dull life. I wish something exciting could happen, as it seems to do with other people. I have not even seen as much of Jamie as I could wish: he is very faithful and calls every week, but last time I was compelled to send him away, for

I could not leave mama's side. I do not think he was very pleased! But then the gentlemen are not so compassionate or so patient as my sex. However, he is always charming and civil to her, and always goes upstairs to see her, the moment he arrives. I am sure that when we are married we will be entirely happy, indeed, I am convinced that with a man of sensibility any woman of tolerable sense *must* be happy. At least, thank God, I am not betrothed to a gentleman like Mr. A. I have written about him so many times. He leads the wildest kind of life. Number 23 opposite is awake till the small hours of the morning, there are endless parties, and I feel that soon I shall have to write to him, begging him, in view of mama's poor health, to be a little more considerate. The things that seem to happen there! They are often most dreadfully elevated, there is gambling and dancing, and there is one very beautiful young lady who comes frequently and seems to stay—

Philadelphia broke off. Her cheeks were flushed. It was true that she was writing all this in her private diary that nobody in the world, not even Jamie, had ever seen, for it was locked away in a drawer, but all this was becoming scandalous, and she wondered if she had the right to destroy a reputation so with a flick of her pen. She scrawled out the last part of the sentence, and continued, without much enthusiasm:

At least my Jamie does not drink or gamble. If he did, I suppose I could not marry him, for the ghost of dear papa would rise to forbid me. He is calling tonight. It is always the best time in the week. How

I wish we could marry—But then, with mama so ill—

She put down her pen. She was suddenly disgusted with her diary, the precious diary that she had kept since she was fourteen years old. If only there were someone she could talk to, confide in, some charming young lady with whom she could exchange confidences. She looked back at what she had written. It seemed somehow flat and priggish, almost complaining, as if she had become an old maid. She thought, I am too old to keep a diary, it is the kind of thing schoolgirls do, it is time I stopped. Yet it was almost her only outlet: there were no friends, she hardly knew her neighbors, and Charlotte, her elder sister, only visited a couple of times a month. She sighed, and picked up her pen again.

"Philly! Philly, where are you?"

The thin, fretful voice came through the open door, and Philadelphia at once slammed her diary shut. She called back in tones that still retained the Scottish accent, "I am coming, mama."

But she did not immediately rise to her feet. Her face, which should have been rounded with the youth of her eighteen years, looked drawn and pale: sleepless nights had smudged her eyes, taken the delicate color from her cheeks. She looked disconsolately at her own reflection, and thought that Jamie was going to find her a perfect sight. The curling brown hair was pulled tightly back over her high forehead, for that was how papa had liked it, and what papa wanted was law, though he had been dead for two years. The gown, modestly high at the throat, was four years old, it had hardly been exciting in its heyday, and now, to Philadelphia, it seemed downright dowdy. She was neither more nor less conceited than any other young girl, but she never could see that she possessed a beauty that fatigue and depression had no power to destroy. "You are the loveliest lass I have ever met," Jamie once told her, in a rare mood of emotion, but Philadelphia took this for lover's talk and simply laughed. She was of course perfectly aware that she was pretty: how indeed could she be anything else, with such magnificent, long-lashed green eyes, the fine, neat features and the delicate skin that the Highland air had given her. But of her quite extraordinary beauty, she was completely unaware: living the life she did, she never met anyone outside the family circle. Charlotte would never have dreamed of flattering her, and the gentlemen in the street who stopped to stare after her were simply behaving as gentlemen did, the whole world over, back in Inverness and here in London.

Papa remarked once, just before he died, "Where do those looks come from? She resembles no one in the family." And he added, almost with apprehension, "It disturbs me. It is almost dangerous."

But he said this secretly to his wife, and Philadelphia never for one moment considered herself to be out of the ordinary. At this moment she thought she looked quite plain. Mr. A.—his name was Atherton, but that was how she always thought of him—would no doubt laugh at the sight of someone so pale and insignificant, and somehow this hurt her, though she deplored her own vanity. Mr. A. was, of course, everything that papa would have condemned, a gambler, a drunkard—Philadelphia had heard him returning in the evenings—and possibly worse, but she still could not bear the thought of his despising her. However, they were quite unlikely to meet, so it hardly mattered: he must be entirely unaware of her existence.

In this supposition Philadelphia underrated Mr. Atherton, whose major vice, apart from gambling, women and all the other sins so berated by papa, was curiosity. He was perfectly well aware of Philadelphia's existence and though he was not particularly interested in this young woman who wore such deplorably unfashionable clothes, he wondered occasionally in his idle moments what sort of life she could lead. It was certainly no life that he could really comprehend, for he knew she looked after an invalid mother, she never seemed to go out—Emma would be driven insane!—and her only outside interest appeared to be a tall, handsome young man who called at the house once a week and who only stayed for about an hour. At least she had a beau, which was something. He had never had the chance to see her face properly, but she seemed to be very young, and she had pretty hair.

It was to be seen that both spent a certain amount of time in wondering about each other and both were unaware of the mutual observation. To each of them the other was something of a curiosity, for though the road that divided them was narrow, and their homes were directly opposite, they lived lives of such complete difference that the road might well have been a sea.

Montagu Road had started life in the sixteenth century. It had then been little more than a country lane barely infringing on London's boundaries: on one side was a small row of cottages and on the other fields much infested by highwaymen. The cottages had never been repaired; they were now dilapidated, shabby and sadly in need of a coat of paint. Dr. Smith, when he came down from Scotland to settle in London six years ago, in 1740, found the place within his humble means. He bought Number 22 for a very small sum and there the family had lived ever since, though Charlotte was now married and lived in the village of Chelsea, several miles away.

However, even by the time of the Smiths' arrival other houses had sprung up opposite, far bigger and far grander, and now Montagu Road, in the way of many London streets, lived two separate lives, with the modest cottages of the even numbers on one side, and the fashionable mansions of the odd numbers on the other. The highwaymen had long since moved away to Marylebone Fields and Hampstead Heath, for the odd numbers tended to carry pistols and proved hard for the plucking, but to Dr. Smith, who belonged to the Church of Scotland and held the strictest religious views, the new inhabitants were not much better. His two daughters thought otherwise. As young girls—Philadelphia was then twelve, and Charlotte seventeen—they were fascinated by the lords and ladies with their grand clothes and carriages: Inverness had never provided anything like that. They were always peeping through the curtains of Number 22 at the brilliantly lit windows of Number 23 and sometimes they would whisper giggling remarks to each other such as, "There's the lady with the high wig," or, "He has a coachman and two footmen." Naturally, as they grew older, they did not behave in such a vulgar fashion, but Philadelphia, despising herself for being so inquisitive, still knew more than she felt she should about the people who wandered in and out, and sometimes, even now, she would watch, a trifle wistfully, the pretty lords and ladies who danced in the vast drawing room that faced their pleasant but simple little parlor.

Mr. Atherton himself had a habit of standing on his own doorstep, especially during the summer months, as if to take the evening air. He was tall and really unnecessarily good-looking, and sometimes it was plain that he had drunk too much wine. Philadelphia, who was a great reader of Mr. Richardson's novel, saw him as the grand seducer, loved by all the young ladies, and sometimes she shivered delightfully, imagining him to be Pamela's wicked master. There was one lady in particular who often appeared in the evenings and, regrettably, was seldom seen to leave before midday the next morning: she was, as Philadelphia noted a little enviously, remarkably lovely, though plumper than fashion demanded, and always most gorgeously dressed. She must certainly be Mr. Atherton's mistress, and what papa would say to that, heaven only knew, but then one had to admit that the *ton* possessed a different code of morals from the neat little families of Inverness.

Now that she was older, Philadelphia no longer watched so blatantly, and certainly Mr. Atherton's affairs, in every sense of the word, were no concern of hers: if she watched at all, it was because she was sometimes lonely and bored and it gave her a little excitement. Not that this provided any excuse for the matter of the tiepin. . . . This was indeed utterly unpardonable, and sometimes Philadelphia would blush at the thought of it, and vow that next day she would run across the road and hand it in to the footman who answered the door. But this she never did, and she never mentioned to a single soul that once, while out shopping, she had seen something gleaming on the roadway, outside Number 23. She stooped to pick it up. It was very pretty, a small tiepin, and at the top of it was a tiny enamelled portrait of Mr. Atherton himself. There was no excuse whatsoever for the fact that she instantly slipped it into her reticule, and that it now lay in a bowl on the parlor mantelpiece. The portrait alone was enough to indicate the owner: it should have been instantly returned. She tried to appease her conscience by telling herself that to Mr. Atherton it would be a mere trinket, that he had probably not even missed it, that dropping it so casually indicated that it had no value for him. All this made no difference: stealing was stealing, and a thief was a thief. But this had happened a year ago; it was surely too late to do anything about it, and the tiepin still lay in the Smith parlor: occasionally Philadelphia picked it up, a little flushed with her own wickedness, yet secretly delighted to own something that belonged to the odd numbers.

That Mr. Atherton sometimes watched her never entered her mind, and on the rare occasions when she saw him in the street, she was always careful to hold her head high and not so much as glance at him. After all, he was nothing more than a kind of fictitious excitement, like a character in a story, and the flashes of melodrama that seemed to occur across the way were like lightning in a dull sky; they held no reality for her. Once, for instance, he had a violent quarrel with his pretty, plump young lady—her name was Emma, for he shouted it at her—and really, they behaved like fighting cats, using dreadful language and screaming abuse: the lady positively hurtled herself into the waiting carriage, while Mr. Atherton stood there glowering after her, his wig awry and his cravat to one side. And on another spectacular occasion there was a brawl in which swords were drawn, and this time Philadelphia was frightened enough to shoot back into the room: when she dared peer out again the two angry gentlemen had vanished, presumably without bloodshed, for there were no bodies lying in the road.

"I have become an interfering old maid," she wrote in her diary, "I have no business to be so interested." Then she was compelled to add:

But how strange, dear Diary, that we live so near and we live such different lives. They have no sense of privacy, they seem to shout out everything at the top of their voices, and they swear so, and they are often drunk. If something happens to us, we keep it to ourselves, we do not even wish the neighbors to know, but they just don't seem to care.

And then she added:

I wonder what would happen if we ever met. I do not imagine we would have much to say to each other—

"Philly!"

The voice came again, and Philadelphia jumped guiltily to her feet. As she ran out into the passage, she saw that Lucy was looking up at her from the landing below, and she flushed a little as if the maid had caught her out in some disloyalty to poor mama.

Her discomfiture made her speak more sharply than she intended. She had never really liked Lucy, though she told herself repeatedly that she should be sorry for her. Lucy was only fifteen and came from an orphanage. She was sluttish and blowsy in person, looking older than her years, and she would have been downright dirty had Philadelphia not insisted on her washing and changing her linen. She did as little work as she could, but then there was hardly any money—the Smith family had lost what income they possessed in the South Sea Bubble—and after all, all she required was her board and lodging, plus five shillings a week pocket money. Sometimes Philadelphia dreamed of having a proper maidservant who would take a little of the burden from her shoulders, who would cook nice meals for mama, and perhaps sometimes sit with her in the evenings. But good maids required good salaries, so it had to be Lucy who did almost nothing, who could not so much as boil an egg without cracking it, who, if she laid a tray, did so with a stained cloth, and a dirty plate with the food spilling over, who would dump this on the invalid's bed so that it knocked against her and soiled the sheets.

Sometimes Philadelphia would wonder crossly what Lucy did with herself all day, but she had lately discovered that her life was not entirely solitary. Followers were of course strictly forbidden, but sometimes Philadelphia would come unexpectedly into the kitchen, and there would be a kind of flurry and Lucy's cheeks would be flushed and hot. Once she even glimpsed a foot vanishing behind the larder door, but she said nothing: she herself was only eighteen, and she had to see that it was a little hard on Lucy to spend her life with an elderly invalid and, as it would seem to her, a prissy young woman for employer.

She said now in a snap that made her instantly ashamed of herself, "You must have heard Mrs. Smith calling, Lucy. Why didn't you go in to her?"

Lucy answered sulkily, "I thought you'd gone in, miss."

Philadelphia looked at the stupid resentful face. She realized suddenly how tired she was. She said wearily, "Oh, very well. Could you please put a kettle on? I think my mother would like a dish of tea."

"Yes, miss."

"And Mr. Sinclair is calling this evening. Did you bake the cake I mixed for you?"

"Yes, miss."

It was probably burnt or had sunk in the middle. Philadelphia felt that she did not really care: in any case Jamie was young enough to be always hungry, and he would wolf it down without noticing. She hesitated, then said, "I suppose this is not much of a life for you, Lucy."

Lucy did not answer. Perhaps she was offended. She was by no means intelligent, but she was quick to take offense, and often was affronted by a perfectly innocent remark.

Philadelphia persisted, wishing to be more friendly, "If you like, I could teach you proper cooking, and then some day, when you are a little older, you could find yourself a better post."

Lucy answered with unexpected energy, "I'm not staying in service all my life, miss."

Well, at least this was almost a conversation. Philadelphia said, "Oh? And what do you want to do?"

But this Lucy would not answer, only a brief sly smile flashed across her face: it was unpleasant and it made Philadelphia, to her own fury, flush, for it said plainly enough: You are just a silly old maid, you wouldn't understand, you with your gentleman who only calls once a week, I've got better things to do with my time than cooking—

Philadelphia gave it up. She turned away and went into her mother's bedroom.

She could see at once that mama was having one of her bad turns, and her heart smote her for her negligence in not coming at once. She knelt down by the bed and took the withered hand in hers. It was very hot, but then so was this September, it was almost like summer, and the air that came through the open window was dry and dusty, there did not seem to be a vestige of a fresh breeze.

She said, "Mama, I think we might ask Dr. Lewen to call. I will send Lucy round for him."

"He can't do me any good."

Philadelphia persisted, "He could give you some of the opium to relieve you. Is the pain very bad, mama? I've asked Lucy to make you some tea. Perhaps there is something else you would fancy—"

Mrs. Smith looked at her daughter, then away. Her head sank back on the pillow. Once she had been a bustling, energetic woman, and pretty too, with a ready smile and Philadelphia's thick, brown, curling hair. But a year back this illness had descended on her. Philadelphia did not know exactly what it was, but it appeared that there was some kind of growth inside her that increased day by day and could no longer be checked. The energy had gone, and the spirit with it, leaving nothing but the thin, frail shell of a woman who had grown querulous with the constant pain, and who said frequently that she wished she were dead.

She muttered this now, only in a strange way that caught at Philadelphia's breath and drove the color from her cheeks. She loved her mother dearly, but sometimes she felt she could no longer bear the burden, and once she had all but quarrelled with Charlotte who, wrapped up in her husband, her home and her spoiled little son, so seldom visited Montagu Road.

"It's different when you have a home of your own," she said. She was much taller than Philadelphia, though not nearly so good-looking; she was what people called a fine figure of a woman. One day soon that fine figure would turn to fat, but now she was handsome enough, with a forceful manner, a habit of telling everyone her most intimate affairs, and an overloud voice with the Scottish accent well subdued. She was only twenty-three, but looked rather older.

"You could spend the day with her occasionally," said Philadelphia in a choked, angry voice.

"And who would look after little Tobias, pray? You never think of anyone but yourself, Philly," said Charlotte. "When you are married, you will find that you can no longer be so selfish. I presume you still are getting married? I have never approved of long engagements, myself, and it seems to me that Jamie takes a deal of time in getting to the point."

Philadelphia did not answer this at all, though she might have pointed out that an invalid mother was no inducement to matrimony, and that Jamie in his own way had been remarkably faithful. She did not say either that Tobias, aged three, had a nursemaid in constant attendance, and that Charlotte's husband, who was in tea, was always away from home until the evening. But then there was never any point in arguing with Charlotte, who was always right, and it was just as well that she did not come too often, for her way of treating mama usually made things worse: she thumped the pillows as if she were using a pestle, and lifted the poor invalid up so energetically that she must have jarred every bone in that fragile body. "Charlotte is so rough," Mrs. Smith once said, "and she shouts so." It was true—to hear what Charlotte was saying, one could stand across the street and be certain not to miss a word.

So Philadelphia did not pursue the matter, and Charlotte still came once or twice a month, bringing with her a little fruit, perhaps a cold chicken, and once even a bottle of wine.

Philadelphia saw the bottle peeping out of the basket. She said abruptly, her accent very Scots, "And what, pray, is that?"

Charlotte had the grace to blush. No strong liquor had ever been permitted in the Smith household, as she was well aware, and if Henry liked to drink, that was his affair: mama would not dream of touching a drop, even though Dr. Lewen had once suggested that a beef broth with a touch of cinnamon and claret would be beneficial.

"You know perfectly well what it is," snapped Charlotte.

"And you know perfectly well that mama never touches wine."

"The Bible says—"

"I know very well what the Bible says. 'The devil can cite scripture for his purpose.' You will put that bottle on the parlor table and take it away with you when you go. It would upset mama dreadfully to see it. I think this is very inconsiderate of you, Char, and I will not have her distressed in such a fashion. You know as well as I do papa's views on drinking, and mama would never dream of going against his wishes."

After this Charlotte could hardly say anything more, but she dumped the bottle down so violently that she almost broke it, then forgot to take it with her when she left, some three hours later.

Philadelphia found it still standing there. She picked it up and looked at it, twirling it round. It struck her that this was the first time in her eighteen years—this had happened two months ago—that she had ever handled a bottle of wine. How Mr. A. would laugh! It was a red wine, and the bottle was an elegant one with some French name upon it. Philadelphia did not speak French, but she assumed this was so; everyone knew that good wine came from France. She had to admit that it did not really look like an instrument of the devil. Exhausted as always by Charlotte's robust vitality, her ears still ringing with the sound of that trumpet-like voice, she wondered for a brief and shameful moment if it really were a sin to drink this attractive-looking stuff. After all, it looked exactly like a superior fruit cordial. For the flash of a second she thought she would like to taste it, if only to know the flavor of damnation. Then she was appalled by her own wickedness, and instantly put the bottle away at the very back of the sideboard cupboard: she turned the key upon it, for Lucy, she was sure, would not share her scruples and would probably finish it at one go.

Kneeling now by her mother's bedside and gazing into that thin, flushed face, she wondered again if drinking wine were so evil: mama looked desperately ill, and perhaps it would put strength into her. But she dared not suggest it, and presently Mrs. Smith said again, "I wish I were dead."

"Oh mama, pray do not say such a thing, it is very wrong of you. You must know that my greatest dream is to have you well again."

"It is a dream, Philly," said Mrs. Smith. She struggled to raise herself up, and Philadelphia instantly put a supporting arm behind her, easing the pillows as she did so. She looked steadily at her daughter. Philadelphia, nearly in tears, suddenly saw that her mother in some extraordinary way, looked more like her old self than she had done for many months. The face was savagely emaciated, the eyes dark with pain, and the thinning hair hung damply down, yet there was a strange, bright spirit to her, and the voice had lost its querulous ring.

She said, putting out a hand to Philadelphia's cheek, "You're a good lass, Philly. And you're quite a beauty too, though I'd not wish to make you conceited. Your papa always wondered where your looks came from. They certainly do not come from either of us. And you are only eighteen. It's hard on you to waste your youth looking after a sick old woman like me. You should be married, my pet, with bairns of your own. You'll make me a better wife than Charlotte, who cares for no one but herself, and as for that Tobias, if I had the strength, I'd give him a good skelp for the ill-mannered little creature that he is."

"Mama!" Philadelphia was both delighted yet frightened, for her mother had not spoken in such a fashion for a very long time. Perhaps a miracle had occurred, perhaps she was going to get better. Yet this was unchancy, it stirred unease and fear within her: when she was downstairs again, she would do as she had said, and send Lucy along to Dr. Lewen's.

"What about Jamie?" demanded her mother.

"He is coming tonight, mama."

"And when are you two getting wed?"

Philadelphia, bewildered, said, "Oh, we do not know. Soon perhaps. He is still teaching in the same school, he does not earn much money, but I am a good manager, I daresay we would do very well." Then she said, almost stammering in her emotion, "Would you like us to marry, mama? Would it make you happy?"

"It would make me happier than anything else in the world."

"He is always asking me—Do you really mean that?

Of course we will always look after you. Jamie knows that I would never marry him unless there was a room for you in our home. He is very fond of you. He says you are so brave. Oh mama, do you really mean what you are saying?"

"Would I say it otherwise? When he comes, you will tell him so. What is that stupid girl bringing in? I don't want it."

The querulous note had returned. Philadelphia jumped to her feet, and took from Lucy the tray she was bringing in. She saw that as usual it was badly laid, and the tea had already slopped over on to the cloth. But she thanked Lucy, wishing she had not heard mama's remark, then, when the door had closed behind her, said, holding the tray in her hands, "I think a hot drink would do you good. If you'll wait while I get a clean cloth—"

"I said no." Then Mrs. Smith smiled, and for that second looked almost young again. "Drink it yourself, pet. It'll do you good. And tell your young man from me that he'll never find himself a better wife if he lives to a hundred. Do you love him, my lass?"

"Yes, mama."

"And does he love you?"

"He is always saying so!"

"I am not sure if he's good enough for you. But I daresay all mothers say the same. He's not a bad lad, but I think he's weak, for all he looks so braw and bonnie. You'll be the strong one, Philly, even if you're half his size. You can never trust these handsome, six foot men; you only have to give them a wee shove and they crumple up like paper."

Philadelphia, for some unknown reason, found herself thinking of Mr. A. She wondered if he would crumple up like paper too: somehow she doubted it.

And, wishing to make her mother smile again, she said, "There is a handsome, six foot gentleman who lives opposite. Sometimes I see him when I do the shopping. Is it not strange that we live such different lives on opposite sides of the street? They are all so rich, and we are all so poor, yet there is only a few yards between us. What do you think would happen if we ever met?"

"You are talking havers," said Mrs. Smith quite sharply. "You know what your papa always said: one should always keep to one's own station in life. Besides, from what I hear, they are wicked people, what with their drinking and their light women. I would not like any daughter of mine to associate with them."

Philadelphia listened to this in a rebellious silence: she could not help thinking that mama was very old-fashioned in her views. After all, this was 1746, this was London; people mixed much more nowadays than they used to, and surely by simply speaking to each other one would not run the danger of the fires of hell. Then she saw that her mother had fallen back against the pillow again, and ran to her side, crying, "Oh, I am a bad girl, and you are so ill. Forgive me, mama. There must be something I can fetch for you. I know—there's the cake I have made for Jamie. It'll still be warm, and you always liked a freshly baked cake. Would you not care to taste a slice and tell me if I have made it properly?"

Mrs. Smith simply said in an exhausted voice, "No, child. I am very tired. I wish to sleep. Tell your Jamie that I cannot see him this evening. And—" The strength returned to her voice so that it rang out with authority. "You are not to fetch the doctor now."

"But mama—"

"You'll do as you're told, Philly. I hope you're listening to me."

"You speak to me as if I'm a child again, mama!"

"You're acting like a child. There is to be no doctor. Is that understood?"

"Yes, mama," said Philadelphia in a rather undutiful tone of voice.

"Then be a good lass now. And give me a kiss. I'll be asleep by the time your young man comes."

"But may I not bring you a little supper?"

"I've said I wish to sleep. I'll be sure to call you if I want anything. Good night, Philly."

"Good night, mama. And don't forget to call out if there's anything, anything at all."

Her mother, to her surprise, put her arms round her daughter's neck as she kissed her. She had never been a demonstrative woman. When Philadelphia, at the door, turned to wave to her, she smiled, then turned a little on her side as if she were already half asleep.

Philadelphia, as she quietly closed the door, thought she spoke one more word. It sounded like "Thank you." She could not quite believe it. She nearly turned back, but it would be a pity to disturb her. It was probably "Good night."

She felt much happier than she had done, partly because mama seemed so much better, and partly because she had this good news for Jamie. It would be wonderful to marry at last, to have a home of her own and a host of children: it would be wonderful to see Jamie every day, not simply for a couple of hours once a week. And she sang a little tuneless song to herself as she went back to her room to change—not that she had much in the way of fine gowns, but at least she could make herself presentable, especially as she had such wonderful news to impart.

She looked in her wardrobe with a faint exasperation, but then Philadelphia, when she was not so tired,
was of an optimistic nature, and there was little point
in lamenting a state of affairs that had after all existed long before papa died. She fingered through a
number of uninspiring gowns, two of them Charlotte's
cast-offs, which had required a deal of altering, Charlotte being nearly twice Philadelphia's size. It was a
pity too that Charlotte's taste was so flamboyant, for
Philadelphia, though she liked pretty colors, had to
see that bright reds and purples were not for her. At
last she selected a gown that she had not worn for
some time: perhaps Jamie would forget and think that
it was new. Gentlemen seldom noticed these things. It
was a soft blue, a little faded now, but a bright silk
scarf would cheer it up and hide the worn bit at the
bosom, and a belt would disguise the fact that it was
a little too large.

She dressed and did her hair, permitting herself a
couple of stray curls that would, she hoped, look as if
they were accidental. She thought that she was in
poor looks, but then sleepless nights and not enough
fresh air were bad for any female complexion.

Perhaps in the soft lamplight Jamie would not notice. And when he heard what she had to say, he
would surely forget about everything else.

Chapter 2

There was still half an hour to go to Jamie's arrival. He always came at the same time, when he had finished with his last class and corrected their exercises. Philadelphia pushed the front door open. It was on the latch, for she always forgot to lock it. In Inverness there had never been any need, and she could not believe that even in London, which was reputed to be such a wicked place, she could be robbed. There was indeed little to steal: such trinkets as she had, had long ago been sold to pay for mama's medicines, and there was nothing else of value in the house.

She stood for a few moments on the top step. It was the first outside air she had breathed during the day. It was still heavy as if there might be a storm, but the dim evening light was soothing, and it was refreshing to be out of the sickroom. She stood very still, her hands folded in front of her, and her eyes moved a little self-consciously to Number 23 opposite.

It appeared to be a moment of drama. There was always drama at Number 23. Philadelphia, whose life was so conspicuously devoid of it, felt an odd pang of envy. In principle of course all these scenes were quite deplorable, but she could not help feeling that perhaps one small scene, one moment of unbridled emotion, would add a little excitement to her normally dull day. Even Jamie, who provided her great moment of the week, was on the whole a predictable young man who seldom said the unexpected, whose conversation mainly concerned his work and his difficult pupils.

"I wish," said Philadelphia aloud, though in a soft, almost inaudible voice, "that something would happen to me."

And, unaware of a malevolent deity above who at this remark invoked the attention of a couple of devils, she gazed with a kind of wistful disapproval at the young woman, whom she now knew as Emma, storming out of the house and crashing the door behind her.

Emma appeared to have quarreled with Mr. Atherton again. She was as always most beautifully dressed and even in her disarray looked magnificent. Her creamy cat-face was wild with temper, and the thick black hair streaked across it. She seemed to be talking to herself. Philadelphia was convinced that she was swearing. There was no sign of Mr. Atherton, but as she ran towards her carriage, which was waiting at the corner, the door opened again. There was nobody to be seen, but perhaps her lover was making certain that she had definitely gone. Only as Emma paused, about to leap into her carriage, she turned her head and looked straight at Philadelphia, who blushed scarlet and wished she were back in the house again.

It was possible that Emma did not even see her, for her face was working with rage and her mind plainly elsewhere, but it seemed to Philadelphia, now both embarrassed and ashamed, that a fierce hostility blazed from her, as if she were aware of being observed. The next instant she was inside, and the horses were trotting away and out of sight.

However, Philadelphia felt that she had every right to stand on her own doorstep, and surely it was natural enough to notice something so dramatic and ill-bred. And, having already committed herself, she could not resist peering inside the half-open door. This was the first time she had had the opportunity. She had always wondered what the house was like. It would certainly be very different from the Smiths' little cottage. The rooms, no doubt, were wide and high, with beautiful furniture and precious porcelain, there would be an elegant winding staircase, with perhaps a balcony on the landing. But there was little she could see except for a small table on which presumably guests left their cards, a lamp that glowed warmly, and what appeared to be a framed portrait on the wall. Perhaps this was Mr. Atherton's father. Then suddenly, as if papa had tapped her on the shoulder, Philadelphia came to her genteel senses, and instantly went inside, almost haughtily as if she were a different person from the vulgar little girl who had been prying into what did not concern her.

She was quite unaware that Mr. Atherton had been watching her, through the half-drawn curtains of the drawing room. He did not realize that she had been peering into his house. He only saw as he had seen before a small little girl in a quite dreadfully unfashionable gown—why on earth did she not buy herself a new one?—with, as he had already remarked, unusually pretty hair and a remarkably trim little figure. It never entered his head that she might have no money for dresses, but then, like many well-off people, he never really considered that other people might not be so fortunate as himself. He was still shaking with temper from his quarrel with Emma, and he found the sight of Philadelphia oddly soothing. She would, he was sure, never scream abuse at anyone, nor would she roar out of the house in such a fashion that all the neighborhood servants would know about it. He wondered what would happen if he came out on the street and spoke to her. She would probably run for her life. He was possessed of a sudden ridiculous idea that he might send across a little note, inviting her—suitably chaperoned, of course—in for a glass of wine. She would certainly not come unattended. From the look of her she was both young and innocent, but something in that small, upright figure intimated that she would behave with the utmost correctness.

He continued to stand there, tapping his fingers on the windowsill, long after Philadelphia had shut the door behind her. He thought idly that it would be amusing to break down that air of impeccable virtue: he had never seen her face clearly, but if the hair were any indication, she was pretty, and something in the look of her suggested that she had spirit.

He found that he was still angry, and he turned abruptly towards the other person in the room, who had sauntered in just before Emma swept out, and who was at that moment sitting there, with his feet up on the sofa and drinking wine. Ferdy, as he was always called, was an old acquaintance. Mr. Atherton did not like him, nobody liked him, but he served as a drinking and gambling companion, and tonight the two of them were going together to a small tavern beyond the boundaries of Holborn, to play hazard in a company of the lowest sort, highwaymen, thieves and professional gamblers. Mr. Atherton had come across this place on one of the long walks that he sometimes took when life bored or disgusted him, and Ferdy on such an errand was the ideal companion, for he was as dissolute and wicked as the men who would hope to prey on him, he did not know what fear was, and crooks and swindlers could only meet their match in him. He had not a friend in the world; high society, to which by birth he belonged, shunned him, but there was no game of chance at which he was not successful, and if there were to be a knife in the back it was certain that the back would not be Ferdy's. His full name was that of a ducal family blazoned in the history books, a family beheaded, impeached, decorated, entwined with royalty. The family did not look upon Ferdy with enthusiasm, and would gladly have repudiated him. Ferdy, to their shame, possessed the family long nose and chin, and the wide gray eyes, even the ginger hair, but otherwise he did his name the utmost discredit. It was unlikely he would ever marry; his father, who was as respectable as his son was depraved, could not endure the sight of him, and paid him a handsome annuity to keep out of his way. Ferdy gambled away the annuity, spent his life in taverns and brothels, and strayed frequently within an inch of the hangman's rope: to his father's intense disappointment he had always managed so far to avoid it.

Mr. Atherton, who was so far considerably less debauched, disliked him and sometimes, like Emma, who could not endure the sight of him, detested him.

But his natural gambling ability was useful to a man who liked gaming above all things, and sometimes it was almost a relief to be in the company of one to whom scruples signified an unknown quantity. Ferdy, with his half-shut, white-lashed eyes, his inane grin and lack of conversation, appeared to be half-witted: those who left the tables, stripped of everything they possessed, sometimes gazed unbelievingly at this young man who smiled at them and pocketed their money.

At least Ferdy's company would be a change from Emma's. Mr. Atherton still felt raw and angry from the scene that had just occurred. There had been many such quarrels, there would be many more, and though at the moment he wanted nothing more than to say goodbye for ever, he knew perfectly well in his heart that when she came back, as she certainly would do within a couple of hours, he would melt before her beauty, her wit and the strange humility that she, the most arrogant of women, could always assume.

Well, tonight he would not be there. Emma could come, as penitent and seductive as she please, and he would not be there. For once she must learn her lesson. He said in a sharp, abrupt voice, "Ferdy!"

"Are we ready to go, Tom?" said Ferdy, in his high-pitched drawl. He had by now finished a bottle and a half of wine. He was perfectly sober. He was only drunk when he permitted himself to be so.

He answered, "Yes, we're ready." He thought Ferdy looked rather more revolting than usual. His eyes strayed again to the window. He said suddenly, "But first I think we'll pay a little call."

Ferdy said, "Oh Christ, no!" His mind was entirely set on the money he was going to win, indeed had to win, for his debts amounted to nearly five thousand pounds, and his creditors were becoming pressing. His only interest in women—he assumed naturally that the person to be called on was feminine—was as bedmates for the night: he had no social graces whatsoever and was bored to death by society ladies. Yet there remained an odd inconsistency in his character, of which Mr. Atherton was unaware: the big houses closed their doors upon him, and this Ferdy savagely resented. It made no difference that he insulted everyone he met, that his manners were worse than those of an untrained dog, that he seldom washed and that his speech was strewn with the vilest of expletives. He still considered that as a duke's son he should be invited, and there was a secret ambition in what was left of his heart, that one day he would contrive to have the entrée to any mansion that took his fancy. However, at this moment, the last thing he wanted was to call on some pretty idiot of a fashionable woman. He had worked out a couple of new and unethical tricks to be tried out at the gaming tables; he was longing to be able to put them into practice.

He went on in his thin drawling voice that Emma always said was like a violin out of tune, "Ah, what the devil. Do we have to pay a bloody social call at this hour? The lady will be dressing for dinner. It would be a devilish waste of time. Let us go straight to Holborn. It was your idea, you son of a whore, what's the matter with you? You can go to bed with her later. She'll like it all the better."

"It will not take long," said Mr. Atherton. His face, which had been creased in lines of boredom, had grown alive and alert. He knew now that he wanted very much to make the acquaintance of this girl who was always standing on her doorstep. She was like no one he had so far met, and it would be a fine novelty to step across the street into what was virtually another world. Besides, it would be doing her a kindness: what a sad and dreary life she must lead, poor creature, with an invalid mama and that dull young man who only seemed to call once a week.

At this particular moment Mr. Atherton had neither ideas nor designs. He was simply bored and inquisitive, and he had quarreled with Emma. It would be amusing to meet someone so different, and of course the young woman would be vastly flattered to find that a gentleman of the *ton* wished to make her acquaintance. He knew exactly how it would go. He would greet her very civilly, making the lowest of bows, suggest that as neighbors they should make each other's acquaintance, and perhaps continue by asking her across one afternoon to take a glass of wine with him. She no doubt would blush and bridle, be covered with confusion. He hoped she did not giggle, but from what he had seen of her, she did not seem the giggling kind. And after that of course the whole matter would be ended. The girl might perhaps fall a little in love with him, but she would soon get over it, and it would be something that she could tell to all her friends, a small point of drama in what must be an intolerably boring life.

He did not really see Philadelphia as a person in her own right: indeed she seemed to him in his mind rather like a superior serving maid.

Ferdy, now really out of temper, snapped, "Where the devil are we going?"

"Across the road!"

"You must be out of your bloody mind," said Ferdy. He shambled over to the window—he had a strange, ungainly way of walking—and peered out at Number 22. The cottages with their even numbers were to him as human as ant heaps. He could not conceive why Tom could possibly want to visit anyone who lived there. The cottage people were common people with no money: they lived extraordinary lives where no one seemed to do anything but be born, marry and die. They were dull as death, they would not recognize a hazard table if they saw it, and the females were all stupid, virtuous and plain. He said, "Who the devil is she?"

"I have no idea," said Mr. Atherton, "but the name is Smith." For he had once received a letter by mistake, which he had returned by a footman. It was from a cousin in Inverness, and Mr. Atherton would not normally have noticed it, except that his eye lit on the first name of Philadelphia, and this was so odd, it had intrigued him. He knew this would madden Ferdy, so he told him this—"She is called Philadelphia."

Ferdy swore unrepeatedly, as if this were a personal insult.

"Well, I understand it is quite a common name, nowadays. It is a trifle over-large for so small a girl, but, so they say, it is becoming popular. Perhaps," went on Mr. Atherton, for all this, in addition to Ferdy's bewildered rage, was slightly going to his head, "we could invent a fashion of London names. What would you say to Marylebone Brown or Chelsea Atherton? I believe I myself could fancy a girl called Piccadilly Fortescue."

Ferdy, to whom this style of conversation was something entirely alien, looked at him sourly and growled, "You're foxed."

"Not at all," said Mr. Atherton, and neither he was, though he certainly would be by the end of the evening: a gaming excursion with Ferdy invariably involved a great deal of wine.

"Ah, Jesus," said Ferdy wearily, "can we not go? Surely you could call on this bitch some other time when I'm not there."

"I wish to call on her now," said Mr. Atherton firmly, "and you are coming with me as chaperon." And he all but dragged Ferdy out with him, gripping him by the sleeve.

The two gentlemen stepped out into the street. There was no sign of life in Number 22, but one of the bedroom lamps was lit, and the curtains were tightly drawn in what was presumably the parlor on the ground floor. The street was silent. The odd numbers were preparing for the evening's entertainment, and the even numbers were having their supper and thinking of bed.

Mr. Atherton, about to cross over, remarked, "Is it not strange, Ferdy? They live there, and we live here, with a few yards between us, and we know nothing of each other, nothing at all."

"I cannot see why we have to know them. I want to go to Holborn," grumbled Ferdy. He was thinking that Tom, God rot him, was in the strangest mood. That bitch, Emma, whom he detested as much as she did him, must have really done it this time. He did not like this sort of conversation, indeed he did not like conversation at all; it seemed to him a waste of energy. He was beginning to wish that he was going on his own.

"You have no soul, Ferdy," said Mr. Atherton, swinging round to stare at him.

"You have no wits," retorted Ferdy, "and either you're coming with me to Holborn, or you are not.

This is a complete waste of time. Does this silly bitch know you're calling on her?"

"She does not, and she is not a bitch. Mind your manners, Ferdy. We cannot let her believe that the odd numbers are so lacking in breeding."

"For God's sake!" muttered Ferdy, defeated.

"Come, sir. Right your cravat and try to look like a gentleman. We are now about to pay our call, and—Damn!" exclaimed Mr. Atherton, with heartfelt conviction.

For, striding along the even-numbered side of the street was the tall young man whom Mr. Atherton recognized well enough, the gentleman who called on Miss Philadelphia so dully and so dutifully once a week. He had forgotten that this was the evening. It was obvious that his little plan was knocked on the head: he would hardly be welcome in the circumstances, and certainly the young man would object most strongly, there might even be a brawl.

He was both disappointed and bad-tempered. He snarled at Ferdy, "Very well, damn you. Holborn it must be. And I hope," he added vindictively, "you lose."

"I'll not lose," said Ferdy, and grinned at him. He might send the ladies screaming from him, and doors might be firmly shut in his face, but at the tables he always won, and would continue to do so until some enraged fellow swindler put a bullet or a knife in him. He was thankful that this whole absurd business was over. He did not give a damn for his friend's temper. His mind was now entirely preoccupied with the entracing games ahead of him, and the two gentlemen walked on, away from Number 22, aiming for a world that Montagu Road did not know, that Philadelphia had never heard of, where lived half the murderers, thieves, highwaymen and doxies of London.

They did not exchange more than a few words on their journey. Ferdy was brooding on his winnings, and Mr. Atherton was discovering to his annoyance that he was genuinely disappointed. He really wanted to meet this young woman, and now that he was thwarted, swore that he would make another and more successful attempt to do so. And he barely thought of Emma who, half an hour later, reproaching herself, yet unable to keep away, drove up to Number 23's door, exactly as her lover had foreseen.

Emma did not wait more than a few minutes. She sat there in the carriage, her face sad and angry and drawn, and from time to time helped herself to a sweetmeat from the candy box she carried in her reticule. She always solaced herself with sweets when unhappy: once when Mr. Atherton made fun of her, she retorted that at least it was better than drinking wine. She had to see that Tom was out for the evening. Perhaps he was with another woman. This thought upset her so much that she could not even swallow her sweet. For the first time in her life she was completely and, perhaps, irrevocably, entangled. She had fallen in love many times before, being twenty-two, wealthy and beautiful: she had never taken it too seriously, and it was the young men who were left sighing on her doorstep. She had met Tom eighteen months ago, and for a year now they had been lovers, with no word of marriage spoken between them. Emma, managing at last to swallow another of the sweetmeats that would in time, if she were not careful, make her fat, had never so much as looked at another man since, and the thought that this last violent quarrel might indeed be the last, was so unbearable that she began to cry. There would be no peace for her until she had made it up, perhaps there would be no peace until she had persuaded Tom, not by any means a marrying man, into wedlock. And so she ate her sweets and moped and sobbed, and determined to visit Tom and beg his pardon.

Before all this occurred, Philadelphia came into the parlor. She made sure everything was tidy, lit the lamp, set the table prettily with the best cloth, some fruit cordial and the newly-baked cake—Lucy must have opened the oven for there was a definite dent in the middle—then curled up on the sofa to read her novel until Jamie arrived.

It was Mr. Richardson's *Pamela*, her favorite. She had read it many times before, indeed there were sections that she almost knew by heart, but it never failed to excite her; it was as if it provided her with all the drama that was so lacking in her real life.

It was all deliciously shocking, and Philadelphia, suppressing a strong conviction that she should not be reading such things at all, found that the first volume opened automatically at a dreadful passage where Pamela's fascinating, yet wicked, master resolved to read her incriminating journals, threatened to strip her to see if they were about her person.

"Now," he said, *"it is my opinion they are about you; and I never undressed a girl in my life, but I will now begin to strip my pretty Pamela, and I hope I shall not go so far before I find them."*

I fell a crying, and said, "I will not be used in this manner. Pray, Sir," said I (*for he began to unpin my handkerchief*) *"consider! Pray, Sir, do!"*

"Pray," said he, *"do you consider, for I will see*

*these papers. But maybe," said he, "they are tied
about your knees with your garters," and stooped.
Was ever anything so vile and wicked?—*

If he did that to me, thought Philadelphia, I would
give him such a box on the ears, he would be deaf-
ened for life. Her eyes moved again to the page, almost sensuously, and she at once shut the volume. She
leaned her head against the back of the sofa and half-
closed her eyes. It was certainly because she was so
tired, but her imagination began to function in a
strange and disgraceful way, the more disgraceful because Jamie was due to arrive in a few minutes, Jamie,
her own Jamie, to whom she had been plighted, almost since childhood, whom she loved so dearly, who
would one day be her husband and the father of the
half dozen children she had already planned to have.

I wonder, thought Philadelphia in the languid fashion of one half-asleep, what it would be like to have a
gentleman trying to seduce you. Naturally, said the
other side of her, papa's side, the strict and Scottish
side, you would never permit it for a second. To try to
strip you—the idea of it! Yet, thought the sleepy Philadelphia, it would at least show that he found you attractive, that he desired you, that he thought you
beautiful. And it would be so exciting. It would be
something to write in my diary—you see, I'm not so
priggish or prim, a gentleman has tried to seduce me,
he undid my garters and took down my hair—

But this was too much, even in a dream, and it was
made worse, much worse, by the fact that this anonymous and disgraceful gentleman was not anonymous
at all: he bore a quite remarkable resemblance to Mr.
A. Philadelphia gave a faint cry of horror, and sat instantly upright, the volume of *Pamela* dropping to the

floor. She put her hands up to her hair as if indeed lustful fingers had pulled it out of its pins. But every curl was in place, as it always was, and at that moment there was Jamie's knock—he always did a special rat-a-tat-tat—on the parlor door, for he had come straight in, the front door being as usual unlatched.

Philadelphia, her cheeks prettily flushed, came to greet him. She and Jamie looked at each other in a smiling silence. They did not kiss. "You must never kiss before you are married," mama always said. "I know it seems just a small, unimportant point, but one thing leads to another, and the gentlemen, while begging for such familiarities, simply despise you once they are granted."

And so they did not kiss, only briefly clasped hands before Philadelphia led her betrothed inside. But it was disturbing how passionately she longed for that forbidden kiss, how she could not help visualizing his mouth against hers, how the longing for him positively hurt her. She instantly released his hand, with its thumb stroking her palm, and sat him down in the chair that was furthest away from the sofa. And, as she sat down herself, she glanced up almost propitiatingly at papa's portrait over the mantelpiece: he looked much sterner than he had ever done in real life, but she hoped that he approved of her.

And, as she was thinking of Jamie's kiss, and sternly pushing the thought away from her, Jamie was wishing that he had the courage to put his arm round her shoulders and draw her close to him. This, in view of what he had to say, disturbed him very much: he sat very upright in his hard-backed chair, and struggled to keep his eyes from dwelling too closely on the beautiful face such a little distance away: she seemed to him lovelier each time he saw her, with the green eyes and the soft, smooth lips. Only, strangely enough, it was the little workworn hands clasped in her lap that moved him more than anything else: he began to think that he could not say what he had come to say, that the whole project was foolish and he had best forget about it.

He was a handsome young man, two years older than his betrothed, and very tall, being about six foot three. The two families had lived next door in Inverness, and he had known Philadelphia ever since she was born. It had always been understood that the two should marry, and Jamie had accepted this with calm if without enthusiasm, until Philadelphia reached the age of fifteen, by which time she was so ravishingly pretty that he fell in love with her. He had followed the Smith family to London, and for a while he stayed with them until he found a teaching job and could support himself.

He had never been a wild boy. He, like Philadelphia, had strictly religious parents, and though nowadays he did not entirely conform, he had always accepted their ruling. It was true that he sometimes drank wine, and occasionally played cards with his friends, but he did not mention such matters to Philadelphia, nor did she know that there had been two other girls. There was no reason to tell her. It was after all one of the accepted things: young men were expected to sow a reasonable crop of wild oats, while young women must remain strictly virtuous until the day they married. He thought privately that Philadelphia would not really mind: the initiatory girl was a roll in the hay and no more, while the next lasted for a month and then was finished. It was Philadelphia he was engaged to, and in the normal course of events they should by now have been married.

But Dr. Smith died, and Mrs. Smith developed this dreadful illness, and here they were, unwed, unkissing, sitting there with the world and one homemade cake between them. Jamie, forgetting his attack of conscience, thought a little wretchedly that Philly could not be so surprised at what he had to say, she was after all an intelligent girl. Jamie's mother disapproved of this, saying that it was not natural for a lassie to have so good a brain, it was not womanly, but Jamie appreciated her ready wit, and knew that it would help him in his career. But he still could not bring the words out, and at one point all but leaped to his feet, so to take his dear, prim, beautiful little girl in his arms and kiss the nonsense out of both of them.

Instead, however, he said, "And how is your mother? I will go up and see her presently. I have brought her a few flowers. And here," he added a little awkwardly, for this in the circumstances seemed wrong, "is a wee gift for you."

"Oh Jamie!" said Philadelphia in a choked voice, and she looked down at the small parcel he had set beside her, instantly moving back to his hard-backed chair.

"Will you not open it?" he said.

Philadelphia believed for one catastrophic moment that she was going to burst into tears. She had never been a crying girl, even as a child: papa did not hold with such emotional displays, and she herself believed that tears were a weakness, so often used by her sex to get their own way. But now there was a great unswallowable lump in her throat, and her eyes pricked ominously: it was all quite absurd, it must be the stormy heat, and of course it had been a very tiring day. But she dared not speak, for fear that a sob would emerge, instead of the grateful yet sensible words she wished to utter. So instead of saying thank you, as she longed to do, she bent her head and simply undid the little parcel: Jamie, chilled by her silence, watched her and began for the first time to think that what he had to say could have been said a long time ago, that he had no reason to be ashamed.

The parcel contained a small silk handkerchief, embroidered with the initial "P" in one corner. It must have cost Jamie a great deal of money, and he did not earn so much with his schoolmastering. She longed to thank him, and once again was possessed of a desire to spring to her feet and hug him. If she had done so, a great many things would not have happened. But the tears still filled her eyes, and she could only say in a choked, subdued voice, "Thank you, dear Jamie. It's very beautiful." Then she did rise to her feet, but only to go over to the table: she was regaining her composure and managed now to speak in a normal voice.

"I have made this cake for you," she said, "but I'm afraid I left Lucy to do the baking, and you know what a silly girl she is, she spoils everything. But I think it must be quite light. May I pour you out some cordial?"

Jamie would have preferred wine, but knew the Smith household too well to say so. He was unaware that the cupboard, just behind his chair, contained a full and unopened bottle. He said that both drink and cake were very good, then suggested again that he would like to go up to have a wee crack with Mrs. Smith.

"I hope she is better," he said. "This weather must be very trying for her." And he stood up, about to go upstairs.

"Oh no!" said Philadelphia quickly. There was an almost frantic note in her voice, and Jamie looked at her in surprise. "No. She has not been at all well to-day, and now I believe she is asleep. She asked especially that she should not be disturbed. I would go up myself to ask her, but I'm so afraid that I might waken her, and the doctor says sleep is essential. Next time, Jamie. She is always so pleased to see you. I'll tell her you were asking for her, and I will put these pretty flowers in water so that she can see them first thing in the morning."

Then she fell silent again, and still the unspoken words burned unhappily within her: Oh Jamie, I do not mean to sound so cold, I am so unhappy, I don't know why, and I do so want to kiss you, it's wicked of me, I'm a fallen girl, but why don't you just pay no attention and put your arms round me, after all we are going to be married, and perhaps sooner than you expect.

There had never before been the least difficulty in conversing. They had of course many friends in common, they knew each other's families, and Charlotte, whom Jamie had never liked—"I can never understand how you two are sisters"—always provoked some dry witticism, especially when she brought Tobias with her on a visit to grandmama, and paraded him in all his finery which was so unsuitable for a child of his age. But now for both of them there seemed absolutely nothing to say, and Philadelphia, bitterly aware that everything was going wrong, cut the cake, poured out two more glasses of cordial, and heard herself making a kind of desperate polite conversation. And he in his turn, usually so quick of speech, spoke back as formally as if they had just been introduced. They sat there, munching cake and taking quick sips of their cordial, and both of them longed to break the misunderstanding, but as neither of them fully understood where the misunderstanding lay, the conversation continued, brittle, sharp and cold.

And how had school been, and were his pupils attentive? No, pupils were seldom attentive, and these were rich boys, spoiled, lazy, accustomed to their own way; he had been compelled to use the rod on young Peterson, whose father was a cavalry captain and who liked to make fun of Jamie's accent.

"And what is wrong with your accent, pray?" demanded Philadelphia, so enraged that she was very Scots and for the first time natural. And Jamie laughed in quite his old fashion, answering, "Precisely what is wrong with yours, my lass."

And for the moment all was well again, but then there was another silence, and Philadelphia was compelled to cut herself another piece of cake, which she did not want and which all but choked her.

He said suddenly, for he knew that the moment was almost on him, whether he liked it or not, he could not postpone it any longer, yet even now could not quite force the words out—"What in heaven's name made them call you Philadelphia?"

She stared at him, and he went suddenly red: he had a delicate skin that flushed easily. He knew the question was a stupid one, but the words were out, he could not recall them. He thought, even in his embarrassment, that she looked very strange, yet the pallor of her cheeks touched him, and he suddenly noticed the two artless little curls on her forehead. Somehow these curls upset him. Philadelphia always brushed her hair straight back as mama had ordered her to do, and this disarming little display which to her no doubt seemed positively coquettish, suggested a vulnerability that she would normally try to hide.

She said in a small voice, "Jamie, you ask me such a

thing, and we have known each other for eighteen years."

"And so we have," he said, smiling at her. The smile was stiff at the corners. "Though," he went on, noting in the academic corner of his mind that embarrassment induced a dreadful kind of playfulness, "I did not mind you so well at the beginning. A young lad of two is not interested in babies, and I daresay I avoided you as much as I could."

"I was a very good baby," said Philadelphia, "but I still do not see why now, after so long a time, you are enquiring after my name."

Jamie said in genuine surprise, "I do not know either. But you must admit it was a strange kind of name to give you, and I do not remember you ever telling me about it."

Philadelphia thought, I want to marry you, mama says we may wed, and it has been too long, it is not good to be engaged for such a while, and I love you so much and I am beginning to think you no longer love me. But she only said quietly, "I find it hard to believe that I have never told you this before. But if you really wish to know, Jamie, my papa as a child met William Penn, the Quaker. Papa was not, of course, of his beliefs, but he greatly admired him, and sometimes he would tell me and Char of the city in the state called after him, with its streets of two and three story dwellings, all in red-pressed brick with white marble steps and white and green shutters on all the windows. So, when I was born, he called me Philadelphia. I hope that answers your question."

"It does indeed," said Jamie, a little dryly, for she sounded to him rather as if she were addressing a class. Then he could bear it no longer. He saw that if he did not speak now, he would never do so, and all this would happen again and again, and perhaps in the end they would no longer love each other, they would have some dreadful quarrel and it would all be over for ever.

He said in a loud voice, "Philly, there is something I must say to you."

And at the same moment she said, "Jamie, I have some news for you."

The two sentences came out at exactly the same time, as if they were well-trained actors on a stage: they both stopped short, staring at each other.

Philadelphia was to wonder wretchedly afterwards what would have happened if she had completed her sentence, if she had said, Mama has given us permission to wed, we will of course take her into our home, but oh Jamie, we can be together, I can look after you, we will not be lonely again. But though Jamie, very flushed again, said quickly, "I beg your pardon. What did you say?"—she only shook her head and said, "You speak first. It is the gentleman's privilege."

"But I would like to hear what you were going to say—"

"It is not so important. Truly it is not. You speak first. I think," said Philadelphia, with a flash of her old spirit, "you have been wishful to mention it from the first moment you arrived—"

"You are an observant lass!" said Jamie, a little bitterly.

"—which is why, no doubt, we are talking to each other as if we were at a polite tea party."

Jamie sprang to his feet. He did not look at all as if he were at a polite tea party. He took a deep breath, saying, "It is not easy to say this," and at once proceeded to say it. In a violent gesture he swung out his hand, and the jug of cordial was swept to the floor, where it lay, a mess of broken glass and fruitjuice.

Philadelphia looked down at it and away. It was cut glass, it had been one of mama's wedding presents. There was scarcely any good stuff left in the house now, and what there was, was precious. But she said nothing, and Jamie did not even notice what he had done.

"You must try not to despise me, Philly," he said, doing what he always forbade his pupils to do, and starting at the end. "It is not that I do not love you. You must believe that. I do love you. I have always loved you. But you must see that this is no life for either of us. How long is it since we were betrothed?" He did not wait for an answer. He told her. "Nearly two years. You were sixteen and I was eighteen. We were going to get married soon. But then everything happened to stop us, and now your mother is so ill, we cannot marry until she is—" He swallowed. "Until she is better. And nobody knows when that will be." He nearly added, "It's driving me out of my mind, just seeing you once a week and not even being able to touch you—" But he did not say this. One did not say such things to females. Philly would never understand, she might be mortally offended and shocked. He said, more quietly, "You must not think I reproach you in any way, or of course her. It is no fault of hers, poor lady, that she is so sick, and you are the most dutiful daughter imaginable, no one could wish for anyone better. But—"

Then he broke off, for his foot had cracked on the glass, and he realized for the first time what he had done. He exclaimed, "Oh my God!" which would normally have earned him a reproach, for papa had never permitted such language. But Philadelphia said nothing.

He looked at her, then down at the broken glass. He said, "I'm sorry."

Philadelphia said in a quiet, composed voice, "I understand then that you are breaking off our engagement."

"No!" The word came out in a shout.

"Then," said Philadelphia, still perfectly calm, "I do not understand at all."

"I am putting it so badly—" Then he began to speak in what was almost a gabble. "I am leaving the school, Philly. I have saved a little money, and I think that if I stay on any longer I shall become—oh, you do not know what it is like. We start at half past seven every day, we continue sometimes till eight in the evening, we always teach the same things, we correct the same exercises, it even seems to me that we have stream after stream of the same boys. You cannot begin to imagine the awful dullness of it all."

Philadelphia could have pointed out that her life was not precisely one of intense drama, that she too got up very early, that she did most of the housework, all the cooking and waited on her mother hand and foot. The friends they had once known were far away in Inverness, there was no social life because she never had the time to go out, and in any case people were not interested in a sick old woman and her unmarried daughter. Philadelphia did not recognize her own beauty, but if she had done, might have seen that it was not always to her advantage: wives were not anxious to invite her home where a susceptible husband might set eyes on her. There was a local curate who had once considered paying court to her, but she never came to his church, and she had too sharp a tongue to please him: after half a dozen visits or so, all on the pretense of inquiring after her poor mama, he had given it up and married someone else. Nowadays the only visitors to the Smith home were Charlotte and Tobias, and rarely, usually at Christmas, Henry. Mr. Bridges, the solicitor, had called once when Mrs. Smith made her will, and Dr. Lewen looked in once or twice a week. As for the neighbors, Philadelphia simply knew them by sight, and occasionally said good morning to them over the garden wall.

But, as she knew only too well, from her experience of papa and friends at home, this was the kind of thing that gentlemen refused to understand. Woman was there to be womanly, and if she were bored to death in the process, it was something she would, if sensible, keep to herself. So she remained silent, only a sickness knotted itself in her stomach: the shock of it all was so great that she could not quite take it in, only somehow knew that worse was to follow.

Jamie was unaware of her reaction. Now that he had at last started, he was entirely concentrated on his own problems. He said, "I have seen what happens to schoolmasters. There's old Dobson—I've told you about him, I'm sure—he's been in the school for twenty years. Twenty years, Philly, imagine! And he's like a dried up old crab. There's no—no *juice* in him, if you know what I mean. And Ferguson, and Mr. Bryan, the head—They are all such old men. They're finished. They don't even earn a decent wage, and what life must be like for their wives, I cannot begin to imagine. Oh my darling, you must see my point of view—"

"I gather," said Philadelphia, this new, cool, detached Philadelphia, "that I am no longer your darling, and so far you have not given me any point of view at all."

He looked at her in despair. He had expected—oh, he did not know what he had expected, tears, recriminations, even swooning, only she had never been the hysterical kind—but the sight of her sitting there so prim and cool and collected was more than he could bear, and this forced him into a violence of speech he had never intended.

He said flatly, "I am going away for six months. I am leaving London. I cannot endure this life any longer. It is not as if we could get married straight away. I could not go on doing the same thing, week in, week out. I am still young, Philly. I want to see something of the world. I am going to travel. The young gentlemen who go on the Grand Tour always take a tutor with them, and I have been fortunate enough to get an introduction to young Lord. But perhaps I should not give you his name. He is very wealthy, he is my own age, and I believe he has taken a liking to me. I received the letter this very morning, confirming the arrangement, and telling me to make myself ready to travel at the shortest notice, probably next week. Oh, you must understand. You could not expect me to miss such an opportunity. And it will mean that we can marry when I come back, for the payment is good, it is more than I could earn in a whole year at the school. And of course I shall improve my knowledge of foreign parts, so I will be able to find a better post. Philly, say you understand. You have always been so good and clever with me. Think of seeing Paris and Rome, with all expenses paid—and my only duties are to accompany my gentleman and give him a certain amount of instruction. It is like a dream come true. I can hardly believe it, myself."

"And what," said Philadelphia, "am I expected to do while you are jaunting?"

There was nothing in her voice to indicate that her whole world had collapsed about her. Looking after mama had trained her to disguise her feelings: often when there had been a bad attack she had been terrified, but it would do the patient no good to show it, and so she had learnt to sound calm and matter of fact. But though she was half-dazed with shock, the wretchedness and despair were devouring her: she could hardly believe that this was really happening.

Jamie briefly closed his eyes. He did not answer directly, for indeed, there was very little he could in all decency say. He said at last, "You will wait for me, Philly, won't you?"

Philadelphia rose to her feet. It was extraordinary and quite shocking, but it came into her mind that the one thing she needed at this moment was a glass of wine. She dismissed the thought immediately. It was all bad enough without adding such wickedness to it. She moved across to the mantelpiece, where papa looked severely down upon her. She had to support herself on something, for her knees were giving beneath her. She said quietly, "I suppose you think I have no choice."

He did not answer this, but of course it was true, he was thinking precisely this. She could almost have spoken for him. He was after all an extremely handsome and gifted young man. A great many girls had set their cap at him, he was not yet earning much money, but then he was only twenty; one day he would have his own school, and certainly, when he chose to exert himself, he had a great deal of charm. Papa, who could be very shrewd at times, had once remarked that James Sinclair would go far, only it was a pity that he never thought of anyone but himself. Philadelphia was beautiful, but the one career open to beauty without a financial backing was not conceivable for a well-bred young woman, and in addition she had a sick mother and no social life whatsoever. There were no other beaux, there were not likely to be either, and Jamie was a good catch, she would be a fool not to wait, and she was too sensible not to know it.

He was of course too fond of her to say any of this, and perhaps too sensitive. He said quickly, "No, Philly. A pretty girl like you always has a choice. But I am hoping with all my heart that you will wait. Six months pass so quickly. And I would make so much better a husband. After all, marriage to a poor schoolmaster would be so dull for you; you would hardly see me, you might be landed with a couple of bairns, and what with that and a husband who is out all day, it would not be much of a life for you."

Philadelphia shot him one despairing glance, then at once lowered her gaze. How could she say that one thing in the world she longed for was marriage to Jamie, and never mind if he were often away from home? As for the two bairns, they would set the seal on her happiness: her only proviso would be that she would prefer half a dozen. Sometimes, daydreaming, she had brooded on these children of hers and Jamie's, with Jamie to cook good dinners for, Jamie to lie beside her at night, Jamie there to comfort her, advise her and protect her.

But there was no point in thinking of such things now, and for the first time it was not so much despair that surged within her as anger. Oh, it was fine for Master Jamie to go abroad, enjoy himself, and improve himself, assuming all the while that she would wait for him. It would not be all historic buildings and statues: he would certainly meet loose women and might even fall in love with them. Philadelphia, despite her enclosed upbringing, knew well enough what could happen to young men in foreign parts, and it was only too possible that after leaving her for six months on her own he would then turn up to say that he did not intend to marry her after all.

She said, "I'll not be waiting for you, Jamie."

"What!" He was utterly astounded. The color left his face so that his normally ruddy complexion turned a yellowish white. "Philly, you cannot mean that! I love you. You know I love you—"

"No," said Philadelphia, "I do not know. It is hardly a proof of love to leave your betrothed for half a year. You are always expecting me to see your point of view. You will now try to see mine. You have planned a fine jaunt for yourself. And I am expected to wait for you like—like Penelope, only she at least was wed, I am to sit there with folded hands, leading the terrible life I lead, with no one to comfort me, no one to help me."

All this melodrama and self-pity was entirely out of character, but Philadelphia was now carried away by the horror of it all and, if she were not entirely displeased by the pallor of Jamie's face, she did not let it stop her. She went on, "I thought you loved me."

"But I do, I do—Oh Philly!"

"Ha!" said this new melodramatic Philadelphia. "A fine sort of love! If that's love, I'd do better to stay a spinster all my days. You really think that you are now going to walk out of this house and leave me, for six months—six months!—and then when it's all over, when you have sufficiently enjoyed yourself and eaten all that horrid foreign food and no doubt made yourself fou on wine and suchlike, you'll come trotting back to me like a good little dog with a stick in its mouth, and you'll say, 'Oh Philly!—'" Her voice soared up to a falsetto. She had always been something of a mimic, though papa had told her it was unladylike. "'Oh Philly, here I am back again, bow wow wow, and you've waited for me like a good lass, so now we might get married, and instead of just cooking for mama and waiting on mama, you can cook for me and wait on me as well. Isn't that lovely for you, Philly, are you not the luckiest of girls?'"

Then, alas for feminine independence, she burst into tears.

Jamie was decent enough to be ashamed of himself but, believing that this was victory, at once made for her, meaning, in defiance of the law laid down by the late Dr. Smith, to put his arms around her and comfort her in the way that young ladies expected. But as his hand slid about her shoulders, hers slid out also, to deal him a resounding box on the ears that, in the astonishment of it, sent him positively reeling back among the broken glass so that it all sounded like musket fire.

He whispered, in a voice quivering with fury, "You did not have to do that, Philly."

Philadelphia was secretly thinking that she did not have to do it either, it was most unladylike and she had never done such a thing in her life, but the shock of it and Jamie's anger, stopped her tears. Her face was still wet with them, but the crying was done. She said, "I believe I did, but I did not mean to do it so hard. Only—only you insult me and hurt me, and then you think that all you have to do is kiss me, and I'll forgive you instanter. That is not right of you, Jamie. You must know it's not right."

Then she stepped forward and laid her hand on his

arm. His face was stubborn with offended dignity, he would not look at her and glowered down at the floor. But he did not move away. She said quietly, "I hope you will be happy. I hope you enjoy your tour. I cannot promise to wait for you, for I do not know if you will ever be back—"

"I said I would be back," mumbled Jamie, still unforgiving. He had from time to time thrashed his pupils, but he did not care for such treatment being meted out to him.

"Six months is a long time," said Philadelphia. "A great many things can change in six months. You may fall in love with someone else, and what kind of a fool does that leave me, sitting here like some old maid, crying my eyes out for a man who doesn't give a rap for me? Besides—" And here she tilted up her chin, managing something that was almost a smile. "Besides Jamie lad, I too might lose my heart to someone else. There was others after me, you know."

And indeed there had been in Inverness, ever since the age of twelve: it was only in London that life had become so lonely. But she could see, not without a certain bitter irony, that this thought had never entered Jamie's head. He exclaimed in a positively righteous indignation, "You could not do that! You are betrothed to me."

"No, Jamie, not any longer."

"But—"

"I wish to give you back your ring."

And she began to tug at it, only the ring in the way of its kind refused to budge. She exclaimed in a wail of temper, "Oh you shall have it back if I have to cut my finger off!"—and at this, the ring as if terrorized slid into the palm of her other hand. It was a thin gold band with one small diamond in it. That diamond had cost Jamie the whole of a month's salary, plus his savings. Philadelphia had treasured it more than anything she had ever owned. She held it out to him.

He refused to take it. He said in a suppressed voice, "Do you really mean this, Philly?"

"Yes, Jamie."

"You are quite sure?"

"Yes, Jamie."

"So it is goodbye then."

"Yes, Jamie."

He was appalled at the way in which everything had roared out of control. He had never imagined it would be like this. And because he was bitterly aware of his own mismanagement, he proceeded to lose his temper again. He said furiously, "Oh very well then, if that is how you want it," and snatched the ring from her, stuffing it into his pocket. He snapped, "You seem glad enough for me to go. I thought you loved me, but I see I was mistaken. I daresay it's as well I'm going after all. I never was one to stay where I'm not wanted."

Philadelphia did not answer this. Her throat was breaking with suppressed tears, but it seemed to him that she looked perfectly calm, as if breaking an engagement were the most everyday affair.

However, despite his temper, he was very ashamed of himself, and he mumbled, "You might at least wait for me."

The gross injustice of this slightly restored Philadelphia. "Oh," she said, "that of course is all women are for. To wait. And wait and wait—You go your way, Jamie, and I'll go mine. I daresay we were never suited to each other, we lived too close; neighbors do not always make the best husbands. You may well come back to find me nicely settled with a couple of bairns and a kind gentleman to look after me."

Jamie did not answer as he might have done that this would be remarkable in the course of six months. But then at that moment such sense of humor as he had was gone beyond recall, and the whole idea of the Grand Tour dusty in his mind. Even the thought of foreign countries was uninviting and, if Philadelphia had then told him that her mother had given them permission to marry, he would possibly have abandoned the whole scheme and put the ring on her finger again.

But she said nothing more, and he looked at her in angry desolation, wanting her with a passion that he did not know existed, thinking bemusedly that if only he had been permitted to kiss her and make love to her, this would never have happened. He said in a subdued voice, "I'll be back, Philly, whether you want me or not."

She answered, making a prim little face, "We'll see. And now you must go, Jamie, for I fear we might be disturbing mama. She may be awake now, and must be wondering why you are here for so long."

He said, "Goodbye. I'll be writing to you."

"No," said Philadelphia in a clear, forceful voice. "No, Jamie. If we are going to break, we will do it properly. There will be no point in sending me letters, for I shall not read them, I shall simply tear them up."

He said in more normal tones, "Christ, you're a perverse bitch, Philly," and as she exclaimed in outrage, "That is no language for a gentleman to use—" he came up to her in a rush, flung his arms round her so tightly that she could not free herself or strike him, and kissed her on the lips three times, each kiss more violent than the last.

Then he released her, shouting, "I will write!" and the next moment was gone, with a banging of doors that would certainly waken poor mama, even if she were sound asleep. Philadelphia heard him tearing down the street as if all the devils of hell were after him—which indeed they might well be, after such lewdness and profanity.

She fell back on the sofa, so bewildered, so miserable, so battered that she hardly knew whether to laugh or cry. She ended inevitably by crying, but her strength was gone, and her tears were weak and sniffling: she simply sat there in a huddle, the water trickling down her cheeks.

Chapter 3

Philadelphia grew aware, not for the first time, of the extraordinary talent of gentlemen for seeming to be in the right when they were really entirely in the wrong. Nothing could excuse Jamie's behavior in leaving her for six months, simply to enjoy himself in the most doubtful manner, especially as he expected her to sit there, placidly waiting for him as if he were the only man in the world. It was disgraceful, it was abominable, it was unpardonable, and this portrayal of herself as a kind of patient Griselda was so outrageous that Philadelphia stopped weeping, and shook with rage instead, sitting there very upright, her hands clenched in her lap. Jamie should have crawled out in abject penitence, and instead of that, had rushed away as if it were he who had been insulted and betrayed. And here she was, bereft, with this blackguard of a boy who said he loved her, gone, and, what was more, convinced she would be waiting for him, despite all that she had said to the contrary.

I probably will be waiting, thought Philadelphia in a fury, then, leaping to her feet, she exclaimed aloud, "No, I will not!" However, this defiance was merely words. Among the *ton*, so she understood, meetings were arranged for nubile daughters through dances and dinners and little teas but it seemed that a girl, even a pretty one, who had no social opportunities, was virtually condemned to spinsterhood. She was now painfully aware that she knew no gentlemen at all.

"I shall have to marry Mr. A.," said Philadelphia and, as she said this in ringing tones, stood up as if she were making some kind of declaration. But her foot caught in the broken glass, and this reminded her that she had not been up to see mama, who would certainly have been wakened by all this noise, who would need her pillows rearranged and perhaps want a hot drink.

The shock of her remissness almost pushed thoughts of Jamie out of her mind. She went softly and swiftly up the stairs, to pause halfway as Lucy came out of the kitchen into the passage.

Lucy's face wore a strange, sly expression, and her wide mouth was curved in a grin. Philadelphia, seeing this, flushed. She was not so stupidly innocent that she could not read that look very well. Jamie had stayed a great deal longer than he usually did, Lucy would have heard all the clatter and banging of doors, and she realized suddenly that she must look horridly disarranged. Those violent kisses had pulled half her hair out of its pins, and the little scarf worn to hide the shabby yoke of her dress, was now twisted round one shoulder. But she said nothing, only raised her chin proudly, and went into mama's bedroom, calling her name as she did so.

Lucy, giggling a little, went back into the kitchen. Who would have thought this stuck-up little miss had such fire in her? Lucy might not know how to boil an egg, but she knew all about goings on, and if there hadn't been goings on in the parlor, then she didn't know what the words meant. She opened the cupboard where she kept a secret bottle of gin, and was about to take a hearty swig to restore herself, when she heard a cry from upstairs and the sound of Miss Philly flying out on to the landing.

She slammed the bottle back and stood there, breathing heavily, her mouth going down at the corners. Lucy knew all about goings on—and she knew about disaster too. The cry and the frantic footsteps told her everything. When Philadelphia's voice, thin and high, came down to her, calling out, "Lucy, Lucy! Oh come upstairs, come at once!" she knew that this was the last night she would spend in the kitchen. If there was one thing she could not endure, it was a corpse, and she would be willing to wager that the old girl had gone at last.

She came heavily and reluctantly up the stairs. Philadelphia's ashen face confirmed her worst suspicions. She stepped fearfully into the bedroom, her eyes swiveling round to the bed.

Mrs. Smith had died quietly. In her dying she had not even disarranged the bedclothes. It was as if she had fallen asleep. Philadelphia, standing beside her and so appalled that she could no longer speak, looked down at her. She had seen death once before, with papa, but he had taken the whole day to die, they had all been at his bedside, and now mama, whom she loved so much, had died alone, with no one even to take her hand.

She turned to look at Lucy, already half out of the door. She whispered, "Oh Lucy, what am I going to do?" then saw even through her grief that there would be no comfort here: Lucy's face was working with disgust, and in that countenance there was neither compassion nor understanding.

Philadelphia thought, I cannot bear it, I cannot, but she spoke in a voice that came out clear and firm. "I would like you to go round to Dr. Lewen, please, Lucy. Tell him what has happened. Ask him to come immediately."

Lucy, backing towards the staircase, answered hysterically, "I'm leaving. You'll have to go yourself, miss. I'm not staying in no house with a corpus. I'm going this minute, and I'll trouble you for my wages."

Philadelphia, aghast, cried out, "But you can't leave me here! Surely a few more days—"

Lucy was now halfway down the stairs. Her voice came out shrill and angry. "I won't stay with a dead 'un, I won't! You couldn't expect it. I'm an honest girl, I am, I do my work, no one's ever complained, but stay in the house with *her*, I won't do it, I won't, I tell you. I know my rights, I'm not a fool. I'm leaving this very instant."

Philadelphia looked at her in silence. It was the first time she had ever heard Lucy utter so many consecutive sentences. She did not believe that Lucy was an honest girl, and the work she did was negligible, but at least she would have been some kind of company, at least it would have meant that she would not be alone with her mother dead, her engagement broken and nobody, nobody at all, to advise or comfort her. Charlotte of course, to do her credit, would fly round immediately, but there seemed to be no means of letting her know. In that moment Philadelphia hated Lucy so much that she was thankful she would be out of the house. A girl like that would not so much as trouble herself to make a hot drink: even if she stayed, she would crawl about the place like a cockroach, exuding the silent insolence that was her greatest attribute.

She said quietly, "Very well, Lucy. If you must—I suppose you could not call on my sister on your way? No. I see you could not. I will fetch my purse."

And this she did, counting out the money into Lucy's grimy palm, knowing that every coin was being scrutinized.

"There's an extra shilling for today," said Lucy.

Philadelphia looked at her. Lucy tried to meet her gaze, but could not: she looked down, her mouth bunched sullenly.

"Here is the shilling," said Philadelphia, and set it smartly down in her palm.

"I suppose," said Lucy in what was almost a grunt, "I could give you a drop of my gin, only you do go on so about such things, you're so mim-faced, you're like them church ladies, you don't hold with such things."

Philadelphia had no idea that Lucy had a bottle of gin on the premises, but really, such things were unimportant now, and perhaps it was a small sign of grace that the girl should offer it to her, even if papa would almost have fainted at the idea of it. She said, "Thank you, Lucy, that's kind of you. I appreciate the offer but, as you know, I never touch strong liquor. You'd best go and do your packing."

Lucy scurried away thankfully. Philadelphia, feeling as if she were immersed in some hideous dream, went back into the bedroom and knelt down by her mother's side. And she wept, silently but making no attempt to stem her tears, so overcome with shock, sorrow and exhaustion that she did not even hear Lucy coming back into the room, a small bundle under her arm.

Lucy mumbled, "I'm going now, miss."

Philadelphia rose to her feet. She moved clumsily like an old woman. Her face was gray-pale and her eyes swollen with weeping. For once her beauty was smuged and blurred. Lucy thought she looked a rare old sight. No wonder the young gentleman had rushed out of the house like that. Yet a faint feeling of shame stirred within her. She never thought of anyone but herself, she had little but contempt for a young woman who seemed incapable of enjoying herself in any way that Lucy could fathom, and the scrimping and pinching that went on in the household, seemed to her ridiculous. There was probably plenty of money, for all miss went on so about it, and in any case all this nonsense about not getting into debt was to Lucy incomprehensible. If she owned a little house like this, she would be buying herself fine clothes and ordering chicken and gin every day, never mind if she could pay for it or not. There was indeed nothing about Philadelphia that she admired: the unrouged face, the scraped back hair—pretty enough, but she made nothing of it—and the dreary clothes, would have made Lucy's friends die a-laughing.

But the stony grief in Philadephia's young face—she was after all not much older than Lucy—stirred a faint compassion within her. She said grudgingly, "Well, I daresay I could leave a message with your young man, miss. I'm sure he'd be round like a shot. I know where he lives, you sent a note round once when the old lady—" She swallowed, then continued, "When madam had one of her bad turns. It's not far from here, and I'll do it to oblige."

This was not entirely provoked by pity or good nature. Jamie was an exceptionally good-looking young man, with his chestnut-brown hair and bright blue eyes, and Lucy had always made a point of looking sideways at him, and brushing against him if they passed in the passageway. She sometimes wondered what a beautiful boy like that could see in such a prim-do-gooding little piece like Miss Philly: she would gladly have warmed his bed for him if he had so much as suggested it, but unhappily he seemed to be unaware of her existence. She thought now that if she went round to see him, he would be impressed by her good nature and might even give her a kiss. It was of course quite different with the doctor, who was a dull old man, and as for Mrs. Charlotte, who lived miles away, she was everything Lucy detested: rude, domineering, and always finding her work to do.

She looked quite hopefully at Philadelphia, then saw to her irritation that her young mistress was in no way impressed.

Philadelphia said in a quiet, flat voice, "No, thank you, Lucy, that will not be necessary."

Lucy exclaimed, "Oh well, if that's all the thanks I get—" and rushed out of the room without even saying goodbye. The haste was not entirely due to bad temper. In the bundle that contained all her meager belongings were several articles that were not hers at all, including a few silver spoons and a pretty brooch that she had had her eye on for some time. She had also looked longingly at the tiepin on the mantelpiece, but she knew that Philadelphia treasured it, and decided it would be too dangerous.

Philadelphia at that moment would not have cared if she had rifled the entire house. She listened wearily to Lucy running down the stairs, heard the bang of the front door. There seemed to be a great deal of door-banging today. The house fell back into its lonely silence. She came back to her mother's bedside. She stood there, saying aloud, again and again, "Oh, mama, mama, what am I to do?"

She longed for Jamie more than anyone else in the world. He would of course have come round immediately. He believed that men were there for crises, and he would at once have taken upon himself the full responsibility of everything. The doctor would be sent for, Charlotte would be informed, and there would be a fine, broad shoulder to weep on. Occasionally Philadelphia, in one of her more analytical moods, had wondered if he would not have preferred her to be more dependent on him. But of course in the circumstances she could not call on him. It would be both feminine and unfair: he would certainly cancel his tour, he would feel it his duty to marry her.

"I'm not going to be married out of duty," sobbed Philadelphia, then she saw that, whether Jamie was at her side or not, she could not stand there crying and doing nothing. She pulled the sheet over her mother's face, shuddering a little at the touch, for she was young and alive, and death was a terrible thing. Then she came very slowly downstairs, thinking bemusedly that somehow she must get to the doctor. It never entered her head to ask the neighbors to help her. She did not after all know them, and this was her responsibility; it somehow seemed essential that she must manage everything by herself. But she was human after all, she felt quite ill from the shock, and she knew that she could not at that moment walk the quarter of a mile that would take her to the doctor's house.

The evening had done nothing to mitigate the storm heaviness, but she thought that a little fresh air might restore her, so she opened the door and stood there on the top step, a sad, desperate little girl who could only see that her whole world had tumbled on top of her and who lacked the strength to do anything about it.

And while Philadelphia stood there, and Emma, now at home, reclined on the sofa, brooding and eating sweets, Mr. Atherton and Ferdy were walking home from Holborn. Their walk was not entirely steady, for they had drunk a great deal of wine. Indeed, Ferdy, who could hold his liquor amazingly when at the tables, had the curious habit of going to pieces once the game was over. He was never drunk, in the sense that he could sober up immediately if the need arose, but he seemed to enjoy letting himself go: he lurched from side to side and sang as he zigzagged on. He had no social graces whatsoever, but he did possess a surprisingly sweet and tuneful voice, only the songs he sang were invariably of an indecorous nature, and the one he had selected now was so obscene that passersby glared at him in disapproval.

Mr. Atherton was not singing: in any case he had little ear for music. Drink did not have on him the amiable effect it had on Ferdy. His head was aching, there was an evil taste in his mouth; the taste was not entirely due to wine. Evenings with Ferdy always ended like this. The tavern at Holborn—it was little more than a bordello—had been dirty and ill-favored, and Mr. Atherton had not cared much for the fat and brassy whores who leered at him, murmuring obscenities in his ear, nor for the hard-eyed men who on seeing them instantly surrounded them, believing them to be animals for the catching. They were, as the evenings progressed, to learn better, and from this Mr. Atherton derived a certain savage amusement. Ferdy was so deceptive-looking. These men, all professional gamesters, murderers and thieves, must have thought he was hardly worth the rooking. His foolish, decadent face, with its gargoyle resemblance to the noble family from which he came, gave the impression that he was not only easy game but an idiot: he giggled a great deal, and the white-lashed eyes flickered from one to the other as if he were trying to appease them.

Mr. Atherton himself played well, but he did not have Ferdy's flair: besides, he played fairly which he always suspected his friend did not do. He had for a long time been convinced that Ferdy was a cheat and a swindler. He did not carry loaded dice, for that would have meant a slit throat, but his sleight of hand was remarkable, his movements unnaturally swift. Mr. Atherton had decided at the beginning that it was better neither to know nor understand. It was certainly nothing that the swindlers ever detected, and they surely must know all the tricks in the calendar.

They stayed for over three hours. Sometimes Mr. Atherton won, and sometimes he lost. In the end he walked out with more than he came in with: if Ferdy had not been at his side he would hardly have carried that sum more than a couple of yards. It would have been lunatic to come to such a place on his own. As for Ferdy, the play played itself out in the usual fashion. It would always be the same until one day he met someone more sly than himself or someone angry enough to stick a knife into his long, gangly back. At first he lost, and each time he lost he giggled, the eyes blinking as if he were surprised and afraid. Mr. Atherton saw the other players nudge each other with little sideways grins. This was easy game, the poor devil had not a chance in hell. Then Ferdy won and lost again, then he won twice and lost once, and suddenly, for all the foolish face did not change, the mouth still open, the eyes still flickering, he went on winning and nobody could stop him. The men, all professionals, stopped grinning. Their faces grew grim and intent, they plied him with wine which he drank down by the bottleful, yet still he won, making little helpless gestures as if astounded by himself: the money beside him grew and grew until at last the other players could play no more.

"One more game," he said in his lisping voice, "Oh, gentlemen, just one more game!"

He always said this. It was the coup de grâce.

But there were no more games, there was no more money. Some of the men slid out through a side entrance, and two of the whores came instantly forward to put their arms round the visitors' shoulders, trying to distract their attention by devices so clumsy as to be immediately obvious.

Mr. Atherton and Ferdy shrugged them off. They strolled out, hands in their pistol pockets. They walked side by side, shoulders touching. Once outside, instead of making for the main street, deserted at this hour, they slipped into an alleyway that they had carefully noted before they came in: there for a while they stood in the dark, backs against the wall. It was a moment that Mr. Atherton enjoyed more than the whole game: sometimes he suspected that it was for this alone that he joined Ferdy in these nocturnal adventures.

Soon—it was always the same—they saw the shadows creeping out of the tavern's side entrance, looking everywhere, their silhouettes expressive of a bewildered fury. And presently Mr. Atherton and Ferdy crept out of the other end of the alley, and soon were walking home, with no more danger than the odd highwayman or pickpocket.

One day someone a little more intelligent would follow rather than wait for them, and that would be the end of such excursions.

"We take a devil of a risk," said Mr. Atherton to Ferdy.

"We win a devil of a lot of money," said Ferdy.

As they came into Montagu Road, Mr. Atherton was thinking not of Philadelphia, who had temporarily slipped from his mind, but of Emma.

He supposed that one day he might marry her. She came, like Ferdy, from a good family, with a cold, correct brother who did not approve of her, and with whom Mr. Atherton had nothing in common. Unlike Ferdy, however, she was plump and beautiful and usually delighted with herself, in a childish fashion that was not unappealing. She was also extremely intelligent, though naturally she disguised this as well as she could, for it was not a feminine asset. Sometimes Mr. Atherton suspected that she was entirely respectable at heart, for all she had been his mistress for nearly a year: it was these contradictions in her nature that fascinated him and always brought him back to her, however badly they quarreled. He told her once that when she married, she would become a matron of awe-inspiring virtue, at which she laughed without attempting to contradict him.

He was never sure how much he loved her, but he was beginning to find that he could not do without her. Even now he found that he was thinking in pleasurable anticipation of their reconciliation. He found himself imagining what form it would take, for Emma was unpredictable and sometimes violent: there might be tears or insults or the sweet humility that never failed to astonish him, all the more so because it was genuine. He knew too that she was entirely faithful to him, which astonished him even more, for he had not by any means been always faithful to her.

He stopped at the corner of the road to see if her carriage were there. He remarked to Ferdy as he did so, "I do not believe I shall ever understand women or be able to do without them."

It was not a particularly intelligent remark, and Ferdy, who considered women to be lower than animals, merely giggled and jangled the money in his pocket.

There was no sign of Emma's carriage. The road was deserted. It was still well before midnight, but the even numbers retired early, and the odd numbers had not yet come home.

There was, however, one even number who was not in bed. Mr. Atherton's disappointed eye caught the glimmer of light. He stopped, then turned to look more closely at Number 22.

The front door was open. The light came from a lamp inside the hallway. Philadelphia stood on the top step, leaning against the wall. Mr. Atherton, for all he was a little drunk, had to see that her attitude was one of the utmost weariness and dejection. He could not make her out very clear, but her head rested against the doorpost as if she were too tired to hold it upright, and her hands were clasped tight before her as if this helped her maintain her balance.

There was no sign of the tall, good-looking young country bumpkin, and Mr. Atherton instantly assumed that there had been some violent lovers' quarrel: he was of course perfectly right, but naturally had no idea of what had happened afterwards. As he himself had quarreled with Emma, he was at once filled with sympathy and, in his inebriated state, felt that this was an ideal moment in which to make acquaintance and perhaps share confidences about difficult lovers.

He laid his hand on Ferdy's arm. Ferdy reacted instantly by thrusting his hand into his coat. Mr. Atherton had noticed this habit before: whatever it signified, it certainly was threatening. However, Ferdy then giggled and apologized: if he had meant murder, he had changed his mind.

"For God's sake," said Mr. Atherton crossly, "do you have to kill me for touching you? Look over there. That girl in the doorway. Can you see her?"

Ferdy looked. He saw her plainly enough. There was nothing wrong with those shifty, gray eyes. She seemed to him completely uninteresting, but then he only saw people in terms of rank and money. The creature's clothes were laughable and she seemed very untidy. He could not see her face properly, but it was plain she was a nobody, a common person: only common people lived in the odd numbers of Montagu Road.

Then he remembered Tom's absurd idea about calling on someone. This must be the girl. He said, with for once no smile, "Do I have to see her? It's just some servant girl taking the night air."

"It certainly is not," said Mr. Atherton. "That is Miss Philadelphia Smith. And," he added, "she has the air of one who's thrown low dice without ceasing for a week."

Ferdy thought she had no air at all, and said so. He also thought his friend must be either touched in the wits or drunker than he seemed. Ferdy detested

Emma who was equally revolted by him, but he could understand why Mr. Atherton was struck on her: she was a good looker and possessed a great deal of money. But this girl obviously had nothing, and why anyone should want to know her, he could not imagine.

"We are going over to comfort her," said Mr. Atherton.

"For Christ's sake, why?"

"Because I like the look of her, and because I believe we are in the same circumstances. And you shall come with me. That kind of girl would never entertain a gentleman by herself."

"That kind of girl," snarled Ferdy, "would probably be enchanted to entertain a gentleman on any terms whatsoever."

"If you say that again, I'll knock you down," said Mr. Atherton in the outraged manner of the intoxicated, and he even went so far as to clench his fists.

Ferdy looked at him unbelievingly, and he went on, "We'll go across now, this very instant," seized his friend by the arm and almost dragged him across the road.

Philadelphia had been standing for some time. She found herself so exhausted that she could not move. She looked without surprise at Mr. Atherton, now walking towards her, though she noticed vaguely through the mist of her misery and fatigue that he was accompanied by a horrid looking fellow who shambled along beside him and who kept on giving her the most unpleasant smile she had ever witnessed. Once the unbelievable prospect of Mr. A.'s actually coming over to speak to her, to smile at her, to bow to her, would have knocked her through the floor, and produced ten pages in her diary, but now she simply inclined her head, her eyes moving away from the pair of them. How could she even consider them when two things were wretchedly entwined in her weary brain: poor mama lying dead upstairs and Jamie, with her ring in his pocket, traveling through Paris and Rome, with no doubt a bedizened harlot on either side of him, and a bottle of wine to his lips.

And so when Mr. Atherton, a little astonished himself, said, "Good evening, Miss Philadelphia," it did not even seem odd that he should know her name. She simply answered, "Good evening," then went inside the house, with the two gentlemen, both now taken aback, and one of them growing more and more bewildered, following after her.

Mr. Atherton was not sober enough to reason clearly, but he had to see that this young woman was acting very strangely. There was nothing even remotely provocative about her, yet it was inconceivable that a well brought up girl should virtually invite into her home two gentlemen whom she had never met before. A faint unease began to grow within him. Perhaps the poor child was out of her wits, perhaps she was ill: it was almost as if she did not know what she was doing.

As for Ferdy, he was already bored to death, yet he too was curious: he and Tom had had some odd adventures in their time, but there had never been anything quite like this.

Philadelphia did not invite them into the parlor, but then she had not really invited them in at all. It was true that the parlor, normally so neat, was a horrid mess, what with the crumby debris of the cake and all the broken glass and fruit juice on the floor, but she did not even think of this, she would not have taken it in if she had seen it. She continued on her way upstairs, for no reason except that it was the only thing in her shocked mind, and the two gentlemen, more and more astonished, followed after her.

She opened the door of her mother's bedroom. Mr. Atherton and Ferdy, standing behind her, looked over her shoulder: as both were a head taller than Philadelphia, it was the natural thing to do. Mr. Atherton did not at first see the sheet-covered body on the bed. He only saw a sparsely furnished, spotlessly clean little room, with a dressing table, a cupboard, a table and a chair. The muslin curtains at the window hung limply in the breezeless air. Then he heard Ferdy make a kind of retching, choking noise, and his gaze moved to the bed.

He said before he could stop himself, "Oh my God!"

Philadelphia said almost inaudibly, "She died this evening. She is my mother, sir. She died, and there was no one with her, but I did not know, I did not know."

And she began to cry again, not even covering her face with her hands. The tears poured down, and her eyes were fixed on the bed.

There was a rushing sound as Ferdy pelted down the stairs, and out into the street. Ferdy would have cheated his own grandmother and shot her afterwards, he had murdered innumerable times, and there was not a streak of compassion in his heart, but, whereas violent death simply made him laugh, ordinary death in a bed was something he could not stomach. The sight of that unmistakable sheeted mound made him feel quite faint, and the one idea now in his mind was to get out of here as fast as he could. What the devil Tom had been thinking of to bring him here in the first place, he could not imagine: it was obscene and ridiculous, and it would be a long time before he accompanied him again.

Once out in the street he was violently sick, then, still shaking with the horror of it, walked as quickly away as his long legs would carry him, to collapse at last into a tavern of his acquaintance where for once he did not even look at the tables, only proceeded with the utmost speed to down a bottle of wine.

Mr. Atherton for a minute remained still and silent. It did not enter his head to run away, besides he could not leave this poor child crying her heart out, without apparently a single soul to help her.

Philadelphia, struggling to control herself, whispered, "I'm so sorry, I do not mean to cry, but I simply do not know what to do."

And at this dramatic moment the storm at last broke, and a great peal of thunder, accompanied by forked lightning cracked through the room: a few seconds later the rain began to fall.

Mr. Atherton, momentarily floodlit, like a devil on the stage, was almost sober now, for the shock had shot the drink out of his brain. But he was still a little lightheaded, and afterwards he could only assume that what with the wine, the shock and the violence of the storm, a temporary insanity had possessed him. He moved towards the still weeping Philadelphia, and slowly sank to his knees. He reached up for her hands and took them in his own. As she bent a bewildered, tear-stained face upon him, he said, "My poor child. I think the first thing you need is a glass of wine. I will take you downstairs, and then we will see what can be done to help you. You can leave everything to me. All I need is the address of your relatives—You do have relatives, I presume?"

"Yes, sir," said Philadelphia, like a child. She was so astonished that she stopped crying.

"And—yes, of course—your doctor. You are not to worry yourself about anything," said this new Mr. Atherton, startling himself afresh with every word he spoke. "This is something for a man to deal with. No young girl should have to cope with such a dreadful situation. I will take my carriage to see to everything immediately. But in the meantime you must on no account stay in this room. You cannot help your poor mama any more, and I am sure she would be happy to think that you are being looked after."

Emma would have laughed—No. Emma would not have laughed at all. Emma might be wild and reckless, Emma might care little for her own sex (who cared less for her) but she was by no means without heart, and in a strange way she was a practical girl. She would at once have taken Philadelphia in her arms and conducted her downstairs, and she would certainly do as Mr. Atherton had suggested—dose her with a large glassful of wine. Ferdy had gone, thank God; one could not see Ferdy comforting anyone, but Emma's heart, far more tender than she chose to admit, would be touched, and indeed, it would be hard for any normal human being to withstand the pathos of this young girl who looked so pitifully unhappy and lost.

Mr. Atherton was still on his knees, illuminated from time to time by the lightning flashes across the sky. He had no idea why he was on his knees. He had never before knelt to anyone. So far he had behaved more like a gentleman than he would have believed possible. The situation was in every way entirely novel to him. Death occurred among the odd numbers as it did among the even, but there were always ser-

vants and physicians in attendance. The whole matter
was decently organized, such unpleasing things as
corpses were quietly removed, and one was left to
dress in black, shed a few tears and attend the funeral, with the loved one nailed securely into a coffin
and shrouded in sweet-smelling flowers.

That a young girl should be left to deal with everything on her own was insupportable.

However, at this moment, preluded by another
crack of thunder, rather different thoughts began to
creep into Mr. Atherton's mind.

Kneeling as he was, with Philadelphia's hands still
clasped in his, he looked up at her from this somewhat
unusual angle. She was dressed in some plain blue
gown that did not suit her, and the hands in his were
rough from housework. Yet, as Mr. Atherton now realized, she had a most delightful figure, the curves of
which were plain to see as he gazed up at her, and her
face, seen close up, was really an extraordinarily
pretty one, despite the reddened eyes; indeed, it was
more than pretty, it was beautiful. The features were
neat, the mouth soft and endearing and the complexion of a delicacy such as he had never seen. And she
certainly had the most enchanting hair, a glossy dark
brown, curling like a baby's about her brow and
cheeks. He seemed to remember that normally it was
pulled back over a high forehead, thus giving her a
prim, almost academic, air, but at the moment it was
in complete disorder, so far out of its pins that it fell
to her shoulders.

Mr. Atherton rose at last to his feet. He found himself quite stiff from his prolonged kneeling. For one
second the two of them were so close that his face
almost brushed against hers. The contact startlingly
excited him so that the thought shot into his mind and

stayed there: I want this girl, she is different, she is like no one I have ever met, I want her, and I am going to have her.

He had to see this was a little unseemly in the setting and circumstances, and he hastily added to himself, not that I wish her harm, but she does not look as if she had had much amusement in life, it will do her all the good in the world to be loved and petted and looked after.

He moved back. This was not the moment to show such emotion, besides, he was genuinely grieved for her, and wanted to do nothing but protect her.

He said gently, "Come, Miss Philadelphia. We will go downstairs, and presently I will fetch your friends."

She only said in a wan little voice that touched him very much, and made it difficult to keep his arms from going round her, "I'm so tired."

"My poor little darling," said Mr. Atherton, forgetting himself, "Let me help you downstairs."

She answered with a dignity that showed him this was not going to be as easy as he hoped, "I am perfectly capable of walking by myself, thank you."

And she proved this by walking in front of him, her back very upright, only as they came down to the hall, she turned and said in that childish way of hers, "I do not usually behave so badly. But you see, Jamie has just left me and I thought we were getting married, and now I think I have nobody left in the world."

You have me, thought Mr. Atherton, and could have embraced the errant Jamie for behaving so helpfully. He demanded, "Who is this Jamie who dares to treat you so? I'll beat him for you, if you wish. Where is he? What is his address?"

"Oh, he is no longer here. And," said Philadelphia, much to his surprise, "he is even bigger than you. Besides, he did not mean to treat me badly. He wants me to wait for him."

"Which I trust you are not going to do?"

They were standing just outside the parlor. The storm was dying down. The thunder had grown fainter and sounded at longer intervals. The air for the first time that day felt fresh and cool. Philadelphia gave Mr. Atherton a faint smile. He saw with a stab of desire and pleasure that in ordinary times she would be a pert and lively girl, this was no little country miss to say, "Yes, sir, No, sir." She was plainly capable of standing up for herself.

She said, almost with regret, "Oh, I daresay I shall. I told him I would not, of course. I gave him back his ring. But then women have their pride, you know, though as a gentleman you would not perhaps admit it." Then she gave a little cry. Perhaps it was the warmth of sympathetic companionship, the awareness that she was no longer alone, but Philadelphia was reverting a little to her normal self. She exclaimed in the utmost dismay, "But everything is so untidy. Oh, I am so ashamed. Pray, sir, if you would leave me alone here for just a few moments, so that I—"

"Don't be silly," said Mr. Atherton, and suddenly smiled at her.

He saw her instantly withdraw, more in spirit than in action. That smile, which was delightful and which had knocked Emma out of her flirtatious dalliance, made her for the first time aware of the person in whose company she was. Up till now she had not really thought of him as Mr. A., the handsome gentleman from Number 23, who drank and gambled and spent his time in the company of loose women. So lost had she been, so wretched, dazed and exhausted, that she could only see him as a kind friend who had turned up miraculously in her moment of greatest need. She now realized that the person who had knelt before her, held her hands, offered to help her, was the wicked and wonderful Mr. A., himself, and at this thought the color swept into her pale cheeks so that she looked quite staggeringly beautiful. And that second of pure beauty took Mr. Atherton's breath away, and the desire, up till now dim and dreaming in his mind, consolidated so that briefly his face became calculating, tough and purposeful.

Philadelphia did not notice this, nor would she have recognized its implication, even if she had done so. She answered, a little coldly, "Very well. We are not usually in such disorder. If you will please come in, sir, and if I am not asking too much of you, I will give you my sister's address, and my doctor's. It is very late, but in the circumstances—" The steady voice quavered. "I still cannot quite believe it. She seemed so much better." She looked up at him and half extended her hand. "I will never be able to thank you enough. I do not know what I would have done, if you hadn't come. Why did you come?"

"I saw you standing in the doorway," answered Mr. Atherton correctly, "and I thought you seemed unwell. I live opposite you, you know."

"Oh indeed," said Philadelphia.

"I have seen you before. I do not suppose you have ever noticed me."

"I so seldom go out," said Philadelphia, "that I have no chance to notice anyone." In making this remark, she was not only obeying papa's precept always tell the truth while at the same time not committing herself, but was also following Mr. Atherton's pattern in leaving a great deal unsaid. She pushed the broken glass away with her foot, and motioned him to sit down in the one armchair.

"Your beau seems to have amused himself," said Mr. Atherton, looking down at the debris.

"He was very upset," said Philadelphia.

"He had no right to upset you. I feel I owe you an apology for my intrusion," said Mr. Atherton, "yet in the circumstances I cannot be anything but happy that I came. I merely intended to ask you if you needed any help—"

Philadelphia said gravely, "I have never needed help more in my life."

"So I should imagine. Though surely your young gentleman could at least have fetched your sister for you—"

"Oh, of course he would have done so. Jamie is not unkind. But this—this happened after he left. I went upstairs and—and—I'm so sorry," whispered Philadelphia, beginning to cry again, "but even now I cannot quite believe it."

"My poor girl," said Mr. Atherton with genuine feeling, for it seemed abominably bad luck to break an engagement and lose an apparently much loved mother on the same evening. He wanted badly to take Philadelphia into his arms, but saw this would be misinterpreted. It was true that his designs were by no means what they should be, but at that moment he was moved by genuine compassion and simply wanted to comfort her. He deliberated the matter briefly and decided against it. He did not think she would scream, but thought it might be possible that she would ask him to leave the house. It would not start their relationship off on the right footing.

He handed her a large, clean handkerchief, then

said in a brisk voice, "A glass of wine, I think. Where do you keep it?"

"I never drink wine," said Philadelphia, blowing her nose.

"But surely—"

"Papa would never permit it. He said it was an invention of the devil. We do not keep it in the house at all," said Philadelphia, forgetting that a whole bottle of the wicked stuff was in the sideboard cupboard, just behind Mr. Atherton's left shoulder.

"But my dear girl, this would be purely for medicinal purposes. Does not the Bible say—"

" 'Use a little wine for thy stomach's sake.' Everyone always quotes that at me," said Philadelphia. "I have never found it an excuse for going against my papa's wishes, even though he died two years ago."

"I cannot believe in the circumstances—let me fetch a bottle over. It will not take me a minute."

"No, thank you," said Philadelphia. There was no doubting the finality of her tone.

Mr. Atherton was silent for a while. This was an unexpected difficulty. He had never so far met a young woman who did not drink at all. It was a pity, for wine—not naturally that he would wish to make her drunk—was a great remover of principles. Emma's principles were somewhat nebulous, and there was no fierce papa in her background, but on the night when she at last consented to stay with him, they had consumed a bottle between them. He foresaw a long and complicated campaign, and his spirits rose joyously to the challenge, for there was nothing more tedious than an easy conquest, and so far in his life he had seldom met a woman who resisted him.

However, all this must wait, and he contented himself with looking round the room, while Philadelphia wrote down the addresses in a neat, round handwriting.

The parlor, like the bedroom, was plain and clean: in normal circumstances it would certainly be immaculately tidy. Mr. Atherton found himself too restless to remain seated, so he rose to his feet and paced up and down during the writing of a small note to the doctor. He gazed up at papa's portrait, his mouth a little wry. The old gentleman looked something of a tartar, with great bushy eyebrows and a firm, unsmiling expression. He would not, thought Mr. Atherton, have much truck with a would-be seducer of his daughter. He would certainly consign the villain to the flames of hell. Mr. Atherton resisted a strong urge to salute him, and turned his attention to a shelf full of books. One of the books had been taken out, and was lying on the table. It was the first volume of *Pamela*. He suppressed a smile. So the little miss who never touched wine had her moments of weakness after all. He moved over to the mantelpiece. There were a few ornaments of little value, two silver candlesticks, and a small bowl, made of some kind of colored stone. It came from Inverness, but of course Mr. Atherton did not yet know she was Scottish, though he had remarked some kind of accent. Being tall, he found it easy to look inside the bowl, and what he saw nearly made him whistle. He picked the object up, dropped it back again, then swung round to stare at Philadelphia, who had now finished, and was tidily closing up the desk.

The object was a small tiepin, with a minute enamel portrait of himself in its head.

Well, well, well, said Mr. Atherton to himself, and who would have believed it? He had been sorry to lose it. It was a pretty thing, not of any particular value, but given him a long time ago by another girl who was now married to someone else. How it had come into Philadelphia's possession he could not imagine. She could hardly have stolen it in the accepted sense of the word, yet she had certainly taken it, and she must know from the portrait that it was his; apart from this, why was it kept in the bowl and in such a prominent place on the mantelpiece?

He saw that he did not know Miss Philadelphia Smith at all. She might not drink wine, and he would have sworn that her virtue was impeccable, but a young woman who had picked up his tiepin—he must have dropped it in the street—and kept it for so long, was, to put it mildly, interesting: it would indeed be worthwhile making her more intimate acquaintance.

You wait, my little madam, said Mr. Atherton softly to himself, you just wait!

Philadelphia rose from her chair and came up to him, the piece of paper in her hand. As he took it from her, he smiled again. It was not quite the smile he had given her before, it seemed to her almost a wicked smile and, though she did not understand it, she had the sudden strange conviction that it was almost like—she could not imagine why the phrase came into her mind—a declaration of war. It brought the color flaming into her cheeks, and at the same time filled her with a strange, unprecedented excitement that was almost fear. Then it was done and he looked perfectly normal and composed.

He said, "I will go to these people immediately, ma'am." He studied the paper. "I believe I know exactly where they are. In any case my coachman will find them easily enough. You can rest assured that I will bring Madam Charlotte back with me, within the

hour. You must be wanting her here more than anyone."

"I think," she said a little nervously, for the strange
tremor still possessed her, "that poor Dr. Lewen
should be informed in the morning. He works so hard,
and he is an old man—I do not like to drag him out at
this time of night. There is after all nothing—nothing
he can do. But I do want to see Charlotte very much
and, though she'll be surprised to be wakened at this
hour, I know she'll come immediately. This is all most
kind of you, I don't know how to begin to thank you."

I'll teach you how to thank me, murmured Mr. Atherton's unregenerate inner voice, but he merely said
with some formality, "Please do not thank me. I am
only delighted to be of service. I will bring your sister
round then, and in the morning I will call again to
help you with the arrangements."

"Oh no," protested Philadelphia in a flurry, "you
have done so much, and I couldn't possibly trouble
you any more."

He took her hand in his. It was done in the friendli-
est manner. Not even Jamie could have objected. "It
will be my pleasure," he said. "And now I will wish
you good night. I dare not urge you to drink a glass of
wine, but at least when your sister is here, let her
make you a hot drink, and then you should go straight
to bed. Have you no maid to help you?"

"She has gone. She would not stay in the house with
someone who is dead. She was never much use. I am
better off without her."

"Then I will see you tomorrow. Don't forget, I am
there to help you in every way possible. You must not
hesitate to ask me."

"I don't know why you are so kind to me," said Philadelphia.

Mr. Atherton, who was in some ways an honest man, wondered for one fleeting second if he would have been so generous to a plain, fat girl with a poor complexion. He hoped he would, but he was not quite sure. However, he simply smiled, kissed her hand, and left, to order his carriage.

Philadelphia felt that in the circumstances she was entitled to watch openly from the window, and she saw him cross the road and step up to his own front door. The rain was still pouring down. He turned before he went in, and sketched her a salute. Despite everything that had happened she was aware of a brief, reprehensible upsurge of happiness.

Then she moved back into the room, to sit on the sofa and wait for Charlotte.

Chapter 4

Philadelphia was unaware that for a girl who normally led so quiet a life she was in this one evening creating considerable turmoil. But then it had been an appalling day, and she knew nothing of Mr. Atherton, except in her imagination. She did not pause to think that it was somewhat unusual for a gentleman of quality, one of Montagu Road's outstanding odd numbers, to concern himself so deeply with a neighbor he did not know, and she did not consider that this might cause a certain amount of speculation among people who so far had never heard of her. She only saw Emma as a beautiful young lady who made violent and unladylike scenes, and as for Ferdy, if she thought of him at all, it was simply as someone quite horrid with his sneering, debauched face and shambling walk. Indeed, he reminded her of Daftie Johnny, who lived in one of the Inverness alleys, and who frightened all the children by shambling up to them, kicking his legs out much as Ferdy did, and poking his vast, dribbling face into theirs.

It certainly never entered her sad, bewildered mind that Mr. Atherton might have any kind of design upon her. Sometimes she saw herself in the mirror, and was innocently pleased that her nose was not as long as Charlotte's, that her skin was free from blemishes, and that her hair, for all she scraped it back, curled charmingly. But then there was the washing to do, and the dinner to prepare, and really, it hardly mattered what one looked like: when it was all done and poor, darling mama settled for the night, all she could think of was bed and sleep.

And now she sat there, so dragged down with exhaustion that she could not fully take in what had happened. Mama was dead. The words rang in her clogged brain, over and over again. What her future would be, she did not know. There had never been any money since the small income was drowned in the southern seas, and Mr. Bridges, who would appear after the funeral, would doubtless tell her that she should look for a post as companion or as a governess for children. Philadelphia thought dimly through her unhappiness and fatigue that she might enjoy working with children, though they said that rich people's bairns were terribly spoiled. Yet it seemed a little dreary that she must spend her life in other people's houses, where she would be nothing better than a kind of superior servant, and from this melancholy reflection her mind drifted back to Jamie who, to do him credit, knew nothing of what had happened, but who had nonetheless abandoned her in her hour of need.

No doubt he was now delighted with himself, free from encumbrances, thinking happily about the loose women he would soon be meeting in France, for everyone knew that France was full of them, indeed the whole of Europe was populated by them. Philadelphia's mind was populated by them too: she saw them with brightly rouged cheeks, frizzled hair and smothered in perfume: there was no place there for a simple mind or virtuous heart. "Oh, I hate you," whispered papa's good little daughter on a sob, then she fell into an uneasy sleep, her cheek cradled against the cushion.

It was the first time in her life that she had slept without saying her prayers.

She did not know that she was doing Jamie an injustice. He was not delighted with anything, much less himself. He had never been particularly interested in loose women, and the few he had run into in the back streets rather frightened him with their flashy clothes and lewd remarks. He found himself remembering things he longed to forget: beautiful, angry eyes shining with tears, a voice saying, "I'll not wait for you, Jamie." He all but rushed back to Number 22, but was too proud to do so. He kicked about his rooms, exasperating his landlady who lived underneath, and then he drank a couple of glasses of wine, for he had long ago broken away from the rules of his boyhood, and kept a bottle by the writing table. If only they could have married—he knew he would never again meet anyone he loved so much, nor anyone so beautiful. But there seemed to be no chance of marriage for perhaps years. The poor old lady lay sick upstairs and might continue so for God knew how long, and the weekly visit had become almost unendurable, when they could not so much as kiss each other, when all they had to do was make polite conversation over the cake and cordial.

Jamie said, "Oh God!" then, "Oh, damnation!" both of which exclamations would have compelled papa to throw him out of the house. At last he flung himself down on his bed with a distempered head and a vast sense of loss: he could not sleep and lay there wakeful till the early morning.

Emma was meanwhile growing more and more afraid. She had always believed that man was the hunter and that no sensible woman should ever pursue her lover: as she was young, handsome and rich, she had never until now had the least need to exert herself. The young men had courted, flirted, languished and mourned, while Emma amused herself, rewarding this one, snubbing that one, knowing that she only had to lift a finger and half the male population would come running.

Tom would never come running. And it was after midnight, and he had not so much as sent her a message. Emma was badly frightened. She grew aware that unless she saw him, she would not be able to sleep a wink. She had finished all her sweetmeats, and she felt a little sick. The tears were trickling down her cheeks, as they had been doing on and off for some time. It must be another woman. Who could it be? She knew perfectly well that he was unfaithful, but up till now it had never mattered, it had simply been the occasional partner for the night. Perhaps at last it was serious. Perhaps her abusive words and ugly screaming had disgusted him. Emma, very pale now, rang the bell and ordered her carriage. It was nearly one in the morning. It was a ridiculous hour to call, and Tom would be angry with her, but she could not bear it any longer, she felt she was going mad. One day, if Tom really left her, or she perhaps left Tom, it might be different, for she could not live without men, but she knew at this moment that she could not live without Tom, and this time he did not seem even to want a reconciliation.

The coachman drove her to Number 23. It was a strange hour for his young mistress to go calling, but he was accustomed to her sudden, wild moods, and hoped that the gentleman—he was perfectly aware of the situation—would receive her kindly.

Emma was informed that Mr. Atherton was out. It was not, however, the first time she had called so late, and the footman led her into the drawing room, to wait for him: she was furious when some ten minutes later Ferdy shambled in, in his usual state of dirt and disrepair.

Ferdy had drunk two bottles of wine, and was quite restored. He had forgotten about that disgusting dead body, and he had quite forgotten that he was never going to see Tom again. His pockets were full of money, for he had won enormously and, as money was the only thing that really interested him, he decided to call back at Number 23, and persuade Tom to have a little friendly game with him so that he could win some more. In any case, whether Tom were there, or not, he dared not walk home with such wealth upon him. He had risked it once already this evening, which was foolish of him: he was lucky not to have been set upon. There was a long journey home ahead of him, for Ferdy had no fixed dwelling, and slept in taverns and brothels and dives on the seamy side of London: if Tom were not there, he would have to leave the money behind him.

He was no more pleased to see Emma than she him, but he saw at once from her pale, melancholy expression that the quarrel was not made up and, as he disliked and resented her, he was delighted.

Emma looked at him with a loathing she made no attempt to conceal. She was reclining there on the sofa and, when she heard the footsteps, believed it was at last Tom. She was too genuinely upset to put on any pretense, and she swung her feet to the ground, her whole body quivering with relief and welcome. When she saw who it was, she could have cried. Ferdy always seemed to her the most repulsive creature she had ever met: the very sight of him made her feel ill.

This she once told Mr. Atherton. "How can you endure him?" she cried. "He is disgusting. He's so dirty. He—he smells. And that face—"

"He can hardly help his looks," replied Mr. Atherton.

"But he can help looking so nasty and evil. You can see he is a thief and a murderer. One day he'll put a knife in your back. You could not possibly trust him. I simply cannot understand why you invite him here. Nobody else does. All my friends bar the door when they see him coming."

Sometimes Mr. Atherton did not understand the acquaintance either. He did not like Ferdy. Nobody liked Ferdy. Ferdy did not have a friend in the world, and it was perfectly true that, for all he was a duke's son, he was never invited anywhere: the few who started off by doing so regretted it most bitterly, for his manners were vile and he was incapable of behaving himself in a seemly manner, even if there were Royalty present. But of course he was an extraordinary gamester, and Mr. Atherton possessed this

strange love of low company, and taverns and brothels on the wrong side of London. Such places could
only be frequented with someone like Ferdy. But it
was true that one day Ferdy might well murder him,
especially if Mr. Atherton won more money than he
did, and perhaps it would be better to make the trips
less frequent, and not encourage Ferdy to call in
whenever he felt like it, always without invitation. Mr.
Atherton did not pursue the matter, only he did his
best to keep Ferdy and Emma apart: it was not after
all his fault that they were now together, eying each
other in mutual dislike.

Ferdy surveyed Emma now. He did not miss the
flash of revulsion that crossed her face, though she
managed to greet him civilly enough. He was in no
way impressed by her beauty, but then the only
women he knew were prostitutes and hussies, and he
regarded them simply as animal conveniences. He
thought Emma was a fat little bitch, and the femininity
that glowed from her, even in her misery, made him
want to vomit. He wanted to beat her, to tear her fine
clothes from her, to reduce her to a howling thing that
begged for mercy. Something of this must have been
betrayed in his smile, for Emma glanced up at him
and involuntarily moved away. There was a new box
of sweetmeats at her side, and she picked out a piece
of pink sugar that she did not really want. One discarded suitor had once described her as a piece of
marzipan, and she knew perfectly well that her
plumpness was dangerous. Yet her figure nonetheless
was beautiful and Mr. Atherton, who enjoyed it and
who in rare fanciful mood had declared that Rubens
would have worshipped her, refused to let her restrict
her eating, which from time to time she struggled to
do. He could not, he said, imagine his Emma, with her

creamy skin and pitch-black hair, becoming fashionably thin and, once, when he saw her picking at a small piece of chicken and pushing away the more exotic dishes, threatened to leave her.

She said now in her throaty voice, trying to ignore the shambling limbs and the weak, vicious face, "Well, Ferdy? Are you looking for Tom too? I have no idea where the wicked fellow can be. Did he not tell you when he was coming home?"

And, as she spoke, she helped herself to yet another sweetmeat, this time a confection in orange and white.

"You're becoming as fat as a sow in litter," said Ferdy with his customary elegance. He lowered himself into the nearest chair, his long legs kicked out in front of him.

"I daresay I am," said Emma.

He swung himself to and fro in the chair. He was incapable of staying still. He said idly, "I fancy Tom will not be back tonight."

"Indeed?" said Emma. Her face was turned from him, and her voice was cool, but the malice in Ferdy's voice was unmistakable, and the alarm signals were beginning to pulse through her.

"I fancy," drawled Ferdy, "that he may not be back for some time."

"And what makes you say that?" asked Emma, still not looking at him. She stretched out her hand for yet another sweet, then drew it back.

"I wonder," said Ferdy, "if you have ever noticed the cottage opposite us?" He pulled some of the money out of his pocket and began to juggle with it: some of the coins rolled on to the floor.

"Why the devil should I?" Emma was genuinely surprised. Nobody ever noticed the even numbers. The people who lived there belonged to another world.

When earlier in the evening she had stared at Philadelphia, she had not really seen her at all, only been dimly aware that some young woman was standing on the doorstep. She had, as it happened, passed Philadelphia several times in the street, but was quite unaware of her. The world was all odd numbers, with fine clothes and bright lights: the dull little mice who scuttled away across the road were nothing to do with her. But she was becoming badly rattled, and Ferdy's play with his money beat on her nerves. She exclaimed angrily, "Oh for God's sake, stop doing that! You're like an old Jew. Are you trying to tell me how rich you are? You are always rich. It's all you care about."

"I won," said Ferdy simply, and fell silent for a while, totting up the exact amount. It was a great deal, even by his standards. By the end of the week it would all be gone. His hands caressed the coins. The fingers, as Emma noticed for the first time, were long and white and elegant. They were the only presentable thing about him. It was the one attribute bequeathed him by the noble family so passionate to disown him.

She waited as long as she could endure it. But she could not stop herself. She burst out, "What is all this nonsense about the cottage opposite?"

The clock said it was half past one. It was not unusual for Mr. Atherton to return late, indeed, sometimes he did not come back till early morning, but never before had he been absent without telling her where he was.

"There is a young lady who lives there," said Ferdy. He returned the money to his pocket, and watched her, catlike, through slitted eyes. "Her name is Philadelphia."

Emma, recovering herself a little, shrugged. The plump white shoulders, one of her greatest beauties, moved gently up and down. "And what is that to do with me?" she said.

"We called on her this evening," said Ferdy. He was vastly enjoying himself. He had wanted for a long time now to get his own back on Miss Emma Slade, with her contemptuous air and her obvious dislike of him. Hers was one of the many houses where he was never invited. Once he had tried to gatecrash, and two of the footmen had thrown him out. Ferdy was enormously strong, but the two of them had overpowered him, and he had landed in the gutter. He had never either forgotten or forgiven and intended one day to shoot both footmen down. He could not very well shoot Emma, though he would have gladly done so, but by Christ he would make her sorry. This was a chance in a million, and he was going to make the most of it.

He saw the color flow up her throat and cheeks. She always blushed easily. He could not see her face except in profile, but this was enough. The long, thin face twisted into a wide, savage smile.

Emma was too astonished to make much pretense. She said unbelievingly, "You called on someone in the cottages! I don't believe it. Why should Tom do such a thing? You're making it up. You're drunk."

"If you don't believe me," said Ferdy happily, "you will have to ask Tom, will you not? I suppose she was quite a pretty girl. I myself abominate these simple country misses, and there seemed to me nothing about her to admire, but Tom was quite *épris,* poor fellow, I have seldom seen him so overcome. She was alone in the house, except for a corpse. I gather that it was her mama, but then I do not care for graveyards, so I left.

I believe I was definitely *de trop*. I have no doubt that Tom comforted her all the better for my absence. He seemed to know her very well."

There was silence. Then Emma whispered, "You're mad. You're a damned liar."

Ferdy rose to his feet. He was still smiling. "I am neither drunk nor mad," he said. "As for me being a liar, I suggest you find out for yourself, my darling—"

"Don't call me that!"

"I think you should investigate. I think you should do so soon. It seems to be quite serious. I wish I could see the battle," said Ferdy. "Well, ma'am, I will now leave you. I will also leave the money I have won. You can tell Tom that it is in his desk. I feel it would be unwise to walk the streets of London at this hour with so much in my pockets."

Emma could have asked for nothing better than to have him knocked on the head and thrown into the Thames, but she knew she had badly betrayed herself, and so she said nothing more, simply watching as Ferdy deposited what seemed to her an extraordinary amount of money in Tom's desk.

She said in her normal husky voice, "You seem to have done remarkably well."

"I told you," said Ferdy. "I won." He added with an air of assumed innocence that contrasted unpleasantly with a face that did not know what innocence was, "I am a most fortunate man."

"So it seems," said Emma, and permitted him to kiss her hand in farewell, though the touch of those wet, loose lips made her flesh crawl: after he had gone she would feel compelled to wash herself.

"Will you tell Tom I have made him my banker?" said Ferdy at the door.

"I doubt I'll be seeing him tonight," said Emma. "It is late, and I think I must go home."

He looked her up and down. He gave her what Philadelphia would have called his daftie smile. "I think you are very wise," he said.

Emma waited until she heard the door close behind him. Then she sprang to her feet and began to pace up and down, twisting her hands together as she did so. Her face was wild with distraction. Ferdy would have been delighted. God knows what all this was about, but obviously it was something that had been going on for a long time. And she had never even suspected! The others had frightened her, but they had proved easy enough to demolish. There was that little bitch from Devonshire, who set her cap at Tom for the whole of one season, and then there had been Lady X, older than he was, divorced, as experienced as Emma herself, and dangerous. But this one—what did Ferdy call her?—this little country miss from the cottages opposite—If Tom were calling on her so late, and apparently helping her in a time of family crisis, this must be serious indeed, this must be dealt with immediately.

Emma swore, stuffed two more sweetmeats into her mouth, then pulled at the bell. She told the footman to bring her carriage round—no, she would not be waiting any longer, it was too late, perhaps he would tell Mr. Atherton that she had called—then came out of the house into the street. The rain had stopped. It was a fine, still night, fresh after the storm. Ferdy had waited to see if she would appear. He was standing at the corner watching, half hidden in the shadows. As Emma stepped on to the roadway, he slid round the bend. Once he was out of sight and hearing, he burst into a great peal of high, falsetto laughter, clapping his hands together, rolling about in an ecstasy of enjoyment. This was worth all the playhouses put together, and serve my fine, bloody lady right. He only wished he could see the meeting between the two girls, for Emma, he was convinced, would seize the first opportunity she could find to take a look at her. They would probably scratch each other's eyes out. "Oh, how I wish I could be there!" cried Ferdy aloud, much to the astonishment of a passer-by and indeed, if he had not walked on so quickly, he would have realized his ambition, for at this moment Philadelphia also opened her front door and came out again on to her doorstep.

Her uneasy sleep had only lasted for a little while. Shortly Mr. Atherton would be back with Charlotte, and perhaps Henry too. Philadelphia, so tired now that she almost dragged herself along, wanted her sister's company and comfort badly. The two of them had never got on particularly well, but Charlotte was not unkind, merely selfish; she was older, she was family, and at such a moment would without any doubt run to take some of the responsibility off Philadelphia's weary shoulders. It was true that Mr. Atherton seemed only too willing to do everything he could, but how lovely it would be to be able to cry without restraint, be cosseted and petted and patted on the back. When she heard the sound of carriage wheels, she assumed immediately that Mr. Atherton was back, and almost ran out to greet her sister.

Then she saw, with a sinking of the heart, that the carriage was not for her, but for someone out of Number 23. She saw vaguely that this was the plump beauty who liked to make hysterical scenes. It did not interest her. It never struck her for a moment that she could interest Emma. She only sighed, praying that

Charlotte would come soon: her mind was filled with thoughts of poor mama lying upstairs, and of Jamie no doubt looking forward to his wicked foreign tour. And the tears filled her eyes again so that she was half blinded: she did not so much as notice that Emma, on the odd number side, was gazing at her with a piercing attention.

Emma saw an exhausted young woman who seemed to have been weeping her heart out. She did not look at all like a glamorous lightskirt, out to seduce a gentleman. In her present state she could hardly have seduced anyone. The clothes she wore were terrible, her hair was untidy, and the hands dangling in front of her untended, as if she had done a great deal of housework. Then Emma raised her eyes to study her rival's face, and her lips tightened, her expression grew intent and fierce.

Philadelphia was tired to death, and her eyes were red and swollen, but the beauty there was such as could not be mistaken. It shone forth through the tears and fatigue, and Emma knew that her suspicions were only too correct: this was serious. Ferdy was a fool to dismiss this girl as a country miss, but then Ferdy knew nothing about women except that for him they were cheats and whores. Certainly this Miss Philadelphia did not come from the upper classes, her grooming was appalling and she probably knew little of the ways of high society—but it was in all these things that the danger lay. Gentlemen like Tom, with looks, breeding and money, met beautiful women by the score, and the courtship game was played out as formally as a minuet; it was all in his way of living and one lovely lady was remarkably like another. Emma's own success was largely due to her being wilder, less conventional, more daringly impudent. But she knew only too well that to the sophisticated, jaded palate, simplicity, if coupled with such extreme natural loveliness, could prove infinitely more seductive than the made-up beauties with their hair piled high and their gowns cut low. The very fact that Philadelphia wore an unmistakable air of innocence made her doubly dangerous: Emma, composed now, a little pale, instinctively prepared for battle.

Her coachman was still outside Number 23. Emma on an impulse told him to wait, picked up her skirts and crossed the road until she stood outside the steps of Number 22.

She said, "Good evening, ma'am."

Philadelphia turned her head slowly to look down at her. She really is a beauty, thought Emma, almost in a panic, it is quite extraordinary. How is it possible that she leads a life that appears to be isolated and virtuous, looking after some old mother and with no gentleman to protect her? Such looks in our world would make her either a courtesan or a queen.

Philadelphia answered her in a choked voice. She had some strange kind of accent, but it was not disagreeable, and her voice was pleasantly pitched. She answered, "Good evening," without astonishment. Once she would have been amazed that the plump, quarrelsome lady spoke to her, but she was long past any such emotion. Indeed, she was almost past caring: her eyes moved away to see if Mr. Atherton was returning.

"The rain has stopped," said Emma. It was hardly scintillating conversation, but she wanted desperately to hear what this girl had to say for herself. However, Philadelphia assented, then fell silent again.

Emma waited, but perceived that the child was too exhausted even to speak. The unhappiness on that

beautiful, drawn face provoked a faint pity in her—
Emma, as Mr. Atherton knew, was not lacking in
heart—but then she remembered that this was her rival, and the compassion vanished. And at this moment
she heard the sound of distant carriage wheels, and
any softness that might have been in her, was swept
away. It was Tom's carriage. She knew the sound of it
well enough: there was a faint squeak to one of the
wheels that she had remarked before. So he was coming back to see his young lady, no doubt hoping to
spend the night with her. Emma, suddenly sick and
shaking, turned away. The last person she wanted to
see just now was Tom Atherton: the confrontation
would come later, this was not the moment.

She did not trouble to say goodbye to Philadelphia,
who would probably not even have heard her. She ran
across the road without dignity, jumped into her own
carriage, then ordered the coachman to take her to the
corner, then pause. He obeyed. This was becoming a
real drama. He sat on his high seat, his back very
straight, and pretended to be taking no notice, but he
saw, as Emma saw, Mr. Atherton's carriage halt outside Number 22, where the gentleman, accompanied
by a lady he had never seen before, stepped down.
There was a highly emotional greeting between the
two women, then, their arms round each other, they
went into the house, with Mr. Atherton following
them.

"You may drive on now," said Emma calmly.

The coachman thought it was all confoundly odd.
He was perfectly aware of the situation between his
mistress and the gentleman from Number 23, and
what all this was about, he could not imagine. However, Emma, if sometimes autocratic and occasionally
disposed to tantrums, was a generous employer who

paid well, and her staff in the big house in Park Lane, where she lived with her brother, were sentimentally disposed to hope that she would land this fine gentleman who appeared to be very much in love with her. The coachman was affronted that Mr. Atherton should be calling on someone else, and made disapproving, clucking sounds to himself as he drove home.

Emma, if he had known it, was as baffled as himself. She could not pretend that the scene she had just witnessed looked like a love nest, yet it must be so, Tom was the least platonic of men, if he were interested in a female, his intentions tended to be perfectly plain. She ate two more sweets from her candy box, and began to consider her campaign: her face was intent and cold, revealing nothing of the terror and rage within her.

Philadelphia, unaware that she had become a small war in her own person, wept gratefully on Charlotte's shoulder, while Mr. Atherton waited a trifle impatiently for the storm to subside.

Charlotte had not been best pleased to receive a caller at that hour of night. She was in bed when Mr. Atherton knocked at her door, and sound asleep: Henry was away, down at the docks, to receive a new consignment of China tea. However, the sight of such an elegant and handsome gentleman at once appeased her rage, and when she heard what had happened, she at once fetched him wine and cakes, begging him to rest himself while she dressed again. Mr. Atherton, waiting in a drawing room furnished in the most excruciatingly bad taste, was cynically amused to note how much money and pedigree counted with females of her kind: if he had been a lower class of person she would have snubbed him into the floor, but one glimpse of him and the carriage outside with its small coat of arms, was enough to provoke the most effusive of thanks and compliments.

He did not of course suspect for a moment that Charlotte was rapidly changing her opinion of the poor little sister. How on earth Philly—Philly!—had found herself so elegant a beau, she could not begin to imagine. It was plain that she had more to her than Charlotte would have believed possible, and amid her genuine grief and sympathy, a kind of bewildered respect surged up: it seemed that the simple little ninny she had always believed Philadelphia to be was not quite so simple after all.

For a time both sisters were so distressed by what had happened that they entirely forgot their differences. Charlotte now became the elder sister, a rôle she had seldom played but which in the emergency she did very well, and Philadelphia, sobbing in her arms, was thankful to have her there and said so repeatedly, much to Charlotte's satisfaction.

At last Mr. Atherton discreetly disappeared. This, from every conceivable viewpoint, including both that of good taste and good sense, was no moment in which to pursue his intentions. He had at least established himself as a friend of the family which, considering that he had made Philadelphia's acquaintance barely a few hours ago, was remarkable in itself. He bowed to both ladies, wishing them good night. He had to wonder privately how Philadelphia could have such a vulgar battle-axe for a sister. He told them that he would be pleased to call the next morning to see what further help he could give them. And then, very exhausted by this time, for it had been an eventful evening, he returned to Number 23.

He was informed by a sleepy footman—it was now

half past two—that both Emma and Ferdy had called.
He was only thankful that neither of them had waited
for him. He never wanted Ferdy's company except on
their gambling excursions, and the thought of Emma
provoked an uneasy guilt, even apprehension, for she
certainly would not accept the prospect of a rival. He
did not immediately go to bed. He poured himself out
some wine—Charlotte's husband might specialize in
tea, but the wine in his home was abominable—then
slumped in an armchair and brooded on Philadelphia.
This would not be an easy campaign. She was young
and she was innocent, but she was by no means lacking in sense: he had the idea that when she was restored to good spirits, she might have a sharp, perceptive eye and tongue. He was filled with a sudden
warmth and affection: she was a lovely little girl and
he did not mean her any harm. And, thinking this, he
dropped off. The last thing that floated into his consciousness was a small tiepin with an enameled portrait of himself in its head.

The two Smith girls sat up talking till nearly four
o'clock. Charlotte, like Mr. Atherton, would have
given a great deal for some wine, but knew her sister
far too well to mention it. She made a hot toddy instead, and sat on the end of Philadelphia's bed while
she drank it.

"You'll not be able to keep on this house," she said.

"I suppose not," admitted Philadelphia sadly. It was
not much of a house from the odd numbers' stand-
point, but it was her home, she had lived here for the
past six years, and the thought of leaving it depressed
her so much that she nearly started to cry again.

"Well, one has to be practical," said Charlotte, patting her shoulder. "Mama had no money at all, as you

very well know. Besides, you cannot live here entirely on your own. We will no doubt see Mr. Bridges after the funeral. Mr. Atherton kindly said he would inform him of what had happened." She paused at this moment. She was dying to ask Philadelphia about Mr. Atherton who seemed, she thought, distinctly smitten. She had noticed the look in his eye. How on earth Philly—But that must wait. The poor child was in no state to discuss anything except the immediate problems. She went on, "I don't suppose there will be a penny, but at least we can sell the cottage. One thing we may be thankful for—there will be no debts. Poor, dear mama never, never ran up debts in her life."

Philadelphia suddenly wished, with a gross lack of gratitude, that Charlotte would go to bed. It seemed so heartless to be discussing money, with mama lying dead next door. But Charlotte always prided herself on her practical nature, besides, money was of the greatest possible interest to her and, as Philadelphia knew, she always counted every penny she spent and regarded extravagance as a major sin. She had briefly allowed herself to be upset and softhearted, but now she was her normal self again. There was after all no point in going on crying, and Philadelphia seemed to be in no condition to look after herself.

She said briskly, "You will of course come to live with us."

Philadelphia was aware of a sinking of the heart. Of course she would have to live with Charlotte. It was a foregone conclusion, and it had already been sticking in her throat like a fishbone. She had never seriously wished to become a governess. But the thought of that house in Chelsea filled her with an ungrateful dismay. For one thing, she had never liked Henry, who seemed to her a gross and stupid man, and who, whenever they met and were alone together, showed a marked tendency to pat her shoulder, stroke her hand and peer quite impertinently at the bodice of her dress. Papa had never liked him, and papa was a perceptive man. Charlotte of course knew nothing of this, and was far too conceited to believe that her husband could have eyes for anyone but herself, but Philadelphia, by no means unobservant, had for a long time suspected that there might be other women. Tea was such a useful excuse, and surely Henry did not have to do business in the evenings and till such a late hour. She knew that if she were unfortunate enough to be Henry's wife, she would have investigated matters a long time ago. It was only too plain that living in the family would provoke the most dreadful difficulties, and of course if anything happened, it would be entirely her own fault. Besides, there was Tobias. Philadelphia could not by nature dislike any children, but he really was a spoiled little boy, over fat, very greedy and always yelling the place down if he did not get his own way. She naturally would be expected to look after him. Charlotte would never miss the opportunity of an unsalaried nursemaid and at this moment, as if she were following her younger sister's thoughts, she went on in an energetic tone.

"Tobias is so fond of you," she said.

Philadelphia did not think Tobias was fond of her at all, but said nothing.

"He always asks for his Aunt Philly-dilly. That is what he calls you. I think it's so sweet."

Philadelphia glanced at her. She thought the designation was revolting, but remained silent.

"Ellen of course is so unsatisfactory. The nursemaid, you know. Sometimes I am worried to death, thinking about what can be happening when we are out of the house—and of course, as Henry's wife, I have to lead quite a social life. I was going to give her notice anyway, and really, it is quite a dispensation that you are coming, for you can look after the little pet until we find someone else."

"Yes, of course," said Philadelphia.

"Naturally, it'll not be permanent."

"I'll be glad to do anything I can."

"Well, that's settled then," said Charlotte, with a sigh of relief. She added encouragingly, "It will be like old times having you with me again. It'll make life so much easier too. You were always the domestic one, Philly."

Philadelphia saw without enthusiasm that not only would she be looking after Tobias but would also be doing most of the housework as well. Charlotte would get herself an unpaid housekeeper-cook-nurse and general factotum. At least with poor mama she had had a little time to herself, with no one to tell her what to do: with Charlotte she would be ordered about and no doubt be kept busy from morning to night. But she did not say anything of this, only smiled faintly, and said that she thought she could sleep now, she was very tired.

"Oh, my poor child," exclaimed Charlotte, genuinely remorseful, and she sprang to her feet in the quick, forceful way that had always upset mama. She was a big woman, and the violence of her abrupt movement shot half the coverlet off the bed. But she was too inquisitive to leave without mentioning what was uppermost in her mind.

"I suppose," she said, her voice artful, "you will now be thinking of getting married. To Jamie. Where is Jamie? I thought this was his evening for coming round."

"I shall probably not be marrying Jamie," said Philadelphia, closing her eyes.

She waited with dread for the outcry, but there was none. If she had looked at Charlotte's face she would have seen an expression half incredulous, half sly, an expression that said, You minx, I would not have believed it possible. But then, as Mr. Atherton was at the moment the last person in her thoughts, she would not have understood. She was only thankful that Charlotte did not overwhelm her with commiserations, and she turned her face into the pillow, hoping that at last she would be left alone.

Charlotte simply said, "Well, I daresay it's for the best. I never cared much for him, myself. I thought him a conceited kind of fellow. Good night, pet. I'll see you in the morning."

Chapter 5

~~~

Mr. Atherton arrived at eleven o'clock the next morning, bringing a somewhat astonished Dr. Lewen with him. He was plainly dealing with everything with the utmost efficiency. "You really are a natural organizer," Charlotte told him, with a merry little laugh. Then she remembered that this was a house of mourning, and all the blinds were already pulled down: she had not naturally been able yet to buy herself the appropriate clothes, but she had tied a piece of black ribbon round her sleeve. She looked instantly sorrowful and begged the gentlemen to come inside. It seemed dreadful not to be able to offer them a glass of wine, but it was no good arguing with Philadelphia who, despite her shock and grief, seemed more strong-minded on the matter than ever.

Then she perceived that Mr. Atherton was carrying a bunch of hothouse roses, and her eyes sparkled despite herself. She still could not imagine how Philly had managed to find herself so fine and rich a gentleman, but it was very exciting, and she was intensely divided between planning a stupendous wedding filled with people of the *ton*, and praying that the marriage would not take place too soon, leaving her with no one to look after Tobias and the house in Chelsea.

Mr. Atherton hardly noticed her: if he did so, it was with distaste. She was a type of woman he disliked. She reminded him of a governess he had had when very young, who had forbidden him to do almost everything then, when inevitably he did it, had beaten him unmercifully. His eyes turned to Philadelphia, who was at this moment coming down the stairs, and he thought with a stirring of the blood that he had never seen anyone so beautiful in his life.

She had apparently discovered a black gown in her wardrobe and, though it was of poor material and badly cut, it brought out startlingly the luminous delicacy of her complexion, the color of her brown hair and green eyes. If she had bought herself some rich, fashionable dress, it would not have suited her half so well, yet Mr. Atherton would have been willing to swear that she was entirely unconscious of the effect she was creating. Charlotte beside her, in her garish clothes, looked like a chambermaid. She was very pale but entirely calm. She looked a little as if she were sleepwalking, not quite aware of the world around her. She greeted Dr. Lewen and asked if he would go upstairs, then begged Mr. Atherton to wait in the parlor, which was now immaculately tidy and clean.

As she spoke, her eyes lit on the bunch of roses. Mr.

Atherton saw the swiftly masked expression, and suspected it was one of disapproval. Perhaps among the even numbers it was not the thing to present bereaved young ladies with flowers. Afterwards he was to marvel at himself, but he heard himself saying in a grave voice, "I thought, Miss Philadelphia, you might wish to lay these on your mother's bed. I did not have the pleasure of knowing her, but I would be pleased if you would accept this as a mark of respect."

He knew at once that he had said the right thing. The color tinged Philadelphia's pale cheeks, and her hand fluttered out at him as if she would touch him. She whispered, "Oh, sir—" and for a moment he feared she would burst into tears. But she did not, only took the flowers and gave him such a loving look of gratitude that he was unexpectedly ashamed of himself: his first thought had been that it was a pity to waste such beautiful blooms on a dead woman whom he did not even know.

He said to Charlotte, as Philadelphia ran upstairs with the flowers, "I think my presence would be an intrusion at the moment, so I will leave you, but in view of the fact that there appears to be no gentleman to help you—"

"My husband is away," said Charlotte, "otherwise he would of course see to everything."

"Naturally," said Mr. Atherton, wondering what kind of man would have the temerity to marry this gorgon, "but as he is not here, I would regard it as a privilege if you would leave all the arrangements to me."

"That is extraordinarily kind of you," said Charlotte, a little taken aback, for it was beyond belief that this fine gentleman should concern himself with funerals, especially as he had never even met mama.

"It seems to me the most natural thing in the world," said Mr. Atherton, thus giving the impression that he spent half his life coping with other people's domestic emergencies. He had in actual fact never dealt with anything like this before, and had not the least idea how to set about it. However, his butler would no doubt advise him: his butler always knew everything, and if not, cook would certainly be *au fait* with funerals, for when she was not preparing excellent meals, she was always holding forth on relatives who had passed over to the other side. Mr. Atherton added a little tentatively, for it seemed to him that the whole situation was becoming a fantasy, "May I suggest that next week, when you are both a little recovered, you do me the honor of taking a glass of wine with me? Perhaps you would like to come after luncheon, about five o'clock, and then we can discuss if there is anything else I can do."

Charlotte, whose mind invariably ran on how to improve her social position, did a little silent sum of addition, and reckoned that the quality could not dine till two or three. The Smiths had always taken their main meal of the day at twelve, and Charlotte and Henry followed suit. This was plainly not genteel. She must mention the matter to Henry. It was the kind of small detail that was so important. He would grumble, of course, but in future luncheon would never be before two. All this meditation took only the fraction of a second, and she replied with an instant eagerness, "Oh, we would be delighted, I'm sure. I am eventually taking Philly back with me, but of course we have to see the solicitor, and there will be a great many things to clear up, so I shall be in and out of the house. It's an elder sister's duty, you know. Philly's a sweet girl, but her head is sometimes in the clouds, and I have always been the practical one. I imagine she will not be here for longer than a month or so."

Mr. Atherton's expression did not change, his smile remained civil and unwavering, but his heart sank. This was not at all according to plan. He had taken it for granted that Philadelphia would continue to live at Number 22, with perhaps a maid found by himself, and then he could call in more and more frequently to comfort her and help her with any business matters that arose. The maid, if discreetly chosen, could be very helpful, and her wages could be privately supplemented by himself. To have her quartered with her sister was an obstacle he had not allowed for, especially as Charlotte lived so far out in the village of Chelsea. It would be natural enough for a friend living opposite to call in frequently: it would be considerably less so if he were miles away. But there was nothing he could do about it, and already little plans were fermenting in his mind. He expressed his pleasure that the two ladies would shortly be coming to see him, kissed Charlotte's hand, which was large and beringed, and begged her to give his compliments to Miss Philadelphia who, as the doctor was still there, would doubtless prefer not to be disturbed.

Then he left for his own home across the way, while Charlotte gazed after him and wondered irrelevantly how he and Henry would get on. Not very well, she thought, as she prepared to drive back to Chelsea, to make sure that Tobias was all right, and to see if Henry had returned.

The funeral took place three days later. The arrangements were made almost entirely by Mr. Atherton's butler, though the two Smith girls did not realize this: it was conducted at the local church, and there was a magnificent wreath of flowers from Mr. Atherton himself, though he could not bring himself to attend the ceremony. It was all something of a play to him. He was not heartless, and Philadelphia's grief moved him very much, but after all he had never so much as set eyes on the late Mrs. Smith, he hardly knew of her existence until it terminated, and the whole business was now so extraordinary that he could not take it quite as seriously as decency and convention demanded. The day after that, when Mr. Bridges the solicitor was due to call, was fixed for the visit, and this interested Mr. Atherton far more; he found himself waiting with an almost boyish excitement to see Philadelphia again, and hardly thought of Emma at all.

Emma was thinking a great deal about him, indeed she was thinking of little else. She did not come back to Number 23. It almost killed her to stay away, and for the first time in her life she grew a little thin, for she was so choked with jealousy, rage and unhappiness that she could hardly eat at all. Her household, who were all very disturbed about her, prepared her delicious little dishes, but she simply pushed her plate away, and indeed for a while existed almost entirely on the sweetmeats that were so bad for her. But she dared not call on Tom. He had after all not even sent her a note: for all the attention he paid her, she might have ceased to exist. She learned that the funeral of the girl's mama had now taken place—she swallowed her pride sufficiently to send her maid along to find out—and it seemed that Philadelphia and her sister were due to call at Number 23 the next day. The thought of Philadelphia, however suitably chaperoned, sitting opposite Tom, talking to Tom, drinking Tom's wine and no doubt being flattered and charmed, was more than Emma could endure, and she burst into violent tears. After this, she recovered a little and permitted a young man she did not particularly care for, to take her to the play. She hardly took in one word of it, and the young man found her exceptionally *distraite* and absent-minded. But then he was not to know that she was frantically working out a plan of campaign, and Emma herself was not to know that an ally was waiting for her in the wings, and certainly the most unexpected person.

Mr. Bridges paced up and down the small parlor of Number 22. Miss Philadelphia had begged him to wait for a few minutes while she fetched her sister, who was in the room upstairs. He found it very inconsiderate of the two ladies to keep him waiting, when he had come all the way from the Temple to read them the will.

He was a smallish man, with red hair that strayed out from under his wig, thus giving him a mildly diabolical appearance. He had of course known the Smiths ever since they came to London, but they were not rich, they were in no way important people, and Charlotte, whom he disliked, was of a litigious nature and always asking his advice on silly problems, besides altering her will regularly once a year. However, the present will had its points of interest, and Mr. Bridges, who possessed a sardonic sense of humor, was quite looking forward to reading it out.

He saw, when the two young ladies at last appeared, that no one was going to offer him a much needed glass of wine. Of course the late Dr. Smith would never permit such a thing to be in the house, but Mr. Bridges always hoped that the daughters might change their ways; besides, Charlotte, as he knew perfectly well, regarded wine as necessary for genteel entertaining. However, Miss Philadelphia was made of sterner stuff, and it was plain that what Dr. Smith ordained, was still law.

She really was a most handsome girl—Mr. Bridges, who was human after all, relented a little, saying, "This must be a most distressing moment for you. If you will sit down, I will read out the will. It is very brief."

Neither girl, he saw, was particularly interested. Charlotte would have been passionately excited if she had thought any money was involved, but was convinced there was nothing. She was also very disturbed about Henry, who had still not returned home. It was true that he had sent her a letter, saying that he was delayed down at the docks, but Charlotte was beginning to grow suspicious. He had never been away so long before, no business could surely take a whole week, and she remembered now the fact that he often stayed out till ten or eleven o'clock, without any satisfactory explanation. She was, therefore, not really thinking about the will at all, while Philadelphia sat there quietly, her hands clasped in her lap, thinking in an apathetic way that this was the end of a period of her life, that nothing would ever be the same again.

Mr. Bridges said abruptly, "I think this will may come as something of a surprise to you."

He saw Charlotte's face grow suddenly intent, but Philadelphia continued to gaze into the fireplace: he suspected that she was not even listening to him. Well, she would be listening in a moment, she was human after all, and not even high-minded young females were entirely oblivious of the power of money.

"Your mother," said Mr. Bridges, "always asked me not to tell you this until after her death, but the investments that your family lost in the South Sea Bubble have during the past five years somewhat recovered themselves. There is, naturally, no vast fortune, but whereas it looked at one time as if there would be nothing, there is now a small annual income which, with proper handling, will increase and which is quite a satisfactory sum. Your mother refused to touch one penny of it. She never regarded it as hers, though I must admit that occasionally I tried to make her change her mind."

Charlotte demanded in what was almost a shout, "How much?"

Philadelphia said nothing at all, though at this information she briefly raised her eyes. She did not look even interested. Mr. Bridges shot her one look—where the devil did she get that astounding beauty from?—then, now enjoying the situation, contrived to rustle his papers as if he were perusing them for some final detail.

Charlotte, who really had no pretensions to gentility at all, repeated roughly, "How much?"

"About five hundred a year," said Mr. Bridges quietly, and folded the papers on his knee.

"Oh my God!" said Charlotte in a gasp. A look of ecstasy came over her face, which entertained Mr. Bridges very much. Who would have believed it possible? Oh, it was not so much as the world would see it, but it was not bad, it was not bad at all. Henry—she had momentarily forgotten her suspicions—would be delighted. It would mean a new carriage, perhaps another servant, and certainly a good tutor for little Tobias, when he reached the appropriate age. Perhaps she could buy a new dinner service—so many plates of the old one were cracked—and then Charlotte began to visualize select dinner parties, with Mr. Atherton and his fine friends complimenting her on her good taste and the excellence of her dinners.

Philadelphia still said not a word.

"It is all left," said Mr. Bridges, who was savoring every syllable of this, "to my dearest daughter, Philadelphia, who has so lovingly looked after me, who has generously sacrificed for me her youth and happiness. I may sometimes have appeared ungrateful, but I can never thank her enough for her love and patience and self-sacrifice. I pray that she will now profit from it in great happiness, and accept it as a small repayment for what she has done for me."

This time it was Charlotte who was silent. She had grown so red that Mr. Bridges feared for an attack of apoplexy. But Philadelphia jumped to her feet. The tears were pouring down her cheeks. She whispered, "Oh no, it is simply not possible. Why, she could have had every sort of comfort—My poor mama! And I did so little for her, so little—"

"She obviously did not think so," said Mr. Bridges.

Charlotte was on her feet too. She dwarfed Mr. Bridges by several inches. She said in a fierce, tight voice—how true it was that wills brought out the worst in people—"I simply cannot believe that mama has left me nothing. What about little Tobias? He was her grandson, was he not? I know she loved him. Surely some of this must be for me."

"I fear not," said Mr. Bridges. His face was decently concerned, but the words danced in his mind: You greedy woman, you hardly ever visited her, you shoved the full burden on to your younger sister's shoulders, serve you right, oh serve you right!

Philadelphia had sat down again. She looked dazed with the shock. She did not speak again, and Charlotte suddenly turned to her, then knelt beside her:

her knees, unaccustomed to such a posture, creaked and snapped.

"I know," she said, patting Philadelphia's shoulder energetically, "you find this as unfair as I do. But then, poor mama, she was so dreadfully ill, and I have thought for a long time now her mind was unhinged. After all, you will have no need for money when you are with us. You know that we would never let you lack for anything. Henry will look after your affairs for you, and we could make you a small allowance so that you can buy pretty ribbons and anything else that takes your fancy. Don't fret, my poor little darling. We'll manage everything for you. You don't have to worry about anything. You can always depend on Henry and me." She stood up again, saying in a different, brisker voice to Mr. Bridges, "How can we arrange for the money to be transferred to my husband? It is surely your business to know about such things."

Mr. Bridges remarked, as he had often done before, how the ill-bred change their voice according to the class of person to whom they are speaking. For Charlotte, a solicitor was plainly of the lower orders, so her voice grew loud and harsh, the Scots accent that she preferred to cover up, much in evidence. When speaking to the upper classes she was gentle and over-refined. He looked at her with ironic contempt. He had never been much concerned with the family, but he suddenly knew that he would fight to the death for young Miss Philadelphia, who was after all both a good girl and a devoted daughter, and who still looked dazed with the shock of it all.

He answered with a chilly satisfaction, "That is a matter for Miss Philadelphia to decide. It is nothing to do with you or me."

"What do you mean? Are you presuming to tell me

it's not my business?" Charlotte's voice was almost a shriek. There was not even a pretense of gentility now.

"I am indeed," said Mr. Bridges, angry enough to speak his mind.

"Philly!" Charlotte rounded on her sister, who was staring down at the floor again, and hardly seemed to be taking all this in. "Oh for God's sake, Philly, pull yourself together. You surely heard what Mr. Bridges has just said. You must agree with me. You do not want the worry of all this money. Besides, you surely wouldn't deprive your poor little nephew—"

"There is no need to blaspheme, Char," said Philadelphia in a cool, calm voice. "We have only just buried poor mama." She looked for a moment at her sister, then turned her gaze on Mr. Bridges. He saw first that she had damned fine eyes, and then that she was by no means as simple as he had feared. She was understanding the situation perfectly well. But he was still not convinced that she would be able to stand out against her sister: besides, she did not seem to him a girl to whom material things were particularly important. She said, "I do not think this is the moment to discuss such a matter. We can talk about it later."

She added to Mr. Bridges, extending her hand, "Thank you for all you have done for us. I am sorry you have had the trouble of coming here, and I wish we had a carriage so that we could drive you home."

"I have my own carriage, thank you," said Mr. Bridges, regarding her steadily. He thought she really had an air to her, and like everyone else wondered where that startling beauty came from. Dr. Smith, though an estimable man, was perfectly ordinary, and as for his wife, Mr. Bridges had really only known her in her illness, when her looks were destroyed.

"Oh, I'm glad," said Philadelphia. "I can assure you that we are most grateful for your help."

"You can always call on me at any time," said Mr. Bridges. He would have liked to say a great deal more, but of course he must not do so, especially as Charlotte, looking anything but grateful, was glowering at him and breathing heavily. The battle would begin in due course, after he was gone. He was beginning not to be quite sure who would win it. He made his salutations and went out of the house.

Charlotte was dying to pursue the matter, but now decided it would be best to wait until her sister was in a better humor. She watched Philadelphia, who, her face abstracted, was moving about the room, setting things in order, then said at last, "We are invited over to Mr. Atherton's house, later on, to take a glass of wine with him."

"I do not drink wine," said Philadelphia.

Really, Philly could be incredibly tiresome, one might almost think she was doing it on purpose. She would certainly never find herself a husband if she behaved in this old-maidish way. Charlotte said, controlling herself with an effort, "Well, you can drink water, my dear, if you prefer it. It is simply a matter of convention. But I think as Mr. Atherton has been so civil to us, it is the least we can do—"

"I do not feel," said Philadelphia, "that we should go out so soon after mama's death."

"Mr. Atherton," said Charlotte, her voice growing tight, "has after all been most generous. I do not know what we would have done without him, especially as Henry is still away. I think it would be very rude not to go, and I am surprised you do not see that. After all, we may need his help again, and if we do not turn up, it is unlikely he will offer it."

"I don't understand why he should take so much trouble over us," said Philadelphia.

"You're playing simple, sister. It is plain that he is smitten with you."

Philadelphia turned so startled a look on her that Charlotte was quite taken aback. But she only said, "Oh nonsense, Char. You are simply imagining things. I never met him until the day mama died. But if you wish me to go, I will do so."

And this unfeminine response baffled Charlotte very much so that, what with this and the question of the will, she was left with nothing to say: the sisters sat down to a rather meager luncheon, with nothing but polite conversation passing between them.

After this luncheon, at the unfashionable hour of twelve thirty—"We really must eat later," Charlotte announced, but Philadelphia simply said, "Why?"—the sisters separated. "I must lie down," Charlotte said, "I am absolutely exhausted. If I do not get some sleep, I shall be in no condition to go out." And she went at once to the spare room, to solace herself with some of the bottle of wine she had secretly brought from home, while Philadelphia washed up and tidied the kitchen.

On the way to her room, she opened her mother's door, and stood there in silence for a while. The vase which had held Mr. Atherton's roses stood on the dressing table. The place, with its neatly made-up bed and drawn curtains seemed utterly untenanted. She thought to herself, Oh mama, why did you have to do this? I do not deserve it, and now Char will never forgive me.

Then she went to her room, but she did not lie down, only sat by the window, her chin on her hand. The diary lay, still open, on the dressing table. Philadelphia thought that she would never write in it again: the young girl who had written so many impassioned pages, night after night, seemed someone from another world.

And then she closed the volume, sighing rather dramatically as she did so. It would probably amuse her grandchildren. Perhaps Tobias would like it, in place of the money that everyone seemed to expect from her. Philadelphia half laughed, then sighed again, and fell into a somber brooding.

Charlotte had, as usual, quite underestimated her. She had always done so since childhood, but then she was a domineering girl who liked to shout and bully, and Philadelphia had quickly learnt the only way to deal with her: she seldom argued, simply vanished from the scene. And went her own way, which was something Charlotte was incapable of understanding. "You are so weak," Charlotte once said to her, and Philadelphia, though she looked surprised, smiled and did not contradict her. She reflected now on Mr. Bridges' astonishing announcement. It had amazed and bewildered her, it had also given her a possibly shameful lift of the heart. The only alternative to being a governess, if she gave up the money, would be to become an unpaid drudge in Charlotte's untidy and ill-managed household. Philadelphia had no illusions whatsoever about Charlotte, and knew that her sister expected everything to be handed over to her, as if it were her right. She supposed she loved her because one always loved one's sister, but that love would die rapidly in the house in Chelsea. Everything would within a week fall upon her shoulders, including presumably Henry, who had always been tiresome, and the adjective "temporary" with regard to her looking after Tobias was stupid nonsense. Charlotte would never part with an unpaid nursemaid.

And with five hundred a year, which was after all a tidy sum for one who had never had a penny, one could preserve one's independence in decency and dignity. One could even—within the prescribed limits, of course—enjoy oneself.

There was also something else. There was Mr. Atherton. Philadelphia up to this moment had hardly considered Mr. Atherton at all, except as the romantic fantasy gentleman who lived opposite and beguiled her imagination, who had for some extraordinary reason arrived at her bitterest hour of need and taken everything upon his shoulders.

He is smitten with you.

That is what Char had said. Smitten! What a horrid, vulgar word. Philadelphia refused to believe something so absurd, yet she had to admit that it was strange that he should take so much trouble on her behalf. He must surely like her a little. And because she was human, if at that moment a trifle battered, she found herself positively beaming, and instantly switched off her smile because she was ashamed of herself.

On an impulse she jumped to her feet and picked up the volume of *Pamela* that she took to bed with her.

She read:

He clasped me to him with great ardour, and said, "Hide your dear face in my bosom, my beloved Pamela! your innocent freedoms charm me! But then say how well—what?" "If you will be good," said I, "to your poor servant, and spare her, I cannot say too much! But, if not, I am doubly undone! Undone indeed!"

Then Philadelphia slammed the book shut, said loudly and firmly, "Rubbish!" and presently, a little later, she and Charlotte set out to cross the road to Number 23.

Charlotte was compelled to wear black, but she had changed her gown for the occasion, having carefully selected it from her Chelsea wardrobe. She had also rouged her cheeks, because black took one's color away, crimped her hair and put on a great deal of the perfume that Henry always brought back from his business excursions. Charlotte was still worried about this long absence, but had by now compelled herself to believe that there could not possibly be another female. It was indeed something of a relief to have him away, for she had discovered long ago that the domestic practices of marriage were not so pleasing as one had been led to imagine, especially as they quarreled so often.

Philadelphia on the other hand wore the same gown she had put on in the morning, and her hat, Charlotte thought, was truly deplorable, being at least six years out of date. But then despite her good looks, she really was a simple girl: it was just as well she would not be on her own, she would never be able to manage without help and guidance.

Mr. Atherton was waiting with an impatience that surprised himself. It was almost as if he were a young boy again. Ferdy had left him an ill-scrawled note, apparently written on a paper that had wrapped up some meat, suggesting that they set out on one of their little excursions this evening. "I no," he wrote, being as incapable of spelling as he was of behaving, "a fine Bordelow were we can Pluck some golden gineas, you will nede a Pistol, it is nere saint Giles, do not Forgett to give me my Money."

"Money" at least was spelled correctly. It was probably the one word Ferdy really knew. Mr. Atherton had no intention of going to the bordello near St. Giles, though once this would have stirred his blood, especially as it was so dangerous. If Ferdy troubled to mention the pistol, it must be a real den of thieves and murderers. He was only thinking of his visitors, and when they were shown in, thought once more that he had never seen a more beautiful girl than Philadelphia in his life. He was still amazed that she could have such a sister, with her over-rouged cheeks, and flamboyant, vulgar gown.

However, he greeted them with the subdued calm fitting for their recent loss, and neither sister had the least idea of the excitement surging up within him as he kissed Philadelphia's hand.

He said, as he poured Charlotte out a glass of wine—she noticed at once the delicate cut glass, and her gaze roamed almost gloatingly over the small but beautifully furnished little room where they were sitting—"There is some fruit juice for you, Miss Philadelphia. I can assure you there is not a trace of wicked alcohol in it." And he smiled at her as he said this, a little mockingly but so charmingly that she had to smile back: the color glowed once more in her pale, exhausted cheeks.

"Such a silly girl," said Charlotte in her most refined tones. As she said this she patted her sister's hand. "But she is very young, Mr. Atherton, and of course we had such a strict upbringing. Dear papa would never permit wine to be in the house. Naturally in my home we do drink wine—in moderation, of

course. One has to move with the times, does one
not?"

"One has to, indeed," said Mr. Atherton.

"You must do us the honor of dining with us one
day," said Charlotte. She added, "We dine at three."

"You used to dine at twelve," said Philadelphia,
speaking for almost the first time. She did not say this
to be tactless or difficult: she simply could not understand why Charlotte had suddenly pushed her hour of
eating on by three hours.

Charlotte went a little red. The natural color looked
strange under the rouge. Mr. Atherton could not make
out what all this was about, but Charlotte's embarrassment amused him, and he wanted to laugh. However, he merely said, "I should be delighted, ma'am, to
renew our acquaintance under happier circumstances," and wondered secretly why this kind of situation tended to make one so pompous.

"I so look forward to it," cried Charlotte. "I believe
we have a couple of friends whom you would enjoy
meeting." She ignored Philadelphia's remark, only said
to her, "It will be quite a treat for you, Philly, to have
a proper social life. She is coming to live with us," she
added, turning back to Mr. Atherton, "as I believe I
have already told you. I could not leave my poor little
sister all on her own in that dreadful house. We have
always been a very devoted family. Besides, she does
so love Tobias. My little son, you know. He adores his
auntie. It will be a very happy home."

At this point two things happened to Philadelphia.
The first was that she met fully and for a concentrated moment Mr. Atherton's gaze, which was fixed
on her. It was filled with amusement, a gentle mockery and something else that made her suddenly feel
breathless. The second was that she now made up her

mind. She was not going to Chelsea. The very thought of that happy home, stuffy, badly furnished and filled with execrable knickknacks, was quite unbearable, what with Tobias adoring her, and Charlotte, for some unknown reason, dining at three. Besides, the reference to that "dreadful house" made her realize how much she loved it, despite its shabbiness and smallness of size. But all this must wait until she was alone with Char, so she said nothing, and Charlotte, who believed that nonstop conversation was a mark of good breeding, went on talking.

"Of course," she said, "my husband will be back soon. I feel quite lonely without him. One does need a man in the house, does one not? You will find that one day, Philly," she added roguishly to her sister who stiffened instantly, and looked down. But Charlotte did not notice this: it was the kind of thing she never noticed. She said, "So sad for Henry to miss the funeral. Poor, dear mama. Somehow I feel I shall never quite get over it."

She dabbed at her eyes as she spoke. Mr. Atherton, hastily pouring her out another glass of wine, could have sworn there were no tears. But then he looked at Philadelphia, and for the first time his heart really smote him, for the grief on her face was such that no one could have remained unmoved. The late Mrs. Smith was fortunate indeed to have had such a loving daughter, and he hoped there had been fitting provision for her in the will, though no doubt the big sister would grab everything she could.

Philadelphia had taken little part in the conversation. It was in any case difficult to slide a word in when Charlotte was in one of her social moods. But she spoke now, looking dry-eyed at Mr. Atherton, saying, "You have been so very kind to us. I do not know how to thank you."

Something in that gaze had an unprecedented effect on Mr. Atherton, who had not blushed since the age of six, when confronted with the theft of a box of sweetmeats. A distinct flush came into his well-shaven cheeks. He said, almost, God forgive him, stammering, "It was the least I could do. If the circumstances had not been so sad for you, I would say it was a pleasure."

Philadelphia's gaze dropped, and she did not answer. Charlotte thought that she was remarkably lacking in the social graces, and promised herself that she would speak to her about it. It was after all an elder sister's duty, and it really was a pity that she seemed to have so little to say for herself, especially in the company of a gentleman who was so plainly *épris*: she would certainly point out to her that the gentlemen did not like dull, silent girls, and if she went on like this, she would probably lose him.

To prove her point, she went on talking. It would at least give Philadelphia some idea of how to make conversation. She spoke, as she always did, in a very loud voice. "We had such a pleasant surprise," she said. "We have been left quite a little fortune, you know. It is a pity that poor, dear mama scraped and scrimped for us, but of course we were all she had to live for. I couldn't believe it when I heard there was so much money. It will make a great difference to us. Not of course that I have ever been poor, but a few luxuries—I daresay you know how it is, Mr. Atherton. I declare I feel quite an heiress."

Mr. Atherton could see that Philadelphia was shaking with embarrassment and, he suspected, anger. He did not know of course that Charlotte always spoke out everything that was in her mind: reticence to her was an unknown quality. He thought she was the most appalling woman he had ever met, and was about to change the subject as swiftly as he could, when at this moment Ferdy, whom he had forgotten about, chose to make his appearance.

Charlotte was still talking. She was saying, "You'll be a rich girl now, Philly—" when she became aware that someone had entered the room, and broke off.

Ferdy rolled in unannounced, as he always did, pushing aside the footman who had tried to prevent him. Mr. Atherton went white with fury. He longed to murder him, and rose to greet him without the faintest pretense of welcome, while Charlotte and Philadelphia gazed at the new arrival in astonishment.

Ferdy looked more disgraceful than usual. He had never given a damn about appearances, and this time he had been riding: his suit was rumpled, his boots spattered with mud and gravel, his cravat was awry and his wig to one side. He was a little drunk, and stank of sweat and wine. He did not trouble to so much as bow to the Smith sisters, but noted, of course, that Tom's acquaintance with the little country miss was going apace. He must tell Emma. He would enjoy telling Emma. His eyes slid over Philadelphia, in her plain black dress, and his mouth curved in contempt, then he looked at Charlotte and burst into a guffaw which, fortunately, she did not know was on her account.

He said to Mr. Atherton in his giggling drawl, cracked and thickened with wine, "What ails you, Tom? We are going out, ain't we? I've been waiting for you, for the past hour. Get your hat on, man. There's business afoot, for Christ's sake, don't pretend you've forgot. And I want my money. Give me my money."

Mr. Atherton had forgotten about everything. He looked at Ferdy with disgust, then went over to his desk and took out the bag of money. He almost threw it at Ferdy, but managed not to, simply dumped it in his waiting hands. The fact that Ferdy instantly started to count it, was the last straw. His little girl, whom he was so determined to impress, would think that he consorted with blackguards and thieves, and indeed, Ferdy fitted well into both categories. He said abruptly, "I am not going out this evening."

Ferdy burst into a volley of oaths. The words were such as the two Smith girls had never heard in their lives, but they understood well enough that they were obscene and profane, and Charlotte's mouth dropped open: for once she was deathly silent. He demanded, "And why the devil not?" He was both enraged and disconcerted. Tom had never refused him before: he was one of the few people who would still keep him company. Besides, it was dangerous to make these excursions on his own, even for a man who was afraid of nothing.

"It may have come to your notice," said Mr. Atherton, longing to seize him by the collar and kick him out of the door, "that I have company."

"Company?" repeated Ferdy, with another oath. He reached out his hand for the wine decanter, and Mr. Atherton, so angry that he forgot all dignity, immediately snatched it from him, and removed it from his reach.

Ferdy looked around him, and the foolish smile that Emma so detested, curled his lips. "Ah," he said, "the little prim miss from opposite—" He lurched towards Philadelphia, who instinctively moved her chair and huddled away from him. She thought he was utterly repulsive: even poor Daftie had not aroused in her such revulsion. She remembered now that he was the other gentleman who had accompanied Mr. Atherton that strange, sad evening, and who at the sight of her mother, had pelted down the stairs and into the street. The sight of him made her feel quite sick, and she could not miss the fact that his smile and light, white-lashed eyes held both derision and hostility.

Mr. Atherton saw clearly that this damned lunatic might well wreck all his plans. If Philadelphia believed this was an example of his friends, she would be entirely justified in never speaking to him again. Even Emma, knowing who Ferdy was, and a great deal more sophisticated, had once begged him never to bring him into her company, for she could not endure the sight or smell of him.

Mr. Atherton walked up to Ferdy, who grinned at him and leaned backwards, balancing himself on his heels. He said, his face taut and grim, "Go away, Ferdy. I am busy."

"That I can see," said Ferdy, his gaze moving back to Philadelphia. He was plainly going to continue, but Mr. Atherton, appalled by the thought of what he might say, gripped him firmly by the arm and led, half dragged him towards the door.

"I have already told you," he said, "I am busy. I cannot accompany you this evening and after your behavior, I have no intention of accompanying you ever again. Now, for God's sake, go. You are in the way, you are drunk, you are filthy, you are half undressed. You are in no state for these ladies to have to look at you and listen to your filthy language. If you do not go, I swear I'll have you thrown out." He saw Ferdy's hand move, and suddenly and completely lost his temper. Did this idiot imagine they could shoot it out as if they were dueling in Hyde Park? He said between his teeth, "I suggest you go, Ferdy, and instanter. If not, I'll have the pleasure of kicking you down the front door steps, and if you threaten me with your pistol, I'll see that you land in Newgate."

He stopped, breathing heavily. Philadelphia by this time must be swooning with fright. He longed to batter Ferdy to pieces, to murder him in some prolonged and agonizing way.

But Ferdy suddenly chose to obey. It was as well, for he was a powerful man, and exceptionally well-versed in the kind of fighting that was not taught at the universities. He bestowed on Mr. Atherton his most foolish and dribbling smile. He did not say another word. He shambled towards the door, rattling the money in his pocket. Only, as Mr. Atherton, who accompanied him every inch of the way, held the front door open for him, he paused and swung round. He gave his former friend one look. He remained completely silent. The next moment he was down the steps and lurching along the street.

Mr. Atherton stayed for a moment in the hall, before returning to the little sitting room. He read that look well enough. Ferdy, as he knew better than most, accepted slights from no one. In a sense he had been slighted from the moment of his birth, and the fact that this was no one's fault made it all the worse. He had received innumerable insults in his time, from distraught hostesses, his own family, angry husbands, infuriated acquaintances who had lost their fortunes to him. Ferdy never forgot, even if the insult were slight. The vapid, foolish face concealed a savagely resentful and vindictive mind. Every rebuff and affront was repaid with a vicious interest, and often out of all proportion. There were gentlemen who had died suddenly for no decipherable cause, ladies whose reputations had been irretrievably ruined, and in one case, though there had never been an actual proof, a house was burned down with three children inside, and everyone believed it was Ferdy who was responsible.

It was wise to keep on the good side of Ferdy, and better to avoid him altogether. Mr. Atherton could not do the latter, and now he could never again do the former either. But he was young and strong, he was no coward, he did not intend to lose sleep over Ferdy's possible revenge. It was the thought that Philadelphia might never see him again that terrified him. He muttered under his breath a few words that the late Dr. Smith would not have liked at all, and came back into the little sitting room.

He had selected a small and cozy room for their meeting: he thought it would be more homely and his guests not overawed. He believed now that nothing would overawe Philadelphia, but was very apprehensive about her reactions, and came instantly up to her.

He had underestimated the parochialism of Inverness and the wild curiosity that the ways of the outside world provoked. Charlotte and Philadelphia were quite drawn together by this meeting with Ferdy. For that moment they were once again the two little Scottish girls from home. Neither had any real conception of life among the *haut ton*. Philadelphia indeed had none whatsoever, except from Mr. Richardson's book, and Charlotte's acquaintance with them was mostly in her dreams when she became a society hostess, and dukes and earls talked dazzlingly at her table.

The sight of Ferdy, so dirty and bedraggled, and above all so shockingly bad-mannered, made their eyes almost start out of their sockets. They looked at each other in amazement, and even drew their heads together as Charlotte, very Scots now and all refinement gone, whispered, "Who's he?" while Philadelphia breathed back, "He's just like Daftie Johnny—Oh, I don't know who he is, but isn't he terrible?"

They moved apart with a jerk as Mr. Atherton reappeared in the doorway.

"How can I apologize?" exclaimed Mr. Atherton. He was so overcome by the horror of the situation that he took Philadelphia's hand in his, then hastily dropped it, begging her pardon. Then he realized that the ladies were not so much affronted as intrigued, and it was to Charlotte that he spoke, knowing by now her weakness.

"He's a sad fellow, Ferdy," he said, "but we have to put up with him. After all, he cannot help his looks. The poor Duke of —— has to endure him, whether he likes it or not, but then Ferdy's his son, for better or for worse, so what can he do? I'm only sorry that he arrived when he did, and in such a pickle. You can depend on it, I shall make my displeasure very plain."

Philadelphia thought privately that he had made it pretty plain already. It must be unusual, even among the odd numbers, to offer to kick your guest from the door. But Charlotte, her eyes sparkling, cried out, "Do you mean to say he is the Duke's son?"

Mr. Atherton was delighted with the way things were turning out, but he answered gravely. "I fear he is. I can assure you that no one is more distressed than the Duke himself."

"And—and he's the heir to the dukedom?"

"He is actually the second son, for which everyone is profoundly grateful. But of course if the eldest son dies—"

"Oh the poor man, how terrible for him." And Charlotte, not making it plain whether she was referring to the Duke, Ferdy or the Duke's heir, fell in a state: Mr. Atherton, much tickled by this, suspected she was thinking, What would they say at home now?

But Philadelphia merely looked perturbed, so he said to her very simply, "I'm sorry, ma'am. I hope you have forgiven me?"

She replied, "After all your kindness, I could not possibly find anything to forgive." And, as she said this, she rose to her feet. She moved as beautifully as she looked, and Mr. Atherton was once again filled with confused longings, coupled—slightly in the background—with a resolve not to injure this young girl.

He said, "May I call next week to find out how you are?" but Charlotte instantly replied, "I am afraid my sister will no longer be there. My carriage will be calling for us tomorrow morning, and we will both be returning to Chelsea." She added kindly, "But naturally we will be seeing you again, and soon, I hope."

"Naturally," said Mr. Atherton without much finesse. Then suddenly he noticed a slightly odd expression crossing Philadelphia's face. It was too brief for him to be certain, but a faint hope stirred within him. It might at least be worthwhile knocking at the door. But he only wished the two ladies a pleasant journey, conducted them across the street, then returned to Number 23.

There was no room for Emma in his thoughts: he was only thinking of Philadelphia.

Chapter 6

Emma had decided that against everything she believed in, she must call on Tom. There was still no word from him, and she was growing desperate. When Ferdy, looking as always quite disgusting, was ushered into her room, she almost gave a moan of despair. He was the last person in the world that she could endure in her present state of mind, and the face she turned upon him expressed pure revulsion.

This in no way distressed Ferdy. He grinned at Emma. He saw that the inevitable box of sweetmeats beside her was almost empty. He sat down, without being asked, and for a time remained silent. He was no good at polite conversation, and he saw no reason to make any effort. A friend of the family had once remarked when Ferdy was still a boy and at that time amusing himself by tearing wings off flies and putting rats in his sister's bed, that he must be a changeling: otherwise there could be no possible excuse for his existence. The old Duke could do little but shake his head, and the Duchess had died with the shock of Ferdy's birth. The eldest boy was perfectly pleasant and normal, and the girl who followed him so detested her brother that the family was compelled to send her to stay with an aunt until Ferdy, at the age of seventeen, left home himself, much to everybody's relief.

His father once remarked bitterly, "I have never known him do a kindly deed, or say a kindly word." And sometimes in the depths of his heart he prayed that Ferdy would meet his just end on the gallows as soon as possible, for that was certainly where he would end, sooner or later. And in the meantime the debts mounted up, the ugly rumors increased, and he never dared refuse his son money, even in excess of a generous allowance, for, if he did so, Ferdy would simply return to the ducal mansion, and that was something that nobody could be expected to endure.

Emma knew about this, as did all her friends. Ferdy was never ashamed of himself, only permanently furious that he was ostracized. He sneaked in, uninvited, to parties and stayed until he was thrown out, he was always to be seen at races and, though White's had forbidden him entrance, was a regular player at all the less reputable clubs. Occasionally, older women, perversely fascinated by his evil reputation, flirted with him, but Ferdy's idea of a flirtation was to hurl them down on the nearest couch, and now they all avoided him and warned their friends.

Emma said again and again to Mr. Atherton that she could not understand how he could endure Ferdy's company. "He is so dirty. I don't think he ever washes, but it is not just that, he is dirty in everything. He makes me physically sick. Why do you go out with him? One day he will murder you, and you must realize that. He does not love anyone. He only thinks of himself."

"You are perfectly right," said Mr. Atherton, who knew this better than she did. If the day came when he won more than Ferdy, he would be very careful indeed on the journey home.

"Then why? You must answer me. It doesn't make sense."

"Oh, you'd not understand, even if I could explain it."

Emma protested, "I'm not such a fool, Tom. Do you think I don't understand the King's English? Explain to me. In simple language."

Mr. Atherton knew well enough that she was not a fool, and this was one of the things that kept him in her company. He had never been a constant man. Emma was beautiful, but there were plenty of beautiful women from good families and with plenty of money. But he had not so far met in someone so young and lovely such a quick mind, as well as a good heart that went oddly with her pert, sharp manner, and which few people suspected besides himself. However, he could not trouble himself to explain something so complicated, and it seemed foolish to talk about a creature as disgusting as Ferdy when Emma reclined there, looking creamy and magnificent, one rounded arm hanging gracefully over the side of the couch. He would look at her and smile, then slide his arms around her. She could not resist this, though she would murmur beneath his kisses that he might occasionally treat her as a human being, talk to her as if she were a man.

"But you are not a man," he would answer without much subtlety.

And now Emma was enraged that Ferdy should come uninvited and fling himself down on the nearest chair, as if he were at home. She exclaimed, "What is all this about, pray? What do you want? Are you hoping to borrow money off me? Because if you are, you are very much mistaken. I'd not give you a penny if you were starving in the gutter."

Most men at this would have sprung to their feet and stalked out. However, this to Ferdy was normal polite conversation, and indeed, the only time he liked Emma at all was when she insulted him: it reminded him of the whores who were his only real feminine acquaintance. He said in his giggling drawl, "Why, darling, I am not in need at the moment. Last night I won a cool three thousand, and tomorrow I shall probably do likewise."

"Then what do you want?" demanded Emma, swinging her long legs off the couch and carefully tucking her petticoats around them, for Ferdy was eyeing them with a grin that made her long to hit him.

"You are still guzzling sweets," said Ferdy.

"And what business is that of yours?" But Emma could not help casting an ashamed glance at the candy box, which had been full this morning and was now practically empty.

Ferdy did not answer this. He simply said, and for once without a smile, "You want Tom, do you not? Well, I'd lay ten guineas to a farthing that you are about to lose him."

And at that moment he looked so like a wolf that Emma could not find words in which to answer him.

The look was ferocious enough to frighten, and suddenly she stopped feeling sorry for herself, and grew calm and wary. She could not bring herself to believe that she would lose Tom to a silly little chit he had only just met—obviously this was what Ferdy was talking about—but she was growing more afraid for Tom than herself. From Ferdy's expression it seemed as if the inexplicable friendship were at last cracking, and she knew perfectly well what Ferdy was capable of doing to people he disliked.

She said quietly, "I have no idea what you are talking about, and whether or not I want Tom is nothing to do with you, but I suspect that you two have quarreled. What happened? I daresay he was drunk. It cannot be of the least importance."

"It is important to me," said Ferdy. Then he gave her a sudden grin that terrified her. "I do not like being insulted."

Emma could have pointed out that he was seldom anything else, considering that everyone he met loathed him on sight, but she was growing too uneasy to insult him herself. She said in what was almost a pacifying tone, "Well, if we have both lost him, we shall just have to find someone else." And, as she said this, a dreadful cold feeling crept into her stomach, and her hand reached out instinctively for another comforting sweet. She could not stop herself from saying, "Why should you think I am about to lose Tom?" She added, clutching to herself what remained of her feminine self-respect, "Not that it matters much to me. There are plenty of gentlemen in the world."

None of this deceived Ferdy in the slightest. He might not have much intelligence as the world rated it, but he was the astutest of observers, especially when there was malice in it: despite his fury with

Tom he was delighted to see this fat, proud little beauty set down. He was also pleased because, believing that everyone was fundamentally evil, he was sure that Emma would now help him in his plans.

He said, "Oh, if it don't matter, I'll not tell you anything more. But I think, Madam Emma, that you should consider the little miss at Number 22, for that is where your dear Tom now spends most of his time. Except of course when she calls on him, as she did yesterday. I fear Tom don't consider me good enough for such a fine lady. He all but threw me out. It is strange what love can do to a man, is it not, ma'am?"

Emma was on the verge of saying that she hoped Tom had followed this up by knocking Ferdy down, but then the full impact of his remarks hit her, and the color left her cheeks: she sat there silent, her head bowed.

"Of course," said Ferdy, seeing that the game was his, "if you wish to give in to a stupid little bitch of no breeding, that is for you to decide, but I daresay something could be done about it. I must admit, ma'am, I've never seen him in such a state. I could not stop myself from laughing. He was behaving like a green schoolboy who's met his first whore and don't know how to set about it. And she of course encouraging him to the hilt—I vow she's all set to marry him. After all, servant wenches don't meet gentlemen like our Tom every day, and she's got her hooks into him all right; oh, no one could miss it, he's a goner unless we do something about it. I think," said Ferdy, meeting Emma's furious, affronted and wretched gaze, "that you owe me a glass or two of wine, sweetheart."

"Don't speak to me like that!" whispered Emma.

"Why not?" asked Ferdy, grinning at her. "Why you

look quite set down, Emma, my pet. I swear I've never seen you look so sick."

He rose to his feet and shambled over to the table where the decanter and glasses lay. Ferdy noticed little of the fine things in a house, for beauty and elegance did not concern him, but he always knew how much money his hosts had, and after that where the wine was kept. He poured himself out a brimming glass, swallowed it down in a couple of gulps, then poured himself out another. He did not offer any to Emma, who watched him silently, the color now high in her cheeks, her foot tapping. Even when he poured out the second glass, she did not utter a word, and Ferdy, who had experienced the weight of her tongue many times, noted this with a sardonic satisfaction.

He crossed the room to stand over her. He stank of drink and dirt, but Emma, her breast rising and falling, did not move back from him. The derision glowed from him, and the very sight of him made her flesh crawl, but she still said nothing and waited, though one tug at the bell would have brought the footman in to get rid of this unwelcome visitor.

He said, "I suggest we remove this young lady for a little while. Tom is hot for her now, but he'll forget her quick enough. It is true she has money—"

"What do you mean?" cried Emma. "Of course she has no money. None of the people in the cottages have money, otherwise they wouldn't live there."

"Oh, she's quite an heiress," said Ferdy. "I understand her mama left a vast fortune—"

"You are making this up!"

"I heard the very words. There was a female with her, some sort of companion, I presume, who said so. I daresay Tom would not be interested, but I am, I can assure you. He is only concerned with her pretty face, but I swear she has no wit or spirit, and she'll smell of scrub soap and dirty linen. It'll never do for him, once he's got her into bed with him and solaced himself."

Emma nearly told him that a little scrub soap would not hurt him either, but the thought of Tom in bed with Philadelphia nearly choked her, so she fell silent again, while he fidgeted before her, slopping the wine on his cravat, and picking at a pimple on his chin with the other hand.

He said, shaking his head from side to side as if he had the palsy, "What do you say, my little darling? Shall we remove mademoiselle, or shall we not?"

"Certainly not!" cried Emma, coming to her senses and jumping to her feet at the same time. The violent movement knocked her against Ferdy's arm, and the wine splashed on to the carpet. But she did not even notice, only raised her voice in almost a scream. "Remove her indeed! Are you out of your mind? What do you propose to do? Murder her?"

"It is just possible," said Ferdy softly.

Then Emma remembered that to Ferdy murder was not an abstract thing, and she went white, saying in a choked voice, "You'll do nothing of the kind. I cannot believe Tom is even interested in her, but—"

"He is, he is, my darling!"

"Don't call me that! God's teeth," cried Emma, "that is something I have never been. Why are you so angry against this girl? Perhaps I have the right, though I cannot believe it, but you—"

"Tom is in love with her."

"Nonsense! Besides, what is that to do with you?"

The grin was wiped off Ferdy's face. "I'll tell you," he said, "I'll tell you, my darling. Oh, I'll tell you—"

Emma said as calmly as she could, "Oh, it's because

he threatened to throw you out. How childish you are, Ferdy. I'm quite ashamed of you."

There was a long pause. Ferdy looked as Emma had never seen him. It was a look that Mr. Atherton knew, and most of those who had witnessed it were no longer there. He looked murderous, he looked mad and he looked evil: this was to Emma, already confused and distraught, the most terrifying expression she had ever seen. The moment he was gone she would swallow her pride and rush over to Tom, to warn him. There was after all little point in being proud about your lover, if your lover were dead. But she did not utter a word and so dreadful was the occasion, she did not even turn to her candy box.

Ferdy spoke at last in a thin drawl, and for once he continued not to smile. "I do not like," he said, "being threatened. I do not like being told it would be a pleasure to kick me down the steps."

Emma liked it very much. The thought of Ferdy being kicked to kingdom come gave her the greatest possible pleasure. But she was cold with fear now, and bewildered too, for this was not like Tom. Tom on the whole was a good-natured man, never involved in any kind of brawl, and who had never to her knowledge involved himself in a duel either: this was rare among fashionable men, who tended to regard the occasional meeting in Hyde Park much as ladies accepted an invitation to dance. She could only think that Ferdy had, in his customary graceless way, insulted this little girl from the cottage, and if amiable Tom lost his temper to such a degree over this same little girl, it was all becoming intensely serious. Emma still remained silent, but her face grew still: the fear that filled her was so keen that it was like being steadied by disaster.

"He told me," went on Ferdy in the same voice, "that he would have me thrown into Newgate. He told me I was filthy and in no state—" His voice soared up to an obscene falsetto. "—for these ladies to see me. Ladies! Common little provincial sluts, as vulgar as dirt." He broke off. He shambled towards Emma, who was still gazing at him in a steady, expressionless manner. "He is going to be sorry. Very sorry, my darling. He'll not see that precious little whore of his much more. I daresay you'll not mind overmuch, Madam Emma. I wouldn't have given her more than a couple of months, but that's time enough to push you out, the way a suet pudding can overwhelm a fine cream cake. They say there's something about these common girls. I daresay it's because they don't know how to conceal anything. Perhaps it's flattering to meet someone so stupid she can't dissimulate, but Tom is behaving like a dog after a bitch and it makes me vomit."

"You still haven't told me what you are proposing to do, Ferdy." Emma's deep, husky voice was perfectly controlled.

"A great many things!"

"Such as?"

"Do you really want to know, my darling?"

"I gather you are going to tell me, Ferdy. What is it this time? Are you really going to murder this girl? Perhaps you are going to murder Tom, too. You might as well throw me in, and make it a trio. And if you have finishing swilling my wine, perhaps you would have the courtesy to pour me out one small glass."

"Pour it out yourself," said Ferdy.

Emma simply looked at him, and perhaps something in that look jerked him back to the days when he was young enough to follow in some desultory manner the conventions of polite society. He did as he was asked, dumping the glass on the table beside her so violently that half its contents were spilled on the polished surface. Then, as if he regretted this concession to the social code, he gave her his witless grin and put the bottle to his lips, finishing the contents in three vast swallows.

Emma did not thank him, nor did she touch the wine. She watched the liquid traveling down Ferdy's throat. He had a very prominent Adam's apple that bobbed up and down in a disgusting manner. She thought that if she could murder him, herself, without anyone finding out, she would do it that very instant: her hatred was passionate enough to astonish herself.

She said, "Well, Ferdy? And what is it to be?"

"There are ways, ma'am."

Suddenly she could endure this no longer. She shouted at him, "Oh, for God's sake! You cannot get away with murder and in any case, this wretched child has done nothing to deserve it. You are only wishing to revenge yourself on Tom. And I don't suppose it's anything more than a flirt, if it's even that—"

"Don't you!"

"No, I do not. She has nothing, neither breeding nor money—"

"I tell you, she has a fortune."

"Well, she doesn't look as if she has," said Emma, almost reluctantly, remembering the poor, unfashionable gown. "Besides, that would hardly interest Tom. I suggest you go to see him and talk the whole matter out. I daresay he did not mean a word of what he said. You can be wonderfully exasperating, Ferdy, and sometimes I could wish to kill you, myself. But there is too much talk of killing—"

"I am not," said Ferdy in what was almost a pontifical tone, "entirely sure I'll kill her. Or indeed Tom."

"Well then," said Emma, turning away from him, "since you have come to your senses and drunk all my wine, I suggest you leave me. I have to go out."

"To see Tom, no doubt?"

"That is none of your business, and you are being grossly impertinent." Emma, as she spoke, rose to her feet. She moved well and lightly, like many plump people, and indeed could dance like an angel, but now her movements had grown clumsy, and she sent the glass of wine flying.

Ferdy noticed all this, as he always noticed anything that was to people's disadvantage, and grinned. He seemed to have recovered his temper, but the mischief glowed from him, and Emma was again aware of a spasm of fear.

"I think," he said, "I will marry her."

Emma cried, almost in a shriek, "You are out of your wits!" Then, forgetting herself, and so enraged that the words tumbled into each other, "Do you think a girl like that would have you? She may be everything you say, but one can see at first glance that she is virtuous. There is no doubt some boy waiting to wed her the moment she says yes, and the idea that someone like you—"

"You did not tell me you had seen her," said Ferdy softly.

Emma, to her own intense fury, flushed. The beautiful, deep color flowed up her throat into her cheeks. She said, "Oh, I caught a glimpse of her once. I found her quite pretty."

"I daresay Tom found her the same."

Emma chose to ignore this. She was beginning to see that she had not distinguished herself. It was so often the way with Ferdy: one believed him to be as witless as he looked, one forgot the shrewd brain beneath the idiot exterior.

"There are ways of marrying," said Ferdy.

"What do you mean? I must go out, so—"

"There is always the Fleet."

Emma stopped and stared at him. She knew of course about the Fleet marriages but, as such a thing never touched her, found this simply amusing in a rather macabre way; sometimes she and her friends had discussed the matter and dismissed it quickly with laughter. Such marriages—if so they could be called—took place in the Fleet prison, under the auspices of clergymen confined there who wished to earn a dishonest penny. There was apparently one William Dare who married monthly up to two hundred couples. There were false names and sham certificates; if bride or bridegroom were not present, the ceremony could be done by proxy. Women in debt married a husband they would never see again, to start new debts under a new name, but more sinister things occurred. Minors were entrapped and married, the weak-minded kidnapped into wedlock, and one midsummer it was reported that a young lady was deluded and forced from her friends, to be married with the aid of a wry-necked, swearing parson to a debauched wretch who ruined her life and took all her money.

Emma had taken none of this seriously, and even now could not quite believe in it, yet the thought of that wretched girl entrapped into a vile marriage with someone like Ferdy, horrified her. She thought, I must tell Tom. She said, "You are quite absurd. What would you do, married to such a girl?"

"The marriage would not last long," said Ferdy. He

added, "I daresay Tom might buy her out. If he did not, it would be no matter. But it would be interesting to see if he did." Then he said in a strange, smiling way, "This is something I have never done." He turned towards the door. "You will let me know what you think of the idea, Emma, my love. I am sure you will agree, once you have thought the matter over. Besides, it would all be so amusing. Do you not think so?"

"I certainly do not," said Emma furiously, her rage increased because the wicked, feminine side of her was tempted. "And I doubt Tom will be very much amused, either."

"So you think you will tell Tom?" said Ferdy softly. He had opened the door. He never waited, as civilized people did, to be ushered in or out, but simply shambled along as the fancy took him.

"Certainly I will! I can promise you that."

"I wonder," said Ferdy.

And that was the last she was to see of him for that day, only before the door closed upon him, the stammering, thin voice said in a drawl, "I do not think you will tell Tom, Emma. I think perhaps, my darling, you will contrive to forget to do so."

Emma did not answer, even to wish him goodbye. She could only hope that Ferdy fell down her front steps into the gutter, to be run over by a passing carriage or eaten up by dogs.

She stood there, hesitating. She must certainly go to see Tom. And of course she must dress at her very best, she must look nothing less than superb: the tear marks must be carefully erased, and the eyes, heavy with lack of sleep, must be remedied with make-up. But as her hand moved towards the bellrope to summon her maid, she paused again to collect herself, then instinctively helped herself to the last sweet. Then she sat down and began once more to cry. She had not seen Tom for so long, and now she could only think with terror that she might not see him again. She had always sworn that a truly feminine woman should never fight for her gentleman: no man was worth the battle and humiliation. Her creamy beauty, which normally needed no cosmetics, coupled with a good family name and an excellent income, had always produced more suitors than she could deal with, and her ballroom card was immediately filled the moment she entered a room. She could, if she wished, have married two Dukes, one Earl and a number of lords, apart from a variety of commoners and hangers-on. She was indeed regarded as the most eligible catch of the season, and was invited to every house of notability in London. During this past week, when she had shut herself off, the cards had arrived without stopping: innumerable gentlemen had called, to be told she was not in, and a pile of unanswered invitations lay outside on the silver tray. At least five gentlemen were pressing her to marry them, and rumor had it that a Royal Personage was interested in her, though not, of course, for marriage.

Emma ignored the invitations and the Royal Personage, who was in any case too fat and did not wash sufficiently. She was learning that one person mattered more than the whole of the peerage. She only wanted Tom, and she wanted Tom more passionately than she had ever wanted anyone in her life, yet so far her pride had prevented her from making the first advance. Even now the prospect of calling on him frightened her, as if she were a little girl again, though her plausible mind had already thought out a dozen excuses. She thought of Philadelphia, and a shudder of jealous fury went through her, then she thought of Ferdy, and shuddered again from pure terror.

However, it was plain that this could not go on and, if she were to continue sulking in her tent, she might well lose Tom altogether. She mopped at her tears, blew her nose and rang the bell.

When her French maid appeared, she said calmly, "Louise, I am going to visit Mr. Atherton. I must look at my very best. I shall wear my newest gown, and you must do my hair in the most fashionable way."

Louise simply inclined her head, knowing perfectly well what had happened, and how important this was. Below stairs they talked of little else. And because Miss Emma was in the main a considerate mistress, very generous in her handouts and once, some time ago, unusually sympathetic in an affair of the heart, Louise was very sorry for her, and agreed with the cook, the coachman and the butler that it was a shame: no one could understand why any gentleman could treat such a lovely lady so badly. And she followed her mistress upstairs, resolved to turn her out looking completely ravishing.

For a time Charlotte and Philadelphia discussed nothing but Ferdy. They were so seldom united that it was only afterwards that it struck them both how unusual this was.

"A duke's son!" cried Philadelphia, wide-eyed.

"His linen wasn't even clean!" exclaimed Charlotte. She had the utmost respect for dukes and their progeny, but she also liked clean linen, and Ferdy's wine-dabbled shirt and filthy breeches were such as would never have been tolerated in Inverness. Why, even the Highland soldiers looked better!

"I think," said Philadelphia sternly, "he was drunk."

Charlotte, who found this less reprehensible, patted her sister's shoulder and said, "You must try not to be so narrow-minded, my dear." She saw from Philadelphia's expression that the moment of accord was passing, and added hastily, "Not of course that I approve of intoxication. Henry is always most moderate in his drinking. Still, one must expect such things among the nobility."

"I don't see why one should expect it from anyone," retorted Philadelphia. "And he swore! He said—Oh, I cannot repeat it."

"Yes indeed," agreed Charlotte, almost in a whisper, for this indeed was shocking. Papa would have thrown such a blasphemous creature out of the house. And this reminded her of something else, for she said wonderingly, "They did not seem very friendly, did they?"

"I would think nothing of Mr. Atherton if they had been so," said Philadelphia.

She was plainly at her most puritanical, and Charlotte, eying her sideways, could not help thinking that if she were to marry this gentleman, she would have to modify her views. However, this was obviously not the moment to say this, so she went back to the subject of Ferdy, and discussed in some detail his fearsome appearance, his horrid voice, his shambling gait and his complete lack of manners, until suddenly Philadelphia exclaimed in a rather shamefaced manner, "Oh Char, it is not perhaps seemly that we should be talking like this so soon after poor mama's death. I believe we should not discuss this poor wretch so. After all, he is so like Daftie Johnny, and it is possible that he is gone in the wits." Then, because this had been on her mind ever since the incident occurred, she said, a little sadly, "I wish, Char, you had not told Mr. Atherton about the money."

"What do you mean?" demanded Charlotte indignantly.

But Philadelphia did not pursue the matter, chiefly because her conscience was stabbing at her, besides Char would never understand. All her life she had always talked of whatever came into her mind and in the loudest possible voice: she would never see that Mr. Atherton could not possibly be interested in such things nor that what she had called a fortune would seem to him something absurdly small.

She did not think that Ferdy had overheard this, nor, if she had done, would it have seemed to her important. But then she had of course no idea of what he was planning for her. She had never even heard of Fleet marriages, and the name to her simply meant a dreadful prison where poor people were locked up and ill-treated. And then, apart from Charlotte's murmuring in an unbelieving voice, "A duke's son too!" the subject of Ferdy was dropped and, while Philadelphia was preparing the supper, Charlotte began to consider something that to her was far more important.

She did not mention it until the supper—a simple one of a little baked fish and vegetables—was over, and Philadelphia did not mention it either. The atmosphere had grown stiff and cold and uneasy, and Charlotte had to feel a little disturbed that her sister was not up in her room, doing her packing.

She wished with a reprehensible fervor that wine was permitted in this household. She had this secret bottle up in her bedroom, but could not think of any decent excuse for creeping out to open it. She said, rather too heartily, "I believe the carriage will call for us early tomorrow. Of course, Philly, you need not stay just now, I thought if you were with us for a day or two you would see how things will be, and how cozy it will be for you. But naturally, I must not leave home for too long. Henry should be back any moment, and I am never happy at leaving wee Tobias for too long." She added in a voice thick with emotion, "Oh, how happy he will be to see his dear Auntie Philly. The child loves you so much, it's quite unbelievable."

Philadelphia thought it was unbelievable too, but she saw that the dreadful moment was now upon her and inescapable. She flushed a little, and remained silent.

"I think," said Charlotte, aware that something was wrong yet not suspecting what it could be, "that I shall put you in the little room on the top floor. It is small, I know, but so agreeable, and the bed has such a pretty coverlet. You will be warm and comfortable, that I can promise you."

"I thought that was the maid's room," said Philadelphia, turning her disconcertingly direct gaze upon Charlotte.

"Oh no, pet, not any longer," cried Charlotte, and made as if to put her arm round her sister, only Philadelphia had moved away, and she was left with her hand flapping in midair. She went on, "It was far too good for a maid. I never believe in pampering servants—it simply gives them ideas. The girl sleeps downstairs now, next to the kitchen. Oh no, Philly, as if I would put you in the maid's room! What an idea! This one has a nice new chair too. I only bought it the other day. You will be able to sit there and read those novels you are so fond of."

Philadelphia moved across the room to stand by the

mantelpiece. She was beginning to shake, but she said very clearly, "Char, I intend to stay on here."

"What nonsense is this?" The color roared into Charlotte's cheeks. She always had an unbecomingly high color. Her voice shrilled, and the accent flew in as it still did in all crises. "You're coming home with me. It's all arranged. You cannot possibly stay here by yourself. It wouldn't be decent. Papa would be turning in his grave. Besides, you won't have any money."

"I shall have five hundred pounds," said Philadelphia. The awful words came out like stones. She had never felt more guilty and wretched in her life. It seemed appalling to be talking like this when mama was newly laid in her grave. But the thought of that cozy little room with its pretty coverlet and the new chair—removed from the kitchen as she knew perfectly well—was somehow the last straw. Philadelphia had seen that room. It was of course the maid's room, whatever Charlotte said: it was dark and dingy, it had a low roof and the smallest possible window, and the draught blew in under the floorboards. Besides, she could see more and more plainly the kind of life that lay ahead of her. Tobias, morning, noon and night, the housekeeping, the shopping, the cooking no doubt when Charlotte held one of her soirées, and herself more and more in the rôle of spinster sister, probably not permitted to meet the guests, an unpaid slavey reading her novels in that horrid little room. Oh, I cannot do it, thought Philadelphia, I just cannot. And though she wanted to cry and at the same time beg her sister's pardon for her frightful conduct, she managed to do neither, and continued to look steadily at Charlotte, praying that her trembling hands were unnoticed.

Charlotte was too angry to notice anything. She too

was on her feet. Her face was ugly with temper. She said, tight-lipped, "I thought we had agreed that the money should be handed over to me."

"It is my money," said Philadelphia. It was all sounding worse and worse, but she knew now that she must go through with it, even if it meant never speaking to Charlotte again. Yet, deep in the tunnel of her disgraceful mind, she was aware that Charlotte would soon be on her doorstep as if nothing had happened: five hundred pounds was a lure she would never be able to resist, however furious she might be now.

Charlotte said in a hoarse whisper, "I would never have believed it—Oh, I have heard from—it doesn't matter where, but I have heard how hard and greedy you have become. Yet to know that you, my own sister, my only sister, could behave so, is something I find impossible to believe. Do you mean to stand there as bold as brass, and tell me that you are hanging on to the full five hundred pounds, when you know we need it so badly, when poor Tobias, your little nephew who loves you so devotedly, the poor, misguided, wee bairn—" She stumbled briefly to a halt. The trouble with emotion was that it tended to entangle. She drew in a heavy breath, then said in her loud, normal voice, "So you are keeping all the money, miss, are you?"

Philadelphia was too choked to speak. She longed to say, Of course I'm not, you can have as much as you please, I'll buy you anything you want—but now she dared not, she could not utter one word, she could only nod.

"You bitch!" said Charlotte.

Philadelphia had never been called by such a name, nor had she ever heard such a word on her sister's lips. Papa, if dead people could really turn in their graves, must be spinning like a top. And Charlotte, who had hardly realized that such an epithet lay in her vocabulary, was equally appalled. The two girls fell silent. It seemed to Philadelphia as if a mountain of money lay between them. She knew now that she must capitulate. She opened her mouth to cry, I didn't mean it, take it all, take anything, only don't hate me so much, I cannot endure it, we are all the family that is left. But then Charlotte spoke again.

She said in an icy voice that Philadelphia had never heard from her, "I cannot imagine what Henry will say. I am sorry to say this, Philadelphia, but you are the most selfish girl I have ever met in my life. You only care for yourself. You care nothing for me, nor for poor wee Tobias. I had hoped we would be happy together. I so looked forward to having you with me again. I imagined you taking Tobias for lovely little walks, and cooking us the nice meals you used to do. I even dreamed of the cozy little talks we could have together, just like the old days. But of course, with your fine gentleman courting you, you've grown far too grand for the likes of us. I daresay you would expect to be waited on hand and foot, and I am sure you wouldn't have the time to concern yourself with a poor wee boy who is misguided enough to love you. I see we'll be better off without you. I wish you joy, I'm sure. Only let me tell you this, my young madam— when you get into trouble as you certainly will, don't come running to me. I don't want to have anything more to do with you. You can just spend your nights counting your money, and no doubt your fine gentleman will be glad to gamble it away for you. I daresay he'll get you with child—"

"Charl"

"Oh ay, you'll not be thinking he'll marry you, will

you? A little country lass like you! You make me laugh," said Charlotte viciously, adding hastily, "that is if you didn't make me weep. You are not only selfish and disgusting but you are also a fool. And now," she said, "I am going to bed. You have made me quite ill. Though I don't suppose that worries you. I have always had a weak heart, though of course I would never fret you with such things. I have always been one to suffer in silence, but now I am sure I am going to have an attack. Oh, how thankful I shall be to leave this place—If I had not sent the carriage away, I'd not stay the night, I can tell you that."

And at this Charlotte made a somewhat unsteady progress towards the door. The tottering steps were caused by temper, not by her heart which was perfectly sound. In the doorway she paused to issue her ultimatum. "If," she said, "you come to your senses, you can let me know. I do not suppose you will, and in the circumstances you cannot expect me ever to come back here again. But one thing I know—God will punish you for your wickedness and hard heart."

And with this she slammed the door behind her.

Philadelphia, sobbing a little, though silently, listened to her sister's progress up the stairs. Charlotte had always been heavy footed, and it sounded very military. Then she buried her face in her hands and wept. There was no need for God to punish her: she had condemned herself to the gallows. She wanted to run after Charlotte, to cry, Forgive me, forgive me, but her legs felt too weak to bear her. But she knew now that tomorrow she must offer Charlotte half the money. She would write at once to Mr. Bridges to tell him so. To live in Chelsea would be utterly impossible, especially now, but she could not stay on such wickedly unfriendly terms with her sister, and perhaps this would pacify her. And of course Char was perfectly right: she had no right to keep such a sum entirely for herself, her needs were small, and half the amount would enable her to live in the utmost comfort.

Perhaps even a quarter of the amount. But unfortunately for Charlotte, Philadelphia, despite her grief and remorse, was a realistic person. In the midst of all this self-flagellation certain unworthy thoughts insisted on swimming to the surface. It was a pity perhaps that Charlotte had visited her sick mother so seldom and, when she did come, stayed for so brief a time. Always, after these visits, especially when little Tobias was running round the house upsetting everything, Mrs. Smith was far worse; occasionally Philadelphia had been frightened enough to send for the doctor. And though the visits sometimes proved unfortunate, it would have been a pretty gesture if Char had from time to time arranged for someone to take over the nursing so that Philadelphia could visit Chelsea and be cosseted and looked after. It was also a little exaggerated to insist so on poverty. Tea appeared to be a profitable business. Henry had his own carriage, the house, though not to Philadelphia's taste, was expensively furnished, and Charlotte never lacked a variety of fashionable new gowns and hats. As for poor wee Tobias, he was spoiled out of all proportion, and it was to his credit that he still remained a reasonably pleasant little boy, though he was so over-fed by his mama that Philadelphia always had to restrain herself from protesting.

In sum, a great deal of all this was both untrue and unfair, yet the picture of herself as hard and greedy had been so luridly painted that she was beginning to believe it herself.

"I am a wicked girl," sobbed Philadelphia, pushing away all realism, and decided she must summon up her strength to go to Charlotte immediately. If she did not do so, she would never sleep a wink. She put up a small, silent prayer for courage, then came towards the hall, wishing that quarrels did not make one feel so ill, and that her head would stop aching.

At this moment there was a knock at the front door.

Chapter 7

~~~~

Charlotte was no happier than her sister. She had to see that she had managed the situation abominably. Henry, who liked money as much as she did, would be furious with her: indeed, there would probably be one of those unpleasant quarrels that occurred now so frequently, when he shouted at her, even struck her, and which always ended by his storming out of the house and staying away for hours. She never knew where he went on such occasions, and so far had not dared to ask. But in this particular instance he would be perfectly right. It was both stupid and vulgar to have spoken as she did. Philadelphia was usually a soft little thing, disposed to give away the food on her plate to a passing beggar, but there was nonetheless a determined core within her, and she would never submit to bullying. Charlotte decided that tomorrow she would apologize, she would be subdued and pathetic. In the meantime she solaced herself with a cupful of wine from the bottle she had brought with her and which Philadelphia must never see.

She too heard the knock. She was at once filled with wild curiosity, and would have rushed downstairs to see who it was, but by now she had drunk another cupful, spilling a little of it on her dressing gown. Wine always thickened her speech, besides, there would be a smell of it upon her breath. Now that Henry was behaving so strangely there was a good deal of wine drunk privately in Chelsea, and Charlotte was finding it increasingly difficult to do without it, though unhappily she had a poor head. She was therefore compelled to stay in her room, though curiosity drove her to open the door and listen, even at one point to creep out on to the landing. But she could not hear a sound except for the closing of a door, and so frustrated was she that she had a third cupful of wine—she had not dared take a glass upstairs—and this after a short while sent her snoring to sleep.

Philadelphia did not answer the knock, for she felt she could not bear visitors at this moment. But she had as always left the door on the latch, and she raised her head to see Mr. Atherton smiling there, a covered jug in his hand.

She said in a choked voice, "You should not be here at this hour, sir," and at the sight and sound of her the smile was instantly stripped from his face. He came up to her and took her in his arms, saying, "My poor child, what has happened now? You have been crying. Your sister should be with you. You should not be left alone like this."

It was all too much after the dreadful quarrel; Philadelphia forgot every tenet that had been drummed into her and abandoned herself to the unprecedented luxury of weeping in a gentleman's arms. She sobbed on Mr. Atherton's shoulder, did not notice that the arms had perceptibly tightened round her, and could only feel that this was the most wonderful thing that had ever happened.

Mr. Atherton was beginning to think the same. The female tendency to tears sometimes had its disadvantages, but in this case he was thanking his Maker for this outburst. He had of course no idea what had happened, and assumed that this was simply a belated reaction to a mother's death, but the soft, young body leaning against him and the sight of that charming, disheveled head just beneath his chin, was so disturbing and magnificent that he only hoped he would be able to control himself and not frighten her away. It had seemed to him that the barrier was almost insurmountable, and now, praise be, the barrier seemed almost dissolved, he had progressed as far in two minutes as he had hoped to do in a month.

When at last she drew away from him, he made no attempt to restrain her. He merely said in a calm, matter of fact voice, "I am thankful that I called. I did hesitate, Miss Philadelphia, for I thought you would prefer me to wait a while, but after all, we are now friends, are we not? I was passing and I saw through the window that you were alone and looked unhappy."

Philadelphia cried out, her hands flying to her lips, "Oh, I have not drawn the curtains!"

"That is easily rectified," said Mr. Atherton, entertained by this sudden modest reaction, and instantly pulled the curtains across. He had his own reasons for this, for it was quite possible that Emma, who had so far miraculously stayed away, might choose this moment to call, or Ferdy might have got over his sulks and turned up on some gambling errand. Then he came back and picked up the jug that he had set down on the table. "I think this will help you sleep," he said. "It is something I drink, myself, when I feel unwell. I asked the kitchen to prepare it for me. You must drink it while it is still warm."

"What is it?" asked Philadelphia. She hastily mopped at her face. It was shocking to have behaved in such a childlike fashion, but despite this she felt extraordinarily happy.

"Oh, milk and cinnamon and—Faith!" said Mr. Atherton, "I do not know. But I can assure you it will do you no harm."

And he filled one of the glasses that stood on the sideboard, and held it out to her.

"It smells very nice," said Philadelphia, sipping at it. "It tastes good too."

He looked briefly away from her. A stab of conscience twinged him. It was true that the drink contained both things he had mentioned, but had not found it necessary to add that it was liberally laced with brandy. This had not been done with any diabolical intent: it was simply that Mr. Atherton was a devout believer in the efficacy of alcohol and could not conceive that a hot drink without it was of the least use. He watched a little guiltily as Philadelphia's sips became more positive swallows, then she smiled at him, saying, "This is perfectly delicious. I have never tasted anything like it. You must ask your cook to give me the recipe."

"I will do that," said Mr. Atherton gravely. His eyes moved to the portrait over the mantelpiece. This must of course be the nonalcoholic papa, and a tough old gentleman he looked too. He wondered if the portrait might suddenly fall off the wall. However, it remained firmly attached, so Mr. Atherton sat himself down beside Philadelphia who looked, he thought, much restored and quite devastatingly beautiful.

"Now," he said in the brisk way he was beginning to adopt, for he was also beginning to know his Philadelphia, "you are going to tell me all about it. I suspect that it was not only the loss of your mama that made you cry."

"You are very clever," said Philadelphia. She really felt unbelievably better, yet a little strange too: it was as if she were enclosed in a soft, warm cloud. She thought she might like a little more of the delicious drink but Mr. Atherton, after a glance at her flushed cheeks, moved the jug out of her reach.

"May I not have another glass?" she asked, surprised.

"Later. Later. You shall have some more before you go to bed, and then you will sleep like an angel. Now tell me all your troubles. I am sure I shall be able to help you."

"It is true," said Philadelphia consideringly, "that gentlemen understand these things better than we do. Only it shows me up in such a shocking light—Oh, I am so ashamed of myself."

"Nonsense. I am sure you have no reason. Well? You know you can always tell me everything. I am an excellent confidant, and I believe I give the very best advice."

Philadelphia hesitated. She glanced sideways at the door as if she expected an avenging Charlotte to appear there in her nightgown. Then she took a deep breath and plunged into the story—how mama had left her this utterly unexpected sum of money, how her sister had taken it for granted that it would be handed over to her, and how she simply could not bear the prospect of living in Chelsea as an unpaid servant.

She said, nearly in tears again, "You see, I do so love this little house. Oh, I know that to you it's a cottage, it's nothing, you have all your big rooms and lovely furniture, but to me it is home. And I like living on my own, Mr. Atherton, I really do. I am sure I would never be lonely or unhappy. And of course with so much money. Do you know, sir, I never dreamed of becoming quite rich. We have always been so poor. It grieves me terribly that mama kept it for me when it could have bought her so many of the small things she required. But then she was good and kind, she never thought of herself. But I do see now that Char—Charlotte is entirely right. I am being entirely selfish. After all, there is my little nephew, and she does so much entertaining, she has to buy clothes, she really needs it. I am going to offer her half. It is only fair. I can manage perfectly well on what is left. After all, I am not an extravagant person."

Mr. Atherton had listened to all this with a very grim expression. He remembered now how Charlotte had referred to the fortune. If she had really appeared at this moment, she would have heard such things as had never been said to her in her life. He said abruptly, "May I ask how much this bequest is?"

"Perhaps to you it is not so much, but to me—Five hundred pounds. A year! Oh," whispered Philadelphia, "it does not seem possible."

Mr. Atherton had been known to lose six times that amount at the gaming tables, and Ferdy twice as much again. Such a sum would not have been sufficient to keep his household for a month. He said with some restraint, "That is a tidy sum."

"It is indeed, and you will understand why I cannot possibly keep it all for myself."

"Now," said Mr. Atherton, ignoring this, "you are going to listen to me, Miss Philadelphia. You loved your mother very much, did you not?"

"Yes, sir."

"And it was you who looked after her?"

This time Philadelphia did not answer, only gazed at him, a little rebelliously. He had a desperate urge to kiss her, but knew that this would lose him all the advantage he had gained. Instead he said, "I think in the circumstances you have no right to go against her express wishes."

"But—"

"I told you to listen to me. Don't interrupt. Do you honestly believe that your sister needs this money?"

Philadelphia longed to say yes, but could not manage to do so. She hung her head, looking like a penitent child. and Mr. Atherton was again so overcome that he had to move a little away.

He said, "I myself do not believe she does. She is married, after all. Her husband—What does her husband do?"

"He is in tea."

"Ah. That settles it then."

"I do not understand you, sir."

"Tea is one of the wealthiest businesses in the world."

Mr. Atherton actually had not the least knowledge of tea for, in his world, it was equivalent to being in trade, and it would have been regarded as impossible to mix with such people. But it sounded very convincing, and he could see that Philadelphia was impressed. He went on, "I imagine your sister is quite wealthy. Of course she wants the money. We all want money. We spend our lives wanting money."

"I don't," said Philadelphia. "Not really. Only if I have none, I must either live with Charlotte, which I could not bear—She is a very good person, you must not misunderstand me—"

"I am sure she is," said Mr. Atherton and, despite the fact that Charlotte belonged to the frailer sex, could gladly have taken his horsewhip to her.

"But," said Philadelphia, "she is much older than I am, and—" She hesitated, then said in a burst of confidence, induced possibly by the milk and cinnamon drink, "we have never done very well together. She does so order me about, and if I live with her, would treat me like a servant. And if I do not live with her, I must become either a governess or a companion. I do not think it would be a happy choice for me."

Mr. Atherton suddenly grinned, and said he did not think so, either. He felt that husbands would welcome her with open arms, literally, but wives, after one glance at that beautiful face, would show her the door.

"So unless I have money I can only do one of two things, and neither pleases me."

"So there can be no more argument. You will keep the money. If you do not," said Mr. Atherton, "I shall be extremely vexed with you. Indeed, I shall go instantly to consult with your solicitor."

"Now you are ordering me about," said Philadelphia, and smiled at him, displaying two beguiling dimples.

Mr. Atherton was discovering something not only strange but alarming. In his time he had fallen in love with a great many women, and slept with most of them. Emma had lasted longer than any, and for her he felt not only desire but also a certain respect. But there had been, as there always was, one pure moonlight and roses romance: he was only fifteen at the time, and the woman concerned nearly twice his age. Never again had he recaptured the intensity of that love, the rapture, the ecstasy, the feeling of complete happiness. He no longer remembered the woman's name, he would not have recognized her if he had met her in the street, but he remembered enough of his ardor to wish occasionally that he could once again experience that innocent passion of love. And now, as he looked at this young girl beside him, it was briefly as if he were back in his youth—and he was thirty-one with such adventures behind him as would have brought papa not only tumbling from the wall, but landing on his dissolute head.

He did not therefore immediately answer. He simply looked, and in that look his innocence faded; his face grew taut and expressionless. Philadelphia had never seen such an expression, papa would not have been capable of it, yet it frightened her, for all she did not understand it. Her smile vanished, and she instinctively reached out for the comforting drink, not because she really wanted it but because it gave her something to do.

This time Mr. Atherton did not stop her. After all, there was only a small glass of brandy in a tumbler of milk: it could not possibly harm her. He said in an abrupt voice, his eyes moving away from her perturbed little face with the milky line round her lips, "It is strange that we have met, Philadelphia."

She whispered, "Yes, sir." And of course it was strange, it had always seemed strange, yet she no longer felt frightened or unhappy, only as if she were back in the soft, warm cloud again, remote, enclosed.

He said—and he had no idea why he was talking like this, he was dead sober, he must be out of his mind—"I live in the odd numbers, and you in the even. And after all, there is only a road between us."

"It is quite a narrow road," said Philadelphia, still in a whisper, and she did not know why she was saying this either: it was as if there were an odd moment of truth between them so that they could only speak what was in their minds.

"It is as wide and deep as the pit," said Mr. Atherton.

"I think," said Philadelphia in her normal crisp voice, "you are exaggerating." For in Inverness one did not talk such nonsense, and this was beginning to disturb her, to make her hair prickle on her head.

"Am I?" said Mr. Atherton. "I am not at all sure. You should be more careful, ma'am, in your choice of friends. We are dangerous creatures, we odd numbers. We have a lot of money—"

"So have I!"

"Oh—! We have a trifle more. And we do all the things your father would not approve of. We are wicked, dissolute people, Miss Philadelphia. We drink and we gamble, we dance and we whore—"

At this last word, which had never before been uttered in the house, except once in a Bible reading, Philadelphia's gaze moved down. But she did not back, nor was the look on her face one of any particular revulsion. She merely said quite calmly, "I think you are boasting, Mr. Atherton."

He laughed, "Perhaps I am. You are a very disconcerting young lady. Why do you not call me Tom?"

"Because I think of you as Mr. Atherton. It is," said Philadelphia, "a wee bit like bairns who are brought up to address people older than themselves as uncle or auntie. It gives them a feeling of security. They like it that way."

"Are you telling me," exclaimed Mr. Atherton, his voice rising, "that you look upon me as an uncle? Because if you do—"

"Oh no!" said Philadelphia, and suddenly giggled. It was a pleasing giggle, soft and not prolonged, but it made Mr. Atherton's eyes turn in some apprehension to the milk and cinnamon drink: she really must not take any more of it. "Of course not," she went on, "I could not possibly think of you as an uncle. You are my friend."

"And uncles," said Mr. Atherton, who was beginning to feel almost intoxicated himself, "are not friends?"

"I only have one uncle. My uncle Menzies. He is not my friend at all. He is rather horrid. He smokes a disgusting pipe. But you are my friend, Mr. Atherton, and from now on I will always remember you in my prayers. I do not know," said Philadelphia, her voice trembling a little, "what I would have done without you. You have helped me so much, you have been so kind, and I will love you to the end of my days. The road you talk about may seem very wide, but I think that for at least a wee while we have crossed it together."

Nobody had ever said anything like this to Mr. Atherton in his whole life. The remarks winded him as neatly as if he had been punched in the belly. The innocent use of the word "love"—it must be innocent—and the announcement that he would be prayed for, rendered him momentarily speechless. He said at last in a hoarse voice, "May I kiss you, Philadelphia?"

"Oh no, sir."

"Why not?"

She rose to her feet. She stumbled a little, but that was pure exhaustion. She said, "Because I am not so silly as you think I am."

"I suppose," said Mr. Atherton rather bitterly, for no man likes to be rebuffed, "that a great many men have offered to kiss you."

"Oh," said Philadelphia, "I have had my offers."

He looked at her. Most women, making such a remark, would have looked smug. Philadelphia merely looked resigned, but then it was reasonable to assume that she was simply speaking the plain truth: Helen of Troy might have said the same. He too rose to his feet. He said, rather helplessly, "I have never met anyone like you."

"Ah," she said, "but then I come from the even numbers. I am going to bed now, Mr. Atherton. I am very tired. It has been a long day. It has been a long time altogether."

"I trust that I may call on you again?"

"Oh, I hope so."

"Soon perhaps?"

"If you wish."

He brooded on this. It was not as enthusiastic as he would have liked. He said at last, "I hope you are going to be sensible and keep that money."

Philadelphia said very mournfully, "Yes, I am." She added, "Of course I will make them all presents. But I see now that you are perfectly right. It is what mama wanted. And you see, I am quite alone. There is no one to look after me, only people to organize me and make use of me. It is not after all the same thing."

Mr. Atherton had been about to say that he would look after her, but the phrase that followed this checked him. He saw that he must leave her unkissed, which was a pity for he wanted to kiss her very much. However, he had at least made some kind of assignation. It was plainly going to be a long drawn-out business, and at this the flame of battle rose high: she filled his eye and heart as someone he must subdue.

He bowed to her and kissed her hand. Philadelphia did not accompany him to the door, but she watched him walk away. When she heard the door close behind him she crept to the window and peered through the folds of the curtains. She watched him cross the road, the wide road that lay between them, and did not stir until he disappeared into Number 23.

A few minutes later she was in her own room, and she knelt down by the bed as papa had instructed her long ago when she was a little girl. She prayed for Mr. Atherton, who perhaps needed her prayers, and then she prayed for Charlotte, though regrettably her heart was not entirely in this. Only as she climbed into bed, she found to her surprise that it was not Mr. Atherton who filled her thoughts but someone else who for some time now had almost slipped her memory.

"Jamie!" whispered Philadelphia, mechanically plaiting her hair. Then the tears descended. He had treated her so badly and still she wanted him, he was after all part of her childhood, she had known him all her life, in his way he understood her as Mr. Atherton could never do. Yet she wanted Mr. Atherton too, and at this shocking thought she sat up very stiffly in bed, her newly plaited hair between her fingers. She said aloud and quite censoriously, "I just do not know what has happened to me."

And this was truer than she knew, for almost immediately she fell asleep: she had no idea that this profound and peaceful slumber was due to the wicked alcohol that she had so happily swallowed down a short time ago.

The two sisters met at breakfast next morning. Apart from the conventional greetings there was an unhappy silence. They faced each other across the kitchen table: the chocolate and rolls lay between them and a great deal more beside. The silence came from desperation as much as anger. Charlotte, who had a headache and a queasy stomach after too much wine, had grown more and more aware that she had handled everything disastrously. If only she had made no protest but simply looked hurt and resigned—Philly was a softhearted little thing. A casual reference to the fact that little Tobias needed a new coat, or that the sheets on Henry's bed were torn, would have at once aroused her conscience, she would certainly have offered to buy whatever was needed. It would all be done without the least unpleasantness, and it would probably end precisely as Charlotte had suggested: Philadelphia would make Henry the trustee and come to live with them.

Even now she half expected Philadelphia to capitulate, or at least reintroduce the subject by excusing herself. But her sister barely uttered a word, only she ate no breakfast, simply swallowed down the chocolate and pushed her roll away.

The carriage, as arranged, drew up at nine o'clock. Philadelphia who by this time was feeling almost hysterical with the horror of this disgusting situation suddenly knew that Mr. Atherton was wrong: she had no business whatsoever to hold on to the money, the very thought of which was beginning to sicken her. At least half must be given over. She could manage after all, as she had decided before, for even that would be

more than she had ever had in her life. She wondered
how she could have been so wicked and weak as to
listen to Mr. Atherton's advice. The very thought of
this decision filled her with relief. She turned towards
her sister who was coming down the stairs, a small
portmanteau in her hand. She thought that Charlotte
looked very angry and very plain, her mouth drawn
down, the protuberant eyes staring ahead. It was obvious that she was deeply upset, and Philadelphia's
conscience stabbed at her like a knife. She opened her
mouth to explain her decision but, as she did so, Charlotte spoke.

"I have no doubt," said Charlotte, exercising her fa-
tal flair for saying everything at the wrong moment,
"that you are delighted to see the last of me. I am only
sorry that I have imposed on your hospitality for so
long. It must have been vastly tedious for you. Of
course I thought that as sisters we should be together
at such a sad time—but I see I was mistaken. I am
going home now. I do not know how I shall be able to
face Henry and poor wee Tobias, but there it is, it's
my problem, it is not my fault that the child's sweet
love is not returned. I don't suppose you will have
much time for us in the future, what with your fine
gentleman and, naturally, all the balls and parties and
elegant new clothes you will be indulging in, but if
you do have a moment of leisure and it will not be too
boring for you to come out to Chelsea, we shall in our
humble way do our best to entertain you. How I shall
ever explain to Tobias that his auntie doesn't want to
be with him, I cannot imagine, but pray do not let
that worry you, you will have enough distraction, I'm
sure, to help you forget us."

She could not, if she had tried, spoken more disastrously, apart from the fact that when in a temper she

always spoke as if addressing a public meeting. Philadelphia had a conscience, but she also had spirit, and the gross unfairness of this attack roused instantly the Smith temper, which the sisters shared. She did not answer one word. She simply looked. The picture of the bereft household at Chelsea, with poor wee Tobias languishing for her, and presumably no dinner to set upon the table, while she herself bought a dozen new gowns and instantly descended upon the town, was such that anything she might have uttered would only have made the situation a hundred times worse. The beautiful color, that Mr. Atherton had so admired, flooded into her cheeks, and at the same time the good resolutions drained away. She watched in silence as Charlotte, her head held high, stepped out into the street. No embraces were exchanged. When Charlotte said, "Goodbye, Philadelphia. I wish you every success in your new life, I'm sure," she merely answered, "Goodbye, Charlotte," and instantly went back into the house.

The coachman, like most of his kind, was observant, malicious and a snob. He did not care at all for his mistress, who was definitely not a lady, and who paid him as little as she could, while speaking to him as if he had come from the gutter. He watched this pantomime with much amusement. It was plain that the two ladies had fallen out, and he would have given a great deal to know the cause. However, he handed Charlotte into the carriage, and presently they set off for Chelsea.

Philadelphia was still in too much of a temper to feel the least remorse. She positively stamped up and down the parlor, thinking such unChristian thoughts that in a short while she grew ashamed of herself, and sat down on the sofa to regain some calm and self-control.

The sound of something being slipped under the door brought her instantly out into the hall.

It was a letter from Jamie. Her dreams had not betrayed her. She recognized the stiff, upright handwriting instantly. He had never been much of a letter writer, indeed, his epistles were brief and matter of fact, unlike Philadelphia's which went on for pages. But she was so enchanted to hear from him that she forgot all the bitterness that had passed between them, ran back into the parlor and there, curled up on the sofa, tore the letter open.

"My Dearest Girl," wrote Jamie in the fine script that he had learnt at school,

> I have taken the Opportunity to send you this Epistle by a Friend who is crossing the Channel. I am well and happy, My Lord is very good to me, and we are now traveling through France after spending two Days in Paris. We will soon go to Rome, and after that, I do not know. We see many Pictures and old Buildings. I like the Foreign Food, tho' it is a Pity that I do not speak the Language. I miss you, Philly, and hope to see you soon. I will write again. I love you, my Dearest. I always think of you. I hope you have forgiven me. Your very own Jamie.

There was no address but then, as Jamie was on the Grand Tour with my lord, it would not be possible. Philadelphia, after reading this through another three times, was so happy that it did not strike her for quite a while that first, it was odd the friend had not called in person, and secondly that it must have been a marvelous journey for Jamie to have seen Paris already.

However, she had no experience of foreign travel, and perhaps in these modern days this was not so extraordinary. It was a shame that the letter was so short. It really told her almost nothing, and she longed to hear about all the small things that made up his daily life. But then that was Jamie's way, he had once declared that she wrote enough for the pair of them, and indeed Philadelphia sometimes felt that she was as bad as Pamela who, from the number of words she produced, could have no time for eating or sleeping. She sighed, reading again the bald statement about Paris and Rome. It somehow sounded quite dull, and she could not help thinking that it was unlikely the two young men should spend their entire time gazing at pictures and old buildings. If this were really so, Jamie must be bored to death, for, possessing an alert and practical mind, he had little patience with things before his time. However, if life were occasionally not so academic, it would not appear seemly to Jamie to tell her about it, and Philadelphia, her face grown prim, considered for a while what the nonacademic life could be like, for this was something entirely outside her experience. Vague pictures of loose women, flowing wine, and cards and dice, flashed through her mind: the irreverent side of her that papa had sometimes deplored, suggested that Jamie would not be much use with loose women, who would surely expect him to flirt gracefully and make a leg. But she would still have preferred to think that there were no loose women at all, and perhaps in Rome, where they probably were by now, there would be so much to see that Jamie would have no time for outside diversions.

Chapter 8

Mr. Atherton, now set on seeing Philadelphia again,
wished that he was as calm as a man of his mature
years should be. He found to his irritation that he was
breathing more quickly than usual and that his pulse
was noticeably fast. That last time when he was crossing the road that led to the odd number of his home,
he had been quite shocked by his own reactions.
There was no denying that he was becoming positively obsessed with this girl; she might be a nobody,
and certainly the two of them had little in common,
but he was behaving like a green boy, and all because
of a startling beauty. He told himself this repeatedly,
and it made no difference at all: he was drunk on
Philadelphia, he could not wait to see her again, he

tossed and turned all night, wishing to God that she were in bed beside him.

And what the prim little Scots madam would think of that was something he preferred not to consider.

Emma had not of course helped, and this was something else he would never tell Philadelphia. She was, he found, waiting for him. She would certainly have seen his emergence from Number 22. Her arrival was not really so unusual, which added to Mr. Atherton's resentment. The hour was barely ten at night, which for the odd numbers was almost the afternoon, and Emma had always had the habit of descending on him as the fancy took her. Indeed, she sometimes arrived in the middle of the night, on her way home from a party: some men might have been alarmed by this, but Mr. Atherton had seldom given a damn for gossip or scandal, and mostly he would laugh, liking the impudence of it, and discovering as always that he needed her.

He did not need her now. She was the last person in the world that he wanted to see, and the fact that she looked at her most beautiful, and was dressed in a more extravagant manner than he had ever seen, somehow made it worse. When he came into his drawing room, to see her reclining on the sofa, he muttered, "Oh, my God!" in an ungentlemanly way under his breath, and though he instantly regretted the words and prayed they had not been audible, he saw that Emma's sharp hearing had caught them.

The betraying color swept up her throat. But her voice and demeanor were calm, and she rose to greet him, smiling as if all were well. She wore a gown that he had never seen, which, as the dressmaker had only finished it a few hours before, was not surprising. It was made of an oyster-colored silk, with a pink rosebud motif round the hem, throat and sleeves, and against it her magnolia skin seemed creamier, the raven hair blacker. He knew she was beautiful, yet at that moment she meant no more to him than the carpet on the floor; his eyes were filled with a young, innocent face, his ears with a soft, Scots accented voice. He wanted none of her, he simply wanted Philadelphia, Philadelphia Smith, who was too young for him, too pure, who came from the wrong class, and with whom he certainly had hardly one idea in common.

"Well, Tom?" said Emma in her low, husky voice. "Is it not time we stopped quarreling? I have just fought a little war with my pride, and my pride lost. I have come to make it up. Shall we kiss and then forget all about it?"

He could not help knowing what an effort this must be for her. Beauties do not have to chase their gentlemen, and Emma, from the time she was in her teens, had barely had to raise a finger to have half London at her feet. He muttered, "Of course, of course, I am delighted to see you," and took her into his arms. He kissed her as lovingly as he could, and that kiss betrayed him more than anything else could have done, for they had been lovers for a long time now, and he kissed her as a stranger.

Emma, suddenly not looking beautiful at all, jerked herself away from him, saying in a harsh voice, "So you think you've done with me, Tom, do you?"

"Look," said Mr. Atherton, as a million gentlemen in his dilemma had said before him, "I am very tired—"

"Is she so exhausting, your little lamb?"

"How vulgar you are, Emma!"

Then she forgot everything she had ever learnt, and began to scream at him. She was more at a disadvantage than most, for she had never before been in such a situation. She had thought sometimes that Tom might never marry her, that their affair might trail to its end as affairs do, but it had never entered her head that she would be so brutally supplanted and by a common little chit who was scarce out of the schoolroom. She spat out two vicious names at him then, beside herself, cried out, "You're not finished with me yet. Can you believe that I'll let myself be pushed out to pasture like some old mare past her prime? We've known each other too well for that. I thought you loved me. God knows, you've told me so often enough. And within a few days you meet someone else, and that is the end of me. But it's not, boy, oh it's not. I'm not being ditched for some common little slut, a trollop from the gutter—"

It was hardly a fair description of Philadelphia, as Emma knew perfectly well, but she was beside herself with shock and misery, and hardly knew what she was saying. When Mr. Atherton swung out his hand and slapped her across the cheek, she fell silent, and so did he. They stared at each other in a kind of exhausted dismay, neither understanding how in a few brief moments their love could fall to such baseness.

Mr. Atherton, who was not by nature a violent man, screwed up his eyes and muttered in a savage monotone, "I'm sorry. I did not mean to do that. It was unpardonable—"

"Yes," said Emma, "it was unpardonable," and at this naturally Mr. Atherton forgot his remorse and wished he had slapped her harder. He looked at her with what seemed to her naked hatred, and she met the look proudly enough, though the tears were bursting behind her eyes, and despair and longing were making her feel physically sick.

She said very quietly, "Am I to be invited to the wedding?"

Mr. Atherton struggled to compose himself and bring some reason to this appalling situation. He came up to her, but she instantly backed away. He made a horrified gesture then said, deliberately moderating his voice, "If you would listen to me for just one moment—I want to explain. I must explain. You cannot believe I am enjoying this—"

"I think you're enjoying it very much," said Emma. She had moved in front of a gilt wall mirror, and was patting her hair into place. All traces of the harridan were gone; this was a composed young lady of fashion who even sounded a trifle bored.

"I assure you I am not," said Mr. Atherton, and this was true enough. He strode over to the decanter, and poured himself out a glass of wine. His hand was shaking. Then he remembered his manners and offered some to Emma, but she shook her head, even managed to smile.

He said, almost imploringly, "Could you not listen to me? I know I have behaved badly, and I never meant to strike you, but if you would just listen—for a few minutes."

"Oh," said Emma, "I'll listen for an hour if it pleases you, but then, you see, I know exactly what you are going to say. Shall I say it for you, Tom? I'll probably word it in a more elegant fashion than you. After all, this is like a play, only of course I am no longer playing the leading role. Let me see now—"

"Emma! For God's sake—"

"Oh, I think we'll leave God out of it. Though she is a religious girl, no doubt. These little misses often are. It makes no difference to their behavior but then, so they say, all good whores say their prayers before falling to their work—perhaps they believe it will spare them a few flames in hell."

Mr. Atherton closed his eyes, and ran a frantic hand across his wig, thus shooting it awry. At that moment he wished all women, without exception, to the devil: the only possible life would be in a monastery.

"How about this?" said Emma, very sweetly. "You must of course remember that I am no longer Emma Slade, this is Mr. Thomas Atherton, damn his poxed soul, speaking. Well now—" Her voice rose to a foolish falsetto. "It is not, my dearest, that I do not love you. I will always love you, as a friend. It is not that I am not grateful for the happy hours we have passed together. I will always remember you, Emma, and I hope and pray you will be godmother to all our little children—"

Mr. Atherton opened his mouth then shut it again. He looked at Emma, who had draped herself over the back of a chair, her head flung back, an expression of what seemed to him idiocy on her face.

"Only," she went on, "you must know yourself that our love was not real love. You should rejoice with me that I have now met this beautiful girl, innocent as a dove, pure as—as—pure as the driven snow. Is that not what they say? You see how poetic I have become. Never before have I experienced such an emotion. I cannot express to you, dearest Emma, the purity of our love. I know that in the kindness and nobility of your heart you will see that we must part as if we had never met. I cannot after all come to my little lamb, sullied and defiled with fornication, lecherous kisses and—"

"I do not think," said Mr. Atherton in a choked voice, "that you have quite caught my style."

"Have I not? Oh surely. I can almost hear you saying it. And at the end you will come up to me and whisper, Let us part friends. I will always remember you, Emma. I could not bear to part in anger. Let us kiss and part—in a pure and decent way, of course—and you must know, sweet girl, that I wish you all happiness, and don't forget to return all the jewels I have given you, all three of them, so that I can pass them on to my sweet new love without involving myself in too much expense—"

For the first time Mr. Atherton appeared to be deriving a certain grim humor from the situation. The glazed look had left his face. He was surveying Emma with a faint smile, and this disconcerted her so that her voice grew more natural, and her words began to fall over each other.

But she managed to continue, saying, "Goodbye, dear Emma. I know you'll understand. You will always have the memory of my gratitude. And now, dear, I must go to my little sweetheart, so pure, so lovely, so innocent, so sweet." Suddenly her voice roughened, and the words flew out like stones. "And once I've got the bitch in bed with me, she can whistle for her ring, and when I've done with her and ruined her and got her with a child, I'll come back to you, Emma, and you will of course be delighted to see me—"

Then she burst into floods of tears.

"I think," said Mr. Atherton, "you had better go."

"I think so too," sobbed Emma, then her poise and sophistication slipped from her as if it had never been, and she burst into the traditional wail of all wronged women, crying out, "to treat me like this after all I've done for you!" She turned a frenzied, tear-blubbered face upon him. "You'll be sorry! You'll not get way

with this. Oh, I could kill you, I've never hated anyone so much in my life—"

And with this she was out of the door, slamming it
behind her with such violence that it might well have
come off its hinges. She had completely forgotten that
the real point of her visit was to warn Tom about
Ferdy and his wicked intentions, and she did not remember this until she was driving off; by this time
she was in such a state that she no longer cared.
Ferdy could do as he pleased, he could cut the bitch's
throat for all it mattered to her: her own life was over,
there was nothing left, she could only wish she were
dead.

And Mr. Atherton, hearing the sound of the carriage driving off, almost fell on to the sofa. The hand
that poured out more wine, shook so badly that he
almost knocked the decanter to the floor. He was, if
Emma had known it, savagely ashamed of himself. It
had never dawned on him before, but he saw now
that it could be possible to love two women at once,
only the trouble was that for a while one wanted one
woman on Monday and the other on Tuesday: no
female in the world would endure such a situation.
And he knew, to his shame and despair, that though
he wanted Philadelphia most passionately, he wanted
Emma too: he was horrified at the prospect of no
Emma at all. She had in her own way become part of
him, and the violence and vulgarity she had just dis-
played was somehow in keeping with her charm for
him. It was as if he needed someone to swear at him,
fight with him, provoke him to insults and blows, and
it was true that the next instant she could become so
soft and loving that it melted his heart.

And presently, a little drunk after too much wine, he
realized two things, one so bizarre that it made him

laugh, and the other sinister enough to go a long way towards sobering him up.

The bizarre thing was that the only person who would ever really understand what had happened to him was Emma herself. He was possessed of an utterly ludicrous urge to follow after her and say, Let me tell you about it, without nonsense or lies or hypocrisy, let me explain what has happened. It is not that I have pushed you out, it is rather that I have crowded the two of you in—

Then the second thought struck him. How the devil did Emma know so much about Philadelphia? She seemed to be remarkably well informed. It did not take him long to arrive at the answer. There was only one other person who could know, and that person was malicious and spiteful enough to enjoy making mischief, especially after what had passed between them.

Mr. Atherton, now very angry indeed, vowed that he would see Ferdy as soon as possible. It did not for one moment enter his head that Ferdy was not confining his mischief-making to words, but then what was now passing through Ferdy's vicious mind was something so inconceivable that Mr. Atherton would probably not have believed it, even if it had actually been explained to him. In a little while he fell asleep on the sofa. No further warning sounded in his bemused brain, and he had no idea that his beautiful little girl was in the utmost danger.

Chapter 9

Philadelphia read Jamie's letter through again for the third time. When she came to the phrase, "I hope you have forgiven me," her eyes misted over. She said, aloud, "Oh, of course I have forgiven you, my darling, how could I ever do anything else?"—then was horrified into a scarlet blush when Mr. Atherton's voice said, "I trust you are speaking of me."

He was standing in the doorway. He was smiling. A big bunch of flowers was in his hand. "May I come in?" he asked, a trifle unnecessarily as one foot was already over the threshold, then he said in a different voice, "You really should bolt your front door, Miss Philadelphia, especially now that you are on your own and a young lady of means. Anybody could come in. There are many evil characters abroad these days. I should like you to give me your word that in future you will always secure the lock."

Philadelphia, her cheeks still very red, answered a little rebelliously, "I have always left the front door off the latch."

"Then that is very foolish of you. After all, you cannot pretend that you heard me come in, yet I made no particular effort to move quietly. I could easily be a thief, knock you down and steal all your valuables."

"There are no valuables!"

Mr. Atherton saw that she was in a difficult mood, and deduced correctly that it was something to do with the letter in her hand. He was not displeased. Young women with temperaments were easier to handle than those without, besides, it gave an added zest to the game. He would soon find out what was the matter and, in a little while, he would contrive to make Philadelphia laugh: from then on she might listen to what he had to propose to her, even perhaps agree.

And now, as he warned Philadelphia about the locking of her front door, it never struck Mr. Atherton how apt the warning was.

"I daresay," he said, "in Scotland you leave the doors ajar all the time."

"We are only simple country folk," said Philadelphia.

She had, as he had already noticed, a certain sharpness of humor. He gave her a look, and she burst out laughing. It was so charming a sound that he laughed back, and after this she waved him to the nearest chair, while marveling over the beautiful flowers he had brought her.

She said, almost wonderingly, "You are so kind to me. I shall never know how to thank you. I have told

Mr. Bridges about you. He does not really trust people very much, I suppose it's because he's a lawyer, but he says he is glad that I have found myself such a good friend. Did you know that he is giving me some of the money in advance? I am now quite rich—at least I shall be within a few days."

"If you are in any immediate difficulties—"

"Oh no." The voice was extremely definite. Obviously papa, as well as keeping his family from the bottle, had warned them about accepting money from strangers. The tone of Philadelphia's voice was such that Mr. Atherton did not dare press the matter. "Besides," she went on, "my needs are so few."

"And what will you do with the money when you get it? Will you buy yourself some fine new gowns?"

She looked at him in surprise. He saw that this idea had not yet crossed her mind, perhaps because until now she had never had anything to spend on luxuries, but it was plain that Philadelphia was as human as the rest of her sex, for a meditative expression flickered across her face, and her next words did not sound entirely sincere.

She said, "Oh no. I hardly ever go out, you see, so it would be a dreadful waste of money." Then she said, quite crossly, "I gather—" (she pronounced the word with a long "a") "—I gather you think I look dowdy."

"Not at all," said Mr. Atherton, glancing briefly at the gray dress she was wearing, with its black armband, "only I believe that most females enjoy new clothes from time to time."

"I am sure," said Philadelphia, "you understand our sex very well."

"I think," he said, "you are a minx." He had almost used a cruder word, but checked himself in time:

Philadelphia was certainly not used to the free language of the odd numbers.

She did not answer this, only looked at him sideways in what he had to see was quite a flirtatious manner. She said, "I would not know where to go."

"Henrietta Street," said Mr. Atherton promptly, then more tentatively, "It would be a privilege and a pleasure to accompany you. Would you permit me to be your escort?"

The color flew into her cheeks. "Oh no!" she exclaimed. "It would not be seemly. What would people think? Why—"

"I'll tell you what people would think," said Mr. Atherton, thinking the time had come for a little firmness. It was all going to be a long, long process, but really, this girlishness must be stopped; besides, he was aware of an increasing suspicion that it was not entirely genuine. Philadelphia might be an innocent, but she was too lovely to be so ingenuous, and there must have been other gentlemen to hint and suggest. "They will think I am your lover," he said. Then he smiled. "There is nothing I would like to be more, but I am sure your papa would never permit me to say so."

She did not bridle or look shocked. She merely said with perfect calm, "I am betrothed, Mr. Atherton. I have just received a letter from him. He will no doubt be returning home shortly. He is accompanying a noble gentleman on the Grand Tour, you know."

"I remember you told me," said Mr. Atherton, rather sourly. He also remembered her telling him that the engagement had been broken, but did not choose to remind her, though the inconsistency was interesting. He was aware of an acute dislike for this young man—what was his name now? Jamie. Jamie! For God's

sake, what a name! He said, "I do not wish to offend
your fiancé, but he cannot after all expect you to live
in complete seclusion while he is away. If I promise
that you will be suitably chaperoned, would you accompany me to the playhouse one evening?"

He saw at once that this had far more effect than
the prospect of a new gown. Philadelphia gave a little
gasp, and said, "Oh, how I love the theater—Do you
know, I have only been once in my whole life."

"I gather that papa did not approve."

"You must not make fun of my father, Mr. Atherton."

"I beg your pardon." He glanced instinctively
at the forbidding portrait over the mantelpiece, and
Philadelphia did likewise: then she realized how both
pairs of eyes were fixed on Dr. Smith's countenance
and began to giggle.

She said, "It is true that papa was angry, but it was
Shakespeare, so in the end he forgave me. It was a
wee company that came to Inverness. I don't think
they were very good, but it was the first play I had
ever seen in my life, and I thought it was wonderful.
It was like going into another world."

"What was the play?"

"*A Midsummer Night's Dream.* Would you really
take me to the playhouse, Mr. Atherton?"

"Upon my honor we will go the moment you wish
to do so."

"And you are sure there would be a chaperone?"

"Two, if you prefer it," said Mr. Atherton, while
rummaging a little frantically in his mind for someone
suitable. It was a pity that the only person he could
think of was Emma. He wondered what she would say
if he asked her.

"Of course," said Philadelphia, "there is no question

of my going now. It would be disrespectful to my poor dear mama's memory. Yet—oh, how lovely it would be."

"And of course you must buy yourself a new gown for the occasion. I would suggest a velvet, a soft crimson or perhaps a golden brown—"

"I did not know," said Philadelphia, "that gentlemen were so knowledgeable on ladies' clothes." She paused and sighed. She said, "How sad it is that I cannot ever go."

"What do you mean?" demanded Mr. Atherton, suddenly angry, for he had not expected this about-face; he believed the matter was settled.

Philadelphia said in a clear, cool voice, "I do not know how it is in your world, Mr. Atherton, but in mine a girl who is affianced to one gentleman never goes out with another. What do you imagine Jamie would say? Why, he would be furious."

He did not answer this directly. He was possessed of a passionate longing to knock Jamie down, or run him through with his sword. He said quietly, "You talk of my world as if it were Cathay. Yet there is only a road between us. It is not even a very wide road."

"You yourself," said Philadelphia, "told me it was as wide and deep as the pit. Have you forgot? I think I argued with you, and you told me I was exaggerating. But now I see you are perfectly right, and I was silly to speak as I did." Then she murmured, beneath her breath, "Oh, I wish you were not right."

"Do you? Do you?" He took a step towards her, and she held up her hands as if to ward him off. But he paid no attention, only gripped her shoulders. He could feel she was trembling, and a shudder of excitement went through him. He said, "I tell you what we'll do, Miss Philadelphia. We'll build a bridge, from Number 22 to Number 23."

"It would break beneath us!"

"Then we'll buy ourselves a little boat and sail from shore to shore, never landing."

"I think both sides would throw stones at us."

He said gently, "What a silly girl you are!" then bent his head and kissed her. She did not move away, though he felt her body stiffen. The lips beneath his were soft and compliant; heaven knows what papa would be saying now, but his daughter was a human being after all. However, he did not pursue his advantage, and after a moment moved away. Only the triumph gleamed briefly on his face until he masked it: if Philadelphia noticed this she said nothing, only whispered after a long pause, "You should not have done that."

"Didn't you like it?"

But this was too much for papa's daughter from Inverness. She said haughtily, "That is nothing to do with it whatsoever, and well you know it. I am surprised at you, Mr. Atherton. I believed you to be a gentleman."

"That was foolish of you," said Mr. Atherton.

Philadelphia said at last, almost in despair, "It's not only that we come from different worlds. We don't even speak the same language. I never understand the half of what you are saying. Oh, Mr. Atherton, please listen to me, instead of fidgeting about the room like that."

"I am listening. And my name is Tom. I told you. It is a very common name. I am sure that both odd and even numbers are called Tom."

"I want you to listen properly," cried Philadelphia, so excited that she banged her hand on the chair.

"And I call you Mr. Atherton because I think of you as Mr. Atherton."

"Yet I call you Philadelphia," said Mr. Atherton. He found this ridiculous conversation wildly exciting. He felt he was beginning to know his little girl from across the road: at least they were not facing each other, making polite conversation. But her next remark so shocked him that it was as if all his advantage had gone.

She said calmly, "That is right and proper. That is one of the differences between us. I cannot address you by your first name, but you are perfectly entitled to call me by mine."

"You confounded little snob!"

"Oh, that is not fair, I am not—"

"Of course you are. Snobbery works both ways. You regard yourself as a kitchen maid, Philadelphia. I am glad you know your place. I trust that next time you visit me you will use the servants' entrance."

She said in a tense, soft voice, "I could kill you!"—and at this singularly non-servile remark, he burst out laughing, checking himself almost immediately for he saw that she was on the point of tears.

He said gently, longing to put his arms round her again, but not daring to, "This is our first quarrel. Now we are really getting to know each other."

She gave him a watery smile: she seemed to have recovered her temper. Emboldened, he went on, "Would it be so wrong to let me take you to the theater?"

"In the circumstances," she answered, "it would be very wrong indeed."

"Yet your precious young man seems to have walked out on you. I do not find that admirable in either of our worlds." Then he remembered what had passed between him and Emma, and did not continue, only looked down, biting a little at his lower lip.

She only said, "No. That is not true. In a sense it would be fairer to say that I have walked out on him."

He said, "Well, I'll not dispute that with you. It is after all entirely your affair. Only you are a singularly pretty girl, Philadelphia, as you know perfectly well—you do know it. Of course you do. Admit it."

"Oh, I do not believe myself ill-favored," said Philadelphia, recovered enough to display her dimples, and indeed, with the bright color in her cheeks and a perceptibly flirtatious turn of the eyes, she was so beautiful that Mr. Atherton moved a couple of paces away.

He said dryly, "Shall we say, you are not precisely plain. I find it strange that your young man, however estimable his motives, should trust you sufficiently to leave you. I myself would not leave you for a single moment. Look at what is happening to you now. You are in the presence of a wicked villain from the odd numbers who is already, after the briefest of acquaintances, trying to entrap you into buying new clothes and visiting the playhouse. Are you not afraid, Philadelphia? For all you know, I might be planning to seduce you."

She answered, to his astonishment, "Oh, I expect you are."

This stripped all words from him and he could only stare at her. At last he said, "I think that is unwise of you. We are alone together, there is no one within call, and I do not think you would have much chance against me."

"Is that a threat?"

"I think it might be more in the nature of a promise."

Philadelphia stared at him. She said nothing. Then

for one appalling and extraordinary moment the thought came to her that instead of running away she would move closer, hold out her arms, smile up at him, pretend to comply. He would surely be so shattered that he would simply gape at her—but then one never really knew with Mr. Atherton, and it was just conceivable that he would not be shattered at all. The sheer wickedness of all this brought the color roaring into her cheeks; it was almost as if papa stood over her, pale with horror at his daughter's iniquity. She moved clumsily backwards, glancing around her as if she were looking for some defensive weapon: it was herself she was running from, but this of course he would never know. But he believed her to be terrified, and this restored his temper: he laughed again and in a derisive fashion that made her scowl furiously. When he spoke, however, it was with perfect calm, and he in no way resembled Pamela's wicked master.

He said, "I have no intention of harming you, but I want you to listen to me. You keep on telling me to listen to you, so now we will reverse the rôles. I think you owe me a few minutes. You insist that we come from different worlds. I think that is true, indeed, I would not attempt to deny it. As to my intentions, I do not choose to deny them either, though I think you must grant me that so far I have treated you with perfect courtesy—"

She said, a little sulkily, "You have been very kind."

"So you keep on telling me. I am beginning to find it tedious. But tell me this, ma'am. Would you marry me if I asked you?"

"No!"

"I wonder," said Mr. Atherton, so softly that she was not quite sure if she had heard him, but then by this time she was in such a state of confusion that she hardly knew what was being said by either of them. Then he said more briskly, "I think perhaps we are both being a little foolish. I feel I am beginning to frighten you—"

"I am not in the least frightened!"

"Well, perhaps you are beginning to frighten me. I suspect that we both need a little time to consider each other. I propose to leave you in peace for a while, Philadelphia." He had to notice her change of expression, and this delighted him: it encouraged him to continue. "I'll not come to see you tomorrow. Indeed, since I appear to have offended you—"

"But you have not—"

"I'll not come at all until I receive an invitation."

Mr. Atherton was unaware that this was a decision he was to regret most bitterly, but then he had no idea of what lay in store. He could only see that he had disconcerted his darling, naughty little girl, and this enchanted him, it proved that she was by no means as impervious as she wished him to believe. Indeed, she was looking quite miserable, but he refused to relent. She deserved it after all, she had presumed to lecture him, she seemed to think that she was in the position of power. With luck, when he returned—he suspected that in spite of everything he would have to make the first move, for she was very proud—she would surely prove far more amenable. He went on, "Goodbye, Philadelphia. You must always remember that I am your friend." His dark eyes moved briefly over her. "I trust we shall meet again soon."

She simply said, "Goodbye, Mr. Atherton."

This time she did not creep to the curtain to watch him return home. She stayed where she was, and presently she sat down on the sofa, with Jamie's letter in her hand. Her face was resentful and bewildered. She was still shocked by her own wicked thoughts, and yet not entirely ashamed of them. She should be glad to see less of Mr. Atherton, but she had to admit that life would lose a great deal of its savor when he was not there: in some ways he was a most immoral man, but he was very exciting and, she had to confess, very attractive. And there was Jamie—The whole situation was like nothing that she had ever met in her life, and what Charlotte would say about it, she could not imagine, but it had become a play, it was almost unreal, and Philadelphia, who had for a long time now led a dull kind of life, could not restrain the shiver of pleasure that passed through her.

She said, as she had said before, "I am a wicked girl," then reached out for a volume of *Pamela* as if this would prove a kind of exorcism.

She opened it at random, and it seemed as if the fates had somehow prompted her hand. Indeed, the passage was so applicable that it made her gasp.

She read:

"Come in," said he, "when I bid you." I did so.
"Pray, Sir," said I, "pity and spare me."
He took hold of my hand . . . "You have too much good sense not to discover that I, in spite of my heart and all the pride of it, cannot but love you. Look up to me, my sweet-faced girl! I must say I love you: and have put on a behaviour to you, that was much against my heart, in hopes to frighten you from your reservedness—"

It might have been Mr. Atherton speaking. Except that he had not called her a sweet-faced girl, he had called her a confounded little snob, and he had certainly not told her he loved her.

Would you marry me if I asked you?

Philadelphia let the book drop to the floor. She was beginning to tremble. Of course she would not marry him, and he had not asked her either, merely put to her this hypothetical question. It was really quite impertinent. Almost as if he expected her to say yes. She looked down at Jamie's letter. She had always been a girl to know her own mind: up till now there had never been any real choice. Jamie had lived next door, they had grown up together, they had everything in common, and she knew she loved him. It was a genuine love, only somehow it was not quite so exciting as being with Mr. Atherton, who seemed to turn the simplest conversation into a battle.

She said aloud—she really must stop talking to herself, it was said that all women who lived alone did so—"I am enjoying myself!" Once she would have written it all down in her diary, but then that was the old, dull Philadelphia, in the pre-Atherton days. To punish herself for her uncontrolled behavior, she set about tidying the little house that was now her own. But she could not, despite everything that had happened, stop herself from breaking into a little gay song, and the knowledge that soon Mr. Atherton would be bound to turn up again on her doorstep, was wonderful, it lent an air of glamour to washing dishes and dusting furniture.

Emma had driven home in a state of near hysteria. She wept furiously throughout the journey. She had quarreled with Tom many times before, but never like this, never like this. The coachman must of course be aware of her distress, but it no longer mattered. In any case, like all of his kind he knew about everything that happened in the household. When she climbed down from the carriage, he helped her as he always did, and she saw the look of pity on his face, as if he were really sorry for her.

She looked up at him before stepping into the house. He had opened the door for her. She gave him a lopsided smile. He thought she really was a lovely girl, despite the fact that she was crying. What the devil was the matter with that Mr. Atherton to treat her so badly? Half the gentlemen in London were crawling after her: how like a female that she had to choose the one who apparently did not want her.

She said, "Well, Jack? What do you think I ought to do?"

He answered warily, "I don't know what you mean, Miss Emma."

"Oh yes, you do," said Emma, tapping his arm with her glove. "Of course you do. You've got eyes in your head, haven't you? My gentleman has jilted me. He thinks he's fallen in love with someone else. Come on, Jack. Give me your advice as a man. What do I do now?"

He hesitated. Miss Emma was always free in her speech, and he knew that her brother disapproved of the way she spoke to the servants, almost as if they were her equals. They had often discussed the matter below stairs. The cook was as censorious as the master, but then she belonged to the old school, she believed that everyone should keep his place.

He said at last, "I think, begging your pardon, ma'am, that you should find someone else. I think you should go to parties and balls and dinners and not stop at home brooding. I'm sure there's a hundred gentlemen would leap at the opportunity to escort you. Why, I daresay you could marry tomorrow, if the fancy took you, a fine-looking young lady like you."

"Perhaps," suggested Emma, comforted by the frank admiration in his eyes, "I could marry in the Fleet."

He exclaimed, so disturbed that he spoke naturally, "You've no call to talk like that, Miss Emma. It's a wicked place. You'll have a grand wedding in church, and all London will come out to see you."

"As if it were a public hanging," said Emma. Really, the mistress sometimes said the most shocking things—then she bestowed on him her lovely smile, and for that smile the coachman, who was a little in love with her, would have lain his length for her to put her foot on. "You have quite restored me," she told him then, just as he was about to close the door, "Have you got a girl, Jack?"

"Yes, ma'am."

"Is it serious? Are you going to marry her?"

"Yes, ma'am."

"Then treat her kindly, and don't suddenly fall in love with someone else."

For the whole week Emma took her coachman's advice. She went out to dinner, she promenaded in Ranelagh, she went to the playhouse, she danced till the sun came up. She flirted outrageously with dozens of bemused young men, she laughed and talked wildly, and returned home to weep into her pillow, because she wanted none of them, she wanted Tom. And at the end of the week she knew she could endure it no longer. She canceled an invitation to a masked ball, and came into her drawing room, to spend the evening on her own. She walked up and down the room like a tigress. She was thankful that her brother was away. He had never approved of her relationship with Tom, but if he discovered how badly she had been treated, he would be threatening all kinds of things, from horsewhipping to a duel in Hyde Park. He would of course do neither of them, for he was terrified of scandal, but it would all be very unpleasant, there would certainly be a lecture, and in the end they would quarrel violently as they had done so many times before.

Emma looked around for her comforting sweetmeats, saw that there were none, then peremptorily rang the bell to demand a bottle of wine. Then she lay down on the couch, and proceeded to drink glass after glass. She knew this was utterly foolish. It was not her custom to drink to excess, it was very bad for the complexion, and Tom would simply despise her, but she was so utterly miserable and ashamed that there seemed nothing else to do.

Once again she brooded on that disastrous conversation. It had indeed never been out of her mind during the whole week: the ugly words rang in her ears while she was laughing and flirting with the faceless cavaliers who had rushed to escort her wherever she pleased. She had of course handled the whole business abominably, no stupid little chit in her teens could have done worse, but then she had not until now permitted herself to acknowledge how violently and senselessly in love she had become. And now she knew that he loved someone else, and it was quite unbearable, it was like something tearing at her entrails. What with jealousy, remorse and wretchedness, in addition to the bottle of wine, she found herself hating Philadelphia with a passion that almost frightened herself. She whispered, "I would like to murder you," and at that moment she meant it: the idea that this provincial little girl with nothing but a pretty face had ensnared Tom, was so unendurable that she longed for a knife with which to cut the usurper's throat.

And it was at this point, after yet another glass of wine, that Ferdy, shambling in, in his usual way, found her lying there, palpably drunk and plainly distraught with misery.

She looked at him in a hazy disgust. She had almost forgotten their previous conversation, but her loathing for him still remained, though the drink had made her feel clogged and stupid and possessed of an irrational anger that made her want to scream at everyone. She was dimly aware that she had drunk far more than she should have done, she was helplessly out of control, and she began to scream at Ferdy.

He looked at her with delighted interest, noting the almost empty bottle and the hectic flush on her cheeks. All this suited him finely for, though he was a secretive man, he had in this instance to make her his ally. There would certainly be trouble later, and he had every intention of thrusting all the blame on her so that Tom's wrath would be deflected.

"I will not," shouted Emma, half raising herself from the couch, then falling back again because her head ached so badly, "have you wandering in and out of my house as if you owned it. My servants tell me you simply push your way past. In future I shall make sure that you are refused admittance."

Even in her intoxicated state she knew this was ridiculous. Ferdy, despite his uncoordinated body, was an immensely powerful man, and he would continue to do as he always did: shove aside anyone who tried to stop him. She shuddered at the sight of him, filthy, crumpled, grinning as always, yet she went on talking, her soft voice now thick and rambling: it was almost as if she did not know what she was saying.

"I want to kill her," she said. "What has she got, this little trollop? She's pretty enough, but Tom never cared much for looks. You've met her. You should know."

"You've met her too," said Ferdy. He did not sit down, only wandered aimlessly about the room. Then he picked up the almost empty bottle of wine, put it to his lips, and gulped the remainder down.

"You're disgusting," said Emma.

"But useful, my darling."

"What do you mean? And don't call me that!"

He continued to grin at her, balancing himself on the balls of his feet. There was something about him that had nothing to do with his ill-favored looks: an evil that came from him like a shadow. Emma fell silent, wishing she did not feel so ill, wishing she had not drunk so much. Vague memories of that past conversation came to her. She longed to tell him to go away, yet was aware that this monster was perhaps the only person who could help her.

He said softly, "I hope you have now thought it over. It has taken a little time to arrange. We would not want it to miscarry, would we, Emma my pet? I am sure you agree with me."

"I don't know what you are talking about—"

"Oh I think you do, darling. After all, you want to kill her. You have just said so. I'll remove her for you. What will you give me for it?"

"I suppose," muttered Emma, struggling to drag herself back to normality, knowing she should not speak to him at all, yet in her desperation incapable of preventing herself, "I suppose you mean money."

"No," said Ferdy.

"Not money?" Her voice rose in shrill mockery. "What has happened to you, Ferdy? I thought money was the only thing that interested you."

He said solemnly, "How unkind of you, ma'am. Why I am the least demanding person imaginable. You should know that. What a terrible thing to say to an old friend."

Emma did not immediately reply. The warning bells were ringing in her befogged mind. *Don't give him anything. Don't listen to him. He is mad and bad, he is planning something dreadful, Tom will never forgive you, and you will never forgive yourself.* Then she heard herself saying—it was as if another person were speaking, not Emma Slade, Emma Slade was sunk in wine—"What is it you want from me?"

"Nothing very shocking. Nothing to alarm a genteel young lady."

"What is it you want, Ferdy?"

"Are you not going to offer me some more wine? The dregs may be sufficient for yourself, but for a gentleman like me—"

Her voice rose to a shriek. "Ferdy, either you tell me what you want, or I shall have you thrown out."

"So you said last time, darling. You and Tom seem to share the same views. I should not say that again, if I were you. I don't like it. I don't think you would care much for me as your enemy, especially as you no longer have Tom to protect you."

"Are you threatening me?"

"You could call it that. It would be so much better to keep me as your friend. If I am your friend. I don't think that little girl will worry any of us much longer."

The ugly memory was beginning to surface through the drink, but Emma was too confused to pin it down.

She said, almost in bewilderment, "You are planning to murder her!"

"No. Not exactly. At least, I do not think so. Not if she behaves herself."

"Then what are you going to do?"

"But I told you last time. I am going to marry her. I could make use of that fine fortune of hers. You tell me I am so interested in money, and that is true enough. But it's not money I want from you, my darling."

Don't listen to him, don't listen! "What is it then?"

"The entrée to your house, ma'am." Ferdy's voice suddenly changed, vibrated with an intense, savage excitement. His eyes were suffused with the vision of all the people who had snubbed him, forced to welcome him, receive him with open arms. "When you give one of your fine parties, you will always, but always, ask me. Me! I will attend your dinners, your soirées, your balls, your picnics, your outings to Ranelagh, the playhouse, the concert hall. And it is I who will be at your side, who will sit at the top of the table, who will be your partner for the dance. Your bloody world don't care much for me, Emma, I'm not good enough for them, but there's pickings there I've always wanted, and though most of your friends are uncivil enough not to ask me, you are going to change all that. I am going to become your most invited guest. I shall enjoy it very much."

Emma thought confusedly that she could always go back on her word, even if she agreed, and it was as if Ferdy could read her mind, for he added smoothly, "If of course you do not do so, I can always have a little word with Tom. And with others too. Our world puts up with a great deal, but I fancy it would look a little askance on a lady who could send a poor girl to the Liberties, just because her gentleman is faithless."

"Tom would kill you!"

"I fancy I might kill him first. Indeed, Emma, if you do not keep to your side of the bargain—"

"I've not yet agreed."

"—I will kill him anyway. I do not take insults kindly," said Ferdy, and at that moment he looked so ugly that Emma, already terrified, nearly fainted, for Ferdy was reputed to have killed a great many times, and not—if one could use such a phrase of murder—in any civilized way.

She said weakly, "Why will you take her to the Liberties? I do not know what you mean."

"It is the area of the Fleet where they celebrate marriages, darling. Did I not tell you? There will be plenty of parsons willing to splice us, and there's not one so particular that he'll mind if the bride says yes or no."

"I thought you were joking," whispered Emma.

"I never joke."

"I could not possibly agree—"

"Then we will attend a wedding, my darling. Not in the Liberties, but a fine grand wedding of Mr. Atherton and Miss—I vow I've forgot her name, something barbaric, I know, the name of a city—Philadelphia. Miss Philadelphia. Perhaps you will, as one of his oldest friends, be a bridesmaid."

The wine was roaring now in Emma's head, mixed with such a turmoil of emotions that she felt as if she were bursting asunder. She said, "You must not hurt her—"

"No. Oh no. I could never hurt a fly," said Ferdy, and suddenly emitted a brief, raucous laugh.

"I don't understand why you have to marry her."

"Because," said Ferdy, "that will hurt Tom more than anything else. She also has a fortune. I need a fortune. But apart from that, I am a subtle man, my darling, and I always get even with people who let me down."

"She's not harmed you," said Emma, almost inaudibly. The words came as if from the far end of a tunnel. She felt so ill that she believed she was about to die.

He did not trouble himself to answer this. Philadelphia to him was no more than an insect he could squash with his hand. He had never thought of people as people: they only interested him for what he could get out of them, for the use he could make of them to further his own devious ends. He only said as if it did not matter, "I think we are now in agreement. We are in agreement, are we not, my darling?"

"I think," said Emma, following her own wretched thoughts, no longer caring that she was betraying herself in front of Ferdy, "Tom will never speak to me again, anyway."

Ferdy could not have cared if Tom had cut her throat. He said contemptuously, "Oh, once the little bitch is out of the way, I daresay he'll return to the old kennel. You'll not forget my party invitations, Emma, will you?"

She shook her head. She was not really taking in what he was saying.

"It would be inadvisable. They tell me you are holding a dinner and dance next month. I understand my august papa will be there. I should like the official invitation."

"Very well."

"Then I will escort the little madam to the Liberties. I believe," said Ferdy, filled with a sudden, strange pride, "that I am a most original man. I do not know if anyone in our circle has ever done such a thing before."

And so he might have spoken of the slitting of a throat, the burning of a house, a knife stab in the back, but now he was simply talking of abduction and rape, in connection with a young girl who had only indirectly crossed his path, who had done him no harm and whom, a short while ago, he had not even seen. He walked quickly out of the drawing room, without another word. He suspected that Emma, when she sobered up, would react violently and differently and, as he came down the steps, leaving the door open behind him, he decided to put his plan into effect tomorrow, at the very latest. He did not trust Emma at all, but then he never trusted anyone: there was after all a possibility that, despite everything that had happened, she might choose to warn Tom, if only to curry favor with him.

He did not think for one moment that she would warn Philadelphia. As a man who had never in his life loved a single soul, he assumed that in this she was like himself. She might tell Tom, for her own personal ends, but she would not give a damn for the girl who had supplanted her.

He strode in his gangling way up to Holborn, where there was a place he knew, filled with the kind of people who could help him. He needed a coachman and a carriage, and a woman to assist him. Once he was in the Liberties he could manage well enough on his own; the woman would keep an eye on Philadelphia, and the men from the Fleet would never think of helping her. It would all be very quick. The parsons wanted the money, they had no scruples and they would not waste time. Tom was unlikely to see his little slut again and, by the time Ferdy had finished with her, he would not want her.

And he would once again have the entrée to society. He would attend a dinner, with his father there, and he would take precedence over the old bastard, be able to shame him, jeer at him, disgrace him in public. Now at last he could get even with his own world that had cut him dead—Ferdy gave a skipping leap of pure joy, and raised his voice in song: the song he sang was obscene, for he knew nothing else, but the clear, sweet notes rang out on the air. It was his paean of triumph.

Emma, overcome at last, fell into a deep, swimming slumber, the walls rocking about her. Louise found her dead to the world, and realized from the empty bottle and glass what had happened. She tried to wake her mistress so as to get her to bed, but Emma did not so much as respond to the pats and taps and shakings. In the end she had to ask the footman to carry her upstairs, and so poor Emma, who had never before in her life drunk so much wine, made an ig-nominious exit to her own bed, to wake up some eight hours later, sick and frantic with headache, with the full realization of what she had done. They said that drunks did not remember what had happened, but this was unhappily not true. She remembered only too well and, almost too ill to stand upright, rang hysteri-cally for her maid.

Chapter 10

Charlotte did not pass a very happy week. She was not proud of herself. She was in no way a bad girl, only a stupid one who, having been brought up in the narrowest of circles with little personal freedom and a veto on extravagance, believed, now that she was married, that money was the key to everything. Henry, in tea, had provided the income, but she wanted an entrée into society as much as Ferdy did, and she had to realize that there was still a long way to go. It was no good pretending that the *haut ton* were crowding on her doorstep, even the back one, and such dinner parties as she gave were peopled with the local curate, a couple of Henry's colleagues (also in tea) and once—this was her peak moment—a minor baronet whom Henry had met somewhere or other, and whom she persuaded to come to dinner. It was true that he simply became drunk and ended up with his face on the table, but at least he was titled and, as Charlotte repeatedly told herself, it was a beginning. But the select little soirées that she had once visualized were a long way from fulfillment, and she comforted herself by thinking that, if only she had more money, they would come into being. The *ton* after all depended on money like everyone else; if she could provide lavish food and wine, they would doubtless come running to her door.

She did not grudge Philadelphia the money, only she was convinced that she would make no use of it. Philly was an odd girl, unlike anyone else in the family. Her beauty, her unmistakable beauty, did not seem to come from anywhere. Most of the Smiths were remarkably plain, and the relatives on her mother's side, the Menzies, were not much better. Where Philly derived her extraordinary looks, no one could make out. Perhaps away back in the centuries some disreputable lady—she must have been disreputable to be so handsome—had bequeathed her those amazing eyes, the lovely complexion and delicate features. Yet Philly was a simple girl who seemed to care nothing for material things: it was plainly absurd that she should have all this money. Charlotte, jolted by the appalling London roads, and holding on to the side of the carriage, thought wistfully of five hundred pounds, and dreamed that Philly, in a fit of conscience, would soon appear to hand it over.

But the week passed, and there was no sign of Philly; there was no sign of Henry either. When precisely seven days later, Charlotte, returning from a boring morning with the ladies at the local church, saw her husband's shadow against the window of his study, she was so relieved that for the moment she forgot her resentment and suspicions. She could not pretend to herself that she and Henry were any longer on loving terms, but she longed for advice and assistance, and the gentlemen, as all good women knew, were much better in crises than their wives.

She came thankfully into the house. She felt very tired with all that had happened and, when little Tobias came running out to greet her, pushed him away, telling him that mama had a headache, and would he ask the nursemaid for her vinaigrette. She ignored the sulky, disappointed look on his face. She always told everyone that she adored Tobias, but she was not really a maternal woman, and his chatter and little ways drove her mad in an hour. She turned away from him. He was beginning to grizzle; it was really quite unendurable, and her temper was not improved by the sight of Henry, who weaved slowly out of the study.

She saw at once that he was drunk. This was in no way unusual, but it was an odd hour for drinking, and she was suddenly furious with him. After all he had dodged a major family crisis—the fact that he knew nothing about it made it no better—and really, if one could not depend on one's husband to be sober at eleven in the morning, it seemed a pity to get married at all.

He said without any enthusiasm, "Well, Char, and how are you?"—then planted a desultory, vinous kiss upon her cheek.

She snapped, ignoring the nursemaid who had now appeared with the vinaigrette and who was, with her free hand, trying to restrain Tobias, "I am not at all well, thank you, I am utterly exhausted. I do not suppose it interests you, but mama is dead. Naturally, you were not there to help us. Where have you been? You have been away a remarkable long time."

He was genuinely shocked, almost to the point of sobriety. He had no particular feeling for his mother-in-law, who was, poor soul, an invalid and, one had to admit it, something of a burden to all concerned, but he had never wished her any harm, and the mention of death invariably had a chilling effect. He said, more gently, "My dear Char, I had not the faintest idea. You must be worn out. Come into the study and I will pour you out a glass of wine, then you shall tell me all about it."

Charlotte, a little comforted, for this after all was how it should be, permitted her husband to conduct her into his study and settle her in the most comfortable armchair. She told Henry what had happened, and how she had been spending days off and on with poor Philly—so exhausting going to and fro, but then one had to do one's duty.

"Philly must be terribly upset," said Henry.

"Why yes, of course, but so am I. We all knew poor mama was very ill, but we did not think for one moment that—oh, it has been a dreadful time. I feel quite ill with exhaustion. I would like the doctor to call, otherwise I know I shall not get a wink of sleep tonight. Oh Henry, how I wished you were there. Of course I had to deal with everything. Philly, poor little soul, she is always inclined to the hysterics, was quite incapable, and it was all left to me, even the funeral arrangements. I just do not know how I managed. Of course I have always been good in an emergency; it seems to rouse the very best in me."

Henry, still rather bemused, both with wine and certain entirely personal problems, thought that Char was dreadful in an emergency, and that he had never seen Philly hysterical in his life. But of course he knew nothing of Mr. Atherton, so he accepted his wife's account, if with certain private reservations. He was secretly thankful that he had been away, and he could not help thinking that with all this happening, it would probably slip from Charlotte's mind that he had been gone for an unusual length of time for investigating a consignment of tea. And, as he thought this and Charlotte sniveled, and sipped at her wine, his eyes turned instinctively to the desk behind him. He saw to his alarm that the letter he had been reading, as Charlotte's carriage drew up, was still lying on the top. He glanced sideways at his wife, and hastily whisked it into a drawer, locking this and placing himself in front of it.

Charlotte had not seen the letter, for her mind was occupied with other things, but she heard the sound of the lock turning, and saw Henry's quick movement. She registered both incidents with instant alarm. All the suspicions she had been nursing flared up at once. She might be foolish in an emergency, and she was not a clever woman, but she had known for some time that Henry was no longer in love with her, and it was ominous that he should have been away for so much longer than usual. She was frightened enough to say nothing about it, only she made a firm resolve to examine that desk at the earliest opportunity. Indeed, she was so alarmed that she became quite clever, and proceeded to mention the one subject that was near to the heart of both of them, and which would certainly distract Henry's attention.

She said abruptly, "You will remember that we all believed mama to have no money—"

Henry at once became so excited that he forgot all about the letter. He exclaimed, "But of course! Are you telling me she did have some money after all? I find it hard to believe. They always seemed so poor."

Charlotte rose to her feet. She said in a quick, harsh voice, "She left five hundred pounds a year, Henry. A year! And it is all going to Philly."

"What!"

"It is all going to Philly. And what is more," said Charlotte, all her submerged fury and resentment roaring to the surface, "she proposes to keep every penny of it. As well as the house, of course. We shall have to be civil to Philadelphia, Henry. She is now a young lady of independent means."

Husband and wife stared at each other. They had almost nothing in common nowadays, except their name and married status. Perhaps they had never had, apart from a brief flare-up of physical passion. That was over a long time ago, and now they did not even particularly like each other: little Tobias, who might have brought them together, and whom Henry surprisingly worshipped, spent most of his life in the nursery at the top of the house. But one thing they still shared, and that was a love of money. To Henry five hundred pounds was no fortune, for he did excellently in tea, but it meant a little more comfort, more indulgence in luxury, and, like his wife, he simply could not understand how Mrs. Smith could so brutally ignore her elder daughter and her family.

He was so outraged that for a while he could not speak. Then he said furiously, "I do not believe this can be legal."

"It is," said Charlotte. "Or so Mr. Bridges assures me. Mind you, I never trusted that man. He is quite old, for one thing, and I think he is a little foolish over Philly."

"But surely Philly sees your point of view. She cannot expect to keep such a sum to herself. What will she do with it? It's not as if she's entirely on her own. There is that young man of hers, I've forgot his name—Jamie. Yes, of course, Jamie, I've never thought much of him myself, but I daresay he earns well enough at his schoolmastering, and now that your poor, dear mama is out of this wicked world the two of them will get married. What could they need so much money for? Oh, I think you will find, Char, that once the shock of it all is over, Philly will come to her senses and hand the money to us. After all, we need it far more than she does, what with Tobias and my business and—"

"If you would kindly let me get a word in edgeways," said Charlotte, a little wearily. After all Henry was only saying what she had been repeating to herself over and over again.

He gave her an ugly look. The moment of rapprochement was over. He thought she looked singularly plain, and he thought too that she must have been very stupid to let Philly get away with it. A more intelligent woman would have played on her sympathies, and the money would then have been handed over with the minimum of unpleasantness.

Then he realized that Charlotte was saying something entirely surprising. She remarked, "I gather that Philly's engagement to Jamie is over."

"You cannot mean that! Though mind you, I never liked him. Such a superior young man. So he's jilted her—Well, it is not so surprising. Young men do not care to wait indefinitely. I daresay he will change his mind fast enough, once he hears about the money."

"I do not believe," said Charlotte rather savagely, "that he has jilted her. It is she who has jilted him."

"Well, well!" said Henry, momentarily distracted. A

sly, displeasing smile lifted the corner of his lips. "And who would have thought it of our Philly? Though she's a deuced pretty girl, one has to grant her that."

"I do not see," said Charlotte, tight-lipped, "what her looks have to do with it. She is a hard girl. I would never have believed it of her, but after this business of the money, I am compelled to recognize that she has no feelings. She has got rid of Jamie for the simplest of reasons—she has found better fish to fry."

"What do you mean by that, Char? She always looks as if butter wouldn't melt in her mouth."

"They are always the worst," said Charlotte, to whom this barrage of culinary clichés was simply normal conversation between husband and wife. "We have never really known her, Henry. When she told me she was keeping the money, I could hardly believe my ears. But now I am beginning to think that Jamie has the best of the bargain. There is another gentleman—" Her voice sank to a reverent tone. Philadelphia might be a hard girl, but a gentleman of the *ton* was a gentleman of the *ton*, and there was no denying that Mr. Atherton was not only excessively good-looking, but also undeniably well-bred.

"And who might he be?" demanded Henry, by this time a little dazed. He himself had had a stirring and difficult time, and to come back to sudden death, small fortunes and the extraordinary behavior of his sister-in-law was a little too much. He sat down, a little suddenly, at his desk. He longed for some more wine, but decided that in the circumstances he had better keep a clear head. He remembered to slide the key into the snuffbox that was its hiding place. He was not a very subtle man. Having done this while Charlotte was rummaging for her handkerchief, he swivelled round to face her with a bright, honest smile.

"He lives opposite," said Charlotte. "He is very wealthy. It is of course only too obvious that marriage is the last thing he has in mind. But I am sure Philly believes what she wants to believe, and she certainly don't listen to me. So it's obvious why she needs the money. A gentleman of that sort expects his ladies to be well turned out." Charlotte having found her handkerchief, began to sob in a dry-eyed fashion. "Oh, I shudder to think what poor papa must be suffering. He'll be turning in his grave, the dear, good, old man, to see his daughter going to the bad."

Henry said dryly, "I think you're jumping to conclusions, Char. After all, his intentions may be entirely honorable, and Philly has always had a good head on her."

Charlotte was a little taken aback by this, for it was perfectly true, she had invented most of this while talking. She had liked Mr. Atherton very much indeed, he had been extraordinarily helpful, and there was no reason on earth to assume that Philly, who had always been a model of propriety, was turning into a whore. But she was not going to be told her business by Henry, especially as she was convinced he was deceiving her, so she said haughtily, "I know my own sister, thank you. You gentlemen are always taken in by a pretty face. Philly is not all she seems to be. I am only surprised that poor, dear mama did not find her out."

Henry, who was not unintelligent, found himself wondering why the dead must always have the adjectives "poor" and "dear" put before their name, but Char's remark about a pretty face had hit home more than she knew, and his own changed involuntarily.

It was over in a flash, but Charlotte, her senses sharpened by exhaustion, saw it. However, she did not pursue the matter, only said, "I think you should consult a lawyer about that will. I do not believe Mr. Bridges knows his business. I cannot conceive that we must be deprived of money that is after all half ours, and I am sure poor, dear mama—" Her voice rose in outrage. "Are you laughing at me, Henry? You're foxed. No decent man could laugh at such a moment."

He said hastily, "Of course I'm not laughing. You are quite mistaken. And I entirely agree with you. I think another lawyer should be consulted instanter. Indeed, I will go this very minute, there is no time like the present. If you will see that the carriage is brought round—"

Charlotte was secretly delighted that Henry would now be out of the way. Then, recollecting herself, she said in a dutiful wife kind of voice, "And how was your little trip? I trust it was successful."

"Oh yes indeed, most successful," said Henry, half out of the room. He wished he was well away. He waited for comments on the length of his absence, but Charlotte said nothing, only continued to sit there, sipping at her wine. He darted back to print a kiss on her cheek, then said, "I may not be in to luncheon."

"I do not see why not," said Charlotte.

"My love, we dine at midday, and it is past that now."

"No, Henry. In future we shall be dining at three."

"For God's sake, why?" demanded Henry, astonished.

"It is the fashionable hour. We owe it to little Tobias to show him the genteel way of life."

Henry began to think that the dramatic events of the past weeks had turned his wife's head. He did not care for the prospect of remaining hungry for three more hours. But he made no comment, and presently Charlotte, still sitting there, heard his carriage driving away.

She rose to her feet. Her color was very high. She tried the top drawers of the desk, and found that they were all locked. However, this did not deter her, and it was only a matter of minutes before she discovered the little snuffbox, concealed under some papers. She took the key out. Then she stepped back to the study door and locked herself in, in case little Tobias should come looking for her: after this she opened all the top drawers, one by one.

Chapter 11

Philadelphia woke up in the morning without the faintest presentiment of disaster. Indeed, she felt remarkably happy. She knew she should not feel so cheerful with poor mama so recently buried, but after all life had to go on, and perhaps Mr. Atherton would relent and call on her, if only to see how she was. After all, a week was a long time. The small, confident smile dimpled her cheeks as she thought this. She did not believe she was really in love with him, and there was always that wicked Jamie, mingling the delights of ancient monuments with other and more modern pleasures, but it was agreeable to have so charming a beau, and surely even papa could not object if she flirted a little in the most modest and restrained manner. As she thought this, dusting round the parlor before she had her breakfast, she remembered the kiss, and glanced up apprehensively at papa's portrait. It was only too plain that he would object very much indeed, for such behavior was positively wanton, and he had always inveighed against fine ladies who behaved like whores. But, thought Philadelphia unregenerately, papa had been dead for a long time, and fashions had changed: it could not be wrong to enjoy oneself, provided one did it with decorum.

And Jamie certainly had no right to protest, walking out like that and leaving her.

Philadelphia finished her dusting. It was all rather dilatory, and mama would have scolded her, but she went singing into the kitchen to prepare her breakfast. Normally, when alone, she ate at the kitchen table, but today she felt in the mood to lay the table in a genteel manner, and eat in the parlor.

If Mr. Atherton did come, she would be instantly aware of it.

While her chocolate was heating up, she unlocked the front door, and stepped outside. It was going to be another fine, clear day, though there was an autumn nip in the air. At this hour the odd numbers were still abed, and she could see in Number 23 that the blinds were still down, the curtains drawn. Mr. Atherton no doubt had led some wicked night of debauchery, dancing perhaps till the small hours and drinking a great deal of wine. Philadelphia was shortly to be enlightened on the subject of debauchery, but at that moment had little conception of it: it was vaguely linked in her mind with music, drinking and fine clothes. Papa had always talked a great deal about hell, but sometimes his daughter suspected that he knew little of the road that led there, never having traveled upon it: he probably dwelt on flames and pitchforks and devils rather as children talk of ogres and witches in fairy tales. He had indeed, despite his forbidding expression in the portrait, been a kind-hearted man, and she was certain he would be the first to run with a drink of cooling water to the damned in their torment.

She stood on the top step for a few minutes, breathing in the sharp morning air, enjoying the empty quiet of the still unawakened street. Then she returned into the house, leaving the door on the latch, as she always did, except at night, when she was in bed. She did not think of Mr. Atherton's warning, and she could not remember locking the door in the daytime, during her whole stay in England.

She carried her breakfast through into the parlor: a bowl of chocolate and a fresh, crusty piece of bread, spread with honey. It was only as she sipped at her drink that an odd feeling of unease suddenly overcame her. There was no reason for it whatsoever, but she could not shake it off, and she found herself glancing nervously over her shoulder.

Then she heard the footsteps in the hall.

She thought for one wild second that it was Mr. Atherton. But the clock told her it was only half past eight in the morning, the drawn curtains across the way told their own tale, and Philadelphia knew enough of the *haut ton* to realize that only a national catastrophe would bring them out at such an hour. She put her bowl of chocolate down with a hand that shook, then rose to her feet. She was about to open the parlor door, when it burst open so violently that she was almost knocked down, and she found herself gazing up into the grinning face of Ferdy.

She knew at once that he meant mischief. She

opened her mouth to scream, but immediately he clapped his hand across it, saying derisively, "Now, now, Miss Philadelphia, this is no way to greet your future husband. Come along, my darling. You are going to be honored. I am about to marry you, and there's a fine, jolly parson waiting to wed us. Come along now—" He broke off with an oath such as Philadelphia had never heard, for her strong young teeth met on his thumb, causing him such pain that for a moment he released hold of her.

She tried to call for help, but she was so frightened that nothing came out but a kind of whistling wail. She backed away from him as he came for her, knocking half the things off the table, then, hardly knowing what she was doing, ran round the little room, throwing at him anything that came to her hand. Nothing touched him, and now he was laughing in a gleeful, falsetto fashion that made her almost faint with terror. She hurled a candlestick at his head, and it flew wide against the wall above the mantlepiece, slicing the cord that held up the portrait, so that papa, to whom all this would be a nightmare as much as it was for her, fell with a clatter of broken glass into the fender, to lie there face downwards.

Ferdy caught her at last, and this time was more careful. His arms came stiflingly round her, and the cloak he was wearing was stuffed into her mouth so that she almost choked. The grinning face that peered into hers was the most revolting thing she had ever seen in her life, and the stink and feel of him sickened her: it was as if she were being held by a corpse.

He picked her up in his arms, flinging the cloak over her head. He was as strong as a gorilla, and her feeble kickings and strugglings were as much use as if she had been a baby.

"Off to our wedding," he told her. "I do not know why you are complaining, girl, you are marrying into a good family. I have a carriage waiting for us outside, and soon we will be in the Fleet. And then, my darling, we will celebrate your nice little fortune. You'll not find me ungenerous. There'll be a good tot of brandy for you, and I daresay your Tom could do no better." The very mention of Mr. Atherton's name enchanted Ferdy so much that he repeated it several times. "Your Tom, your Tom, your Tom—Poor fellow, his heart will be broken, but no one wants shop-soiled goods, and I doubt he'll ever look at you again." Then Philadelphia's frantic struggles suddenly angered him, and he slammed her across the cheek, shouting, "Stop that, you bitch, or I'll wring your bloody neck, and there'll be no wedding for you ever again."

Philadelphia fell instantly still. No one had ever struck her in her life. When she was young papa had sometimes threatened her with the rod, but it had only been words, he was incapable of striking either of his children, however badly they behaved. And what with her panic and disgust and the fact that the cloak was almost choking her, she was on the verge of fainting: the world was going black and swimming ominously about her. But she knew she must not faint: if she were to have any chance of escaping this monster, whose touch and smell revolted her, she must somehow retain her senses, and struggling would not only do no good but simply weaken her.

She prayed that someone was abroad, but could see through the folds of the cloak that the street was empty. Ferdy must have read her thoughts, for he said jeeringly, prodding his hands into her, "No Tom, my darling. Tom's abed still, sleeping off the wine and Emma. Tom will be no good for another three hours, and by that time, sweetheart, we'll be wedded, you and I, starting a happy life together." And saying this, he came up to what she could dimly see was some kind of carriage. Another man, who was plainly as much a villain as Ferdy, opened the door, and she was dumped unceremoniously on the seat, with Ferdy beside her. The cloak was whisked away, but instantly a scarf was wound round her face so that she could not utter a sound. Her eyes rolled desperately up to Ferdy, who broke into one of his whinnying laughs and paddled his hand against her cheek. His arm was tightly round her shoulders so that she could not even move, and the man driving the carriage was plainly in league with him: there was no chance of appealing to him even if she could have spoken a word.

She thought she would go mad, but managed to lie still, conserving her strength for the moment when the carriage door was opened. She could not believe this was happening to her. Such things did not happen to ordinary people. She knew well enough that London was a wicked city: there were daily accounts of robbings and murders, and there were parts where no decent woman could possibly go. It had all seemed to her quite remote, no concern of herself or her friends. Sometimes she had been shocked and saddened by what she read, but the next moment had forgotten all about it. And what was all this talk about marriage and the Fleet? Surely nobody could marry her against her will, this was not the Middle Ages. Philadelphia seemed to remember hearing once about Fleet marriages, but it had not registered in her mind, it meant nothing to her. One thing was certain: she could not marry this monster who was plainly a lunatic: even if he found some disgraceful parson to perform the ceremony, it would surely be completely illegal. Then the terror engulfed her again, for Ferdy had sounded so sure of himself, and the tears oozed out from under her eyelids, and she dug her nails into the palms of her hands to try to control herself.

Emma set off for Number 22 in as frantic a state as she had ever been throughout her life.

It never entered her head that she might already be too late, but she knew only too well the urgency of the situation. Whatever her feelings about Philadelphia—and these were compounded of hate, fury and resentment, together with a seasoning of pure astonishment—she could not in all conscience endure the thought of a young girl being abducted and carted off to the Fleet. No normal decent person should be left to the mercies of Ferdy, Ferdy who had no respect or consideration for anyone, and who would, apart from the ghastly marriage, subject her to every insult and indignity. The thought that she in her drunkenness had connived at this made Emma sick with self-disgust. What Tom would say to her if he found out, God only knew, but then surely Tom would never know, he must never know, and even Ferdy at his most diabolical would find it hard to convince him when Emma had set off deliberately to warn her.

For once in her life Emma did not trouble with her toilet. Firstly, she felt too ill, and secondly, despite the fact that she was sure she would be in plenty of time, there was an ominous sense of urgency that twisted in her belly worse than the sickness of too much wine. When Louise, expecting to find her young mistress stricken in bed, saw her already dressed in a gown that for her was not particularly becoming, and trying to screw her hair up, she could hardly believe her eyes.

"But madam—" she began, but Emma merely snapped, "Help me with my hair. No, I do not want breakfast." Then she screamed out, "I said, No! Where is my hat? Oh Louise, you're a stupid bitch—can't you see I'm in a hurry?"

Louise looked at her in despair, but had the sense to do as she was asked, and ten minutes later, Emma, with her hat slightly crooked, ran down the stairs and jumped into the carriage hastily brought round.

"She has gone mad," Louise told the kitchen staff, tapping her head, and cook remarked, "It's love. It's that Mr. Atherton. I hope he comes to a bad end, that's all I can say—upsetting such a nice young lady."

At that moment there was a possibility of everyone coming to a bad end, but nobody recognized the truth of this remark, and Louise went upstairs again to put Miss Emma's room to rights: she was unaccustomed to dressing herself, and everything was scattered about the floor.

Emma, on arrival at Number 22, sprang from the carriage without waiting for the coachman to help her. It was at this point that she began to wonder if she were not perhaps being foolish. She hesitated on the top step. The house looked perfectly normal. The curtains were still drawn, but perhaps Philadelphia rose late or perhaps this was still a sign of mourning. She decided to knock. There was no answer. She called out crossly, "Miss Smith! Miss Philadelphia!"

There was still no answer, so she pushed fretfully at the door, only almost to fall her length in the hall, for it was off the latch.

Mr. Atherton could have told her that this was quite usual in the Smith household, but Emma, when she had righted herself, saw with a dreadful sinking within her that it was not usual at all.

She was so horrified that, what with the wine last night and the nausea still overcoming her, she thought she would faint. There was every mark of disarray. Ferdy had kept his word. Ferdy had gone, and so had Philadelphia. The hall rug was scuffed up, a picture had been knocked from the wall, and a couple of ornaments were smashed. Emma, now shaking from head to foot and beginning to sob, ran into the parlor. Here it was plain the main struggle had taken place. Philadelphia must have been having her breakfast when Ferdy arrived. There was a broken cup, with chocolate spilt over the table and floor, and a half-eaten piece of bread still lay on the plate. It was obvious too that Ferdy had not had an easy victory. Philadelphia might be young and slight, but she was sturdily built in her own way, and she seemed to have fought as hard as she could. The room looked like a battlefield, and a big portrait over the mantelpiece had fallen on to the fender, with its glass smashed to pieces.

The room began to turn round before Emma's appalled vision. She sank on to the sofa, muttering, "Oh my God, my God!" She had never swooned in her life, but the shock of it all, coupled with feeling so ill, made her temporarily loose consciousness. She recovered the next instant, but felt so weak that for a while she could not bring herself to her feet. She looked wildly round her, the tears pouring down her cheeks. Whatever the girl was she did not deserve this. There was now only one thing to do. She must cross the road immediately and tell Tom. She had no choice. And what Tom would say, defeated imagination. *I got drunk. I have sent her to the Fleet with Ferdy.* Emma, who boasted that she was afraid of no one, was so overcome by terror that she longed to die. She wailed aloud, "I can't, oh I can't! He'll kill me. He'll never forgive me. He'll think it was all my fault."

She had quarreled with Mr. Atherton a hundred times, though never so viciously as at their last meeting. Both were hot-tempered, quick-tongued, violent people, and mostly the quarrels had been invigorating, with no holds barred and a glorious reconciliation to follow. It was their pattern of living. Mr. Atherton had once remarked, "We'll be quarreling on our deathbeds." He added, "I swear you'd snatch my shroud from me if the fancy took you."

Well, after this, they would never quarrel again. There would be bitter, savage words spoken—and Mr. Atherton had, when he chose, an ugly tongue—but this time there would be no reconciliation. It would be the end, for good and all. Emma, feeling already as if she had been beaten, tottered to her feet and prepared to cross the road to Number 23 and damnation. Her face was ashen-pale, her eyes swollen with weeping, and the beautiful black hair, over which she took so much trouble, fell in straggling witchlocks over her shoulders.

For a second she closed her eyes. She had never loved Tom so much in her life. She knew she would never love anyone so much again. Oh, she would recover, one always recovered, and one day she might fall in love again, but it would never be quite like this, she loved him so much and wanted him so much, and in the next few minutes that love would be smashed to pieces like the glass on that portrait in the parlor.

Then she stopped crying. It was too late for tears. She made no attempt to tidy herself, for after all it no longer mattered what she looked like. She went quietly out of the house and across the road to Number

23. It was unlikely that Mr. Atherton would be up at such an hour, for like herself he seldom went to bed until early morning, but she must insist on his coming down and, once he heard what she had to say, he would be wakeful enough.

She tugged at the bell pull. She felt as if she were going to her hanging. She informed the startled footman that she had to speak to Mr. Atherton immediately, and she just missed Charlotte by one minute as the door closed behind her.

The even numbers had never seen so many carriages. Emma's coachman looked contemptuously at Charlotte's, recognizing its inferior nature: like all his kind he was a vast snob, and to him this tall, badly-dressed female who ran up the steps to push open the door, could only be some superior kind of servant. When five minutes later she reappeared, exclaiming hysterically that she must find Philly, where was she, the ungrateful girl was never there in a crisis, he simply thought that the world had gone mad, then was confirmed in this belief when the stupid female dashed across to Mr. Atherton's house at Number 23.

Mr. Atherton was in his room partaking of a quiet breakfast, a simple affair of roast beef, a dish of stewed kidneys and a bottle of wine. He was feeling perfectly at ease with the world, and had just decided that he would not keep his lovely little girl waiting more than a week after all. First of course he must find Ferdy. He had already tried once or twice, but had not been successful. It did not seem to him a matter of much urgency, and in the waiting period his temper had somewhat cooled. However, he must certainly see him, then he would call upon Philadelphia this afternoon and suggest a gentle drive through the Park in this fine autumn weather: she would enjoy the fresh air and the sight of the pretty leaves. It would all be entirely decorous, it would also be reasonably brief. He was prepared to capitulate up to a point, because he could not bear to be away from her: however, he was not going to prolong it. When the drive was done, he would bring her home, hand her out of the carriage and politely leave her. He did not think she would refuse. He would make no further rendezvous. It would be delightful if she looked disappointed, and somehow he believed she would. Everything was turning out most agreeably, and last night he had spent a quiet evening at home so that for once he was in no way fatigued or heavy with too much food and wine.

He had naturally not the faintest idea that downstairs a distraught and terrified Emma was waiting for him. He certainly did not suspect that beside her was the sister he so disliked, who after the most cursory of glances had simply decided that Philadelphia was out, and who was entirely concerned with the discovery that her husband had been unfaithful to her for years, carrying on with a plump and disreputable widow for whom he had found a little lodging in the village of Marylebone.

He looked up in some annoyance when the footman tapped at the door. He was a reasonable and amiable employer, but it was understood that nobody disturbed him until eleven o'clock. He said, making no attempt to hide his irritation, "Well, what is it?"

"There are two visitors for you, sir."

"What! Who the devil are they? No one has any business to call at such an hour."

The footman entirely agreed with him, and thought privately that if his master had a glim at what was going on in his drawing room, he would drop his beef and kidneys to the floor. He said, "Miss Slade, sir—"

Mr. Atherton's face changed. The very last person in the world he wanted to see at this moment was Emma, and indeed it was extraordinary of her to call at such a time in the morning. When the footman went on to inform him that Miss Philadelphia's sister was also there, he began to think he was going mad. Indeed, he was outraged enough to exclaim, "What the hell is she doing here?"—and the footman, normally trained to self-control, was equally disturbed enough to answer the truth: "She says her husband is unfaithful to her, sir."

For Charlotte, always disposed to blurt everything out, and now nearly driven out of her mind by the frightful discovery of a packet of vulgar and revealing letters, followed by a shattering scene with Henry, had wailed out to Emma, who was standing tensely by the mantelpiece, "My husband has a mistress! He's had her for years and years. Oh, I could kill him. I don't know what to do, and after all I've done for him, giving him the best years of my life, nobody could have had a more devoted wife, I'm sure I think all men are abominable. Do you think Mr. Atherton can help me?"

The footman, hearing all this, which was shouted out the moment Charlotte entered the room, was so aghast that he nearly fell over an occasional table. He remembered Charlotte perfectly well, and at first had placed her as the companion of the beautiful young lady who appeared to have supplanted Miss Slade. He learnt later that she was the sister, but this did not interest him, and he never expected to see her again. And now she was bawling out the most ridiculous details about her husband, and to Miss Slade too, who looked entirely distraught and who could not possibly be interested.

Emma stared at Charlotte as if she were some prostitute off the streets. She was thinking of nothing but the awful thing she had to tell Tom, and this strange, wild, screaming creature, telling her all the intimate details of her private life, was simply an additional horror. What was it to do with her if the woman's husband had betrayed her, and why was she expecting Tom to help her? She simply stared at Charlotte, and something in that stare brought the wretched lady to her senses: even in her hysterical state of mind she had to be aware that well-bred people did not shriek out their woes to complete strangers. She struggled to pull herself together, patted her hair which was wildly disordered, and tried to right her dress which had tucked up at one side.

She said with a pitiful attempt at a smile, "Oh, I know I should not talk like this, but it has been such a dreadful time, and I'm very highly-strung, you know, and now to find Philly gone—oh, I daresay she's just out on some little jaunt or other, so thoughtless, young girls, why, she didn't even bother to tidy the room—but I did think she would be there at such an early hour, and if one cannot expect help from one's own sister, I just do not know where one is supposed to turn. After all—"

Emma spoke at last. She was thinking, in so far as she could coordinate her thoughts at all, that this woman would make everything worse: somehow she must be got rid of before Tom came downstairs. She said, "Are you Miss Philadelphia's sister, ma'am?"

"Of course I am," retorted Charlotte with some indignation, though why Emma should be expected to know this she could not have said. She added, "Do you know Philly? If so, perhaps you could tell me where she is."

I wish to God I could, thought poor Emma, but she managed to answer with reasonable calm, "I have not the faintest idea, ma'am. I do not really know her at all, but after all she is of an age, and I daresay she is visiting some friend—"

"We have no friends! Poor mama was so ill, and Philly has always been a quiet girl."

"Well," said Emma who, what with the horror of it all, and the knowledge that in a minute Mr. Atherton would appear in the doorway, was aware of an hysteric temper surging within her, "it is none of my business, and surely none of yours either."

"She is my sister! And," cried Charlotte, forgetting her good resolutions, "I am in the most shocking trouble. To think that Henry—we have been married for five years. Of course I married very young. I can assure you that no man could ask for a better wife. I have given up my whole life to making him happy. Why, I could have married a dozen others wealthier, I could really have bettered myself, but no, I was always a fool, I married for love. And now—"

I hope you fall down dead, thought Emma passionately, if I were married to you, I'd slit your throat. She said, her voice shaking with dislike and rage, "Ma'am, I am truly sorry for you, but I really must ask you to leave."

"Why should I leave?" demanded Charlotte. "I want to see Mr. Atherton. If he can help Philly, he can surely help me. After all, if he is going to marry her—"

She broke off. She was not a sensitive or perceptive person, but something emanated from Emma that even she could not miss. For the first time she looked closely into that beautiful, fevered face, and that beauty and Emma's presence at so early an hour, at least made an addition in her mind. This woman must be Mr. Atherton's *mistress*, no wonder she spoke as if she owned the place. Oh, one knew that the *ton* had the morals of cats, but really, it was quite disgusting, and what Philly would think—of course she would let her know immediately, it was her duty. This prospect quite cheered her, then she met the look in Emma's eyes and began instinctively to back towards the door.

Emma said, "I will tell Mr. Atherton that you called. I have no doubt that he will go to see you as soon as possible. Perhaps you will leave him your address."

"He knows my address, thank you," said Charlotte coldly.

Emma suddenly realized that this would not do. Certainly the woman must be got rid of, she was already hysterical and, if she discovered that her sister had been abducted, would doubtless scream the place down. She managed to submerge her own emotions, stepped forward and began to speak in a low, confiding voice.

"I know," she said, "that I should not tell you this, but I can see that you are a person of discretion, and I am sure you will never mention it to a soul. I have to speak to Mr. Atherton on a most private and unhappy matter. You yourself have a sister, madam, so you will understand this only too well. Mr. Atherton has a young sister too, and I have just learnt that she has been abducted, and may even be compelled into marriage at the Fleet prison."

"Good God!" exclaimed Charlotte, suitably horrified.

"Yes, indeed. She is, I fear, a wild girl, but no one deserves such a wicked fate. You will understand of course that this is something that must be kept within the family. It would be impossible for a stranger to remain here, even someone as understanding as yourself. I do not wish to seem impertinent, ma'am, but if you would leave us to discuss this most unhappy matter in private, I should be eternally grateful."

"Of course, of course," said Charlotte, blissfully unaware that most of which she had just been told was the truth, if applying to the wrong sister. She felt quite happy and important, and forgot that she was speaking to a fallen woman. When Emma rang for the footman to show her out, she went meekly enough, only pausing to say, "You will tell Mr. Atherton, will you not? I am sure he will be able to advise me."

Emma promised that she would do so, waited until she heard Charlotte's carriage driving away, then once again began to cry: in a moment the full horror of it would be upon her. Divided between a wild desire to postpone her confession and a passionate feeling of urgency about Philadelphia, she paced up and down, sobbing, and had barely arrived at even a pretence of self-control when Mr. Atherton came down, a quarter of an hour later.

Mr. Atherton was in a very bad temper. He always enjoyed his quiet mornings, and he had refused to hurry. Emma had no right to call at such a ridiculous hour, and as for that other appalling woman, she had no right to call at all. What the devil did she think she was, burdening him with her wretched domestic troubles? It was nothing to do with him if her husband took a dozen mistresses, he had only met her a couple of times, and it was intolerable that she should expect him to act as mediator. At this rate, what with burying the mother, and intervening between erring husband and wife, he would shortly be expected to look after the child, or perhaps solve Charlotte's cooking difficulties.

Emma was never to know this, but it was at this moment that Mr. Atherton began to see the difficulties of conducting a liaison with someone from a different class of life. Philadelphia was entirely delightful, but Philadelphia's sister was not, neither was Philadelphia's sister's husband: it seemed that he would shortly be invaded by the entire Smith family.

He strode into the drawing room, looking as angry as he felt. He saw that Emma seemed to be alone. It was a minute before he took in that she looked distraught and untidy: the gown she was wearing did not suit her, and the beautiful black hair on which she always expended so much attention, was falling over her shoulders. Then he perceived that she had been crying, and he closed his eyes in exasperation. She was going to make a scene. It was the last straw. For that moment he positively detested all women, even Philadelphia.

He said sharply, "Where is Charlotte? That, I believe, is her name."

"She has gone home," said Emma, now shaking uncontrollably. "Tom—"

"What the devil did she want? I have never heard of such a thing. I gather her husband has left her. I am not at all surprised. It's a miracle he married her in the first place. Why—"

"Tom, please, please! You must listen to me."

He eyed her warily, but something in her tone brought his brows together. "Well, Emma?" he said, sitting down and crossing his legs. "What is it?"

She said in a gasp. "Ferdy's taken your Philadelphia away. I think he proposes to marry her. In the Fleet."

Mr. Atherton received this broadside in complete silence. The only indication of emotion was that the color receded from his cheeks. He simply looked at Emma, and waited.

It was worse than a flood of invective, but now that she had started, Emma could only continue. She made no attempt to cover anything up, though she realized that every word put her in a worse light. She had said that this would be like going to her hanging. It was much worse. If one were hanged, that was the end of the matter: this was something that would stay with her till the end of her days.

She came nearer Mr. Atherton. She spoke in a swift, monotonous voice. "It's all my fault, Tom," she said. "If anything happens to her, I am her murderer. I knew about this some time ago. I never took it seriously. I did come to see you, but then—then we quarreled so badly, and I forgot all about it. And last night Ferdy came around and told me it was all arranged. I was drunk. I was terribly drunk. I just listened to him. I don't think I even protested. Of course I should have come to you at once, but I was too drunk to care. He wants to revenge himself on you. I do not understand what exactly has happened, but it seems you insulted him. I think you threatened him. And of course there is her fortune. I don't know how he found out about that, but I understand she is now very rich, and to Ferdy that is more important than anything else."

Mr. Atherton, now on his feet, spoke at last in a voice that Emma had never heard from him. "Her fortune!" he said. "Do you realize how much that is?"

"Oh," said Emma on an exhausted sob, "how should I? Such things do not interest me."

"Five hundred pounds," said Mr. Atherton in a voice like a whiplash.

"Oh no!"

"Five hundred pounds. For that and a drunken slut's vicious temper she is to be ruined and possibly murdered." He shot Emma a look that seemed to her one of pure loathing. He said harshly, "When did he take her away?"

Emma answered quietly, "It must have been early this morning. Not very long ago. I—I went round to warn her. I found the house all upside down. I could see there had been a struggle. There was no sign of her, no message. I think she was having her breakfast when he came. The door was off the latch."

He said in a savage whisper, "I warned her. The damned little idiot, I warned her." He looked full at Emma. "I hope you are proud of yourself. To think that I ever imagined I loved you—You are a whore and a bitch. You have ruined a young girl who never did you the faintest harm." As he spoke, he was rummaging in his desk. He produced a box that held a brace of pistols. He slammed one into his pocket. "I can only hope," he said, "for everyone's sake, that I am not too late."

His words to her were so monstrous that she felt almost stripped of emotion. She whispered, "Are you going to the Fleet?"

"Where the devil do you think I'm going?" As he spoke he was striding towards the door.

"I am coming with you," said Emma.

"What?" He had opened the door. He swung round to face her. The anger in him blazed like a roaring furnace. "You come with me? To gloat, I suppose. To laugh at the damnation of an innocent young girl. Or perhaps you wish to see how the other side of the world lives. Though for you the world is not so different, for you will meet sluts and whores with whom you will be entirely at home—"

"That is not fair of you, Tom," said Emma. She moved over to the desk and picked up the second pistol. This startled him so much that he spoke in a more natural way.

"What do you think you are doing?" he said.

"I am coming with you," repeated Emma, her voice tight and cold. "I may need this."

"You cannot shoot!"

"I can."

"I did not know—"

"There is a great deal you do not know. You are a brave man, Tom, but if the Fleet is what I hear it is, you may be glad of an ally."

"An ally!" he repeated, and in the same breath called out to the footman, who was outside and who had doubtless heard the whole exchange, "Bring round my carriage immediately." He looked at Emma with a contempt that was like a blow in the face. "With such an ally I might as well go straight to hell."

She repeated for the third time, "I am coming with you." Then she cried out, ignoring the startled look on the footman's face, "You cannot stop me. I will come! If you throw me out of your carriage, I'll hold on to the back of it and be dragged along. I will not stay here, thinking of what may happen—"

He saw that he could hardly stop her. However furious he was, he could not push her into the gutter in front of the whole street, and Emma, as he knew to his cost, was not easily deflected when she chose to do something. He glared at her, then shrugged. He turned to step out of the house, and she followed him, thrusting the pistol into her reticule as she did so.

In a few moments they were driving in the direction of Ludgate Hill, going at as fast a speed as the horses could manage. Mr. Atherton and Emma sat silently side by side. She said only one thing: "He spoke of the Liberties. That is where she will be. I do not know what the Liberties are, but that is where we must go."

He did not answer, but turned his head to look at her. He was already ashamed of what he had said to her. She had behaved outrageously, but at least she had done her best to make up for it. It must have required enormous courage, and she did not in all fairness deserve to be called slut and whore. And it was strange that in the midst of his horror and fear and outrage he had to see that she looked more beautiful than he had ever seen her, and in a different and more touching way. For him she had always dressed splendidly, her black hair immaculate, her magnolia skin only slightly tinted from her rouge box. Now she was in complete disarray, even bedraggled, her hair down, her cheeks stained with her weeping and, as he looked at her, to his own amazement he stretched out his hand and laid it on her own.

When he did this she closed her eyes, and the tears began to fall again. She did not move or look at him. And presently they arrived at Fleet Street. Mr. Atherton stopped the carriage, told the coachman to wait for him, then leapt out and ran over Fleet Bridge in the direction of Bell Savage Yard, where already they could see the prison: Emma moved easily and swiftly at his side.

Despite her panic and desperation Philadelphia was still sure that when the carriage stopped, she could somehow leap out and appeal to some passer-by. But soon this hope was to be destroyed. She could see that the neighborhood around her looked far rougher than anything she had so far met, and the people who were walking there did not look as if they cared about anyone but themselves. Philadelphia did not know her

London, for so far she had never had time or occasion to go far from her own home. She shuddered and prayed silently to herself; as she did so Ferdy began to sing, in the sweet, tuneful voice that was so at variance with his personality. The words that beat against her ears were so vile that she could hardly believe what she was hearing, yet it was somehow a suitable background to this appalling situation. Ferdy sang about some dissolute girl who lost her virtue to a sailor in Wapping, and it rang like a bell in Philadelphia's dazed mind that she too was about to lose her virtue, and to this filthy, stinking creature who obviously never washed, who did not know the meaning of pity, who was so brutal and debased as to be no longer human. And her courage all but failed her, only despite her slightness she was of a stubborn disposition: she even contemplated killing him if he attempted to ravish her.

Papa, face downwards in the fender, would be appalled. Not even Pamela could have visualized a fate like this. Pamela! Suddenly Philadelphia hated Pamela who was simply a designing hussy who used her virtue as a bargaining counter then lamented to high heaven when matters got beyond her control. She knew that she would never read *Pamela* again. And as she brooded on this and her chances of escape, the carriage stopped: she prepared instantly to throw herself out, to fling herself into the arms of some complete stranger, tear away the scarf and scream her lungs out.

But the door did not open her side, and Ferdy did not remove his restraining arms that were now almost choking the breath from her. It was the coachman who dismounted, and presently there was a waft of cheap, sickly perfume and the sound of a shrill, female voice: to her horror this person sat heavily down beside her so that her exit was now blocked on both sides.

"Your maid of honor, darling," said Ferdy in a crow of triumph. "Can't have a wedding without a bridesmaid. This is Doll, sweetheart, an old friend of mine who is going to look after you. In case you get any idea into your little head about running away—not that I can understand why you should want to run, with such a handsome husband panting to lay you. Most girls would be delighted, and my papa a duke and all—"

It is the end, thought poor Philadelphia, and then again, Why has this happened to me, what have I done, what does he want with me? I have only met him twice, he is nothing, he cannot have any grudge against me, and why should he choose me? I have no money, I am just a girl from the even numbers. And frantically she turned her gaze round, to see who the newcomer could be, thinking that surely as a woman she would feel some pity and help her.

She saw at once that there was no pity or help here. Doll was large and blowzy and flashily dressed, with a grotesquely made-up face. There were great blobs of red upon her cheeks, and her lips were scarlet, so that she looked like some macabre doll. It was plain, even to Philadelphia's inexperienced eye, that she was a woman of the looser sort; it was plain too that she was an old acquaintance of Ferdy's, for she nudged him familiarly, spoke to him with lewd jests, and seemed to regard the whole business as a vast joke.

Ferdy said, "You keep an eye on her, Doll. There's a great many folk touting round the Liberties, and we don't want to lose our little darling, do we?"

"She's a lucky girl," said Doll, speaking in a crude London accent that Philadelphia had never heard before. "We never thought we'd get you spliced, Ferdy, and now she's actually hooked you. How did you do it, sweetheart? You'll have a fine old time. He's a grand old performer, Ferdy, I can vouch for that myself, and—" Here she embarked on a description of so gross a nature that Philadelphia's head swam in horror. She had sometimes in a faintly self-conscious and ashamed way visualized her married life with Jamie, but the thought of this appalling creature taking her into his arms and making love to her was so shocking that she feared she might really go out of her wits.

As they came into Fleet Market—Philadelphia naturally did not know the name—she saw that the carriage was surrounded by people, and at first this gave her hope. Then she realized that they were touting for marriages in the way that theaters were besieged by vendors of playbills. There were laughing cries of, "A parson, sir!" and, "I am the clerk and registrar of the Fleet," and, "This way, my pretty madam, that fellow will carry you to a little puddling ale house," or, "Come with me, sir and madam, he will take you to a brandy shop."

The carriage stopped. Philadelphia found herself lifted out by Ferdy, and the next instant Doll's horrid arm was tight around her. The scarf was removed, but she had to see that even if she could summon up the strength to call for help, there was nobody here who would answer her. She gave a weak cry, and looked round frantically for a kindly face, but all the countenances she saw were avid, lecherous and derisive. Before she could speak one word, Doll announced, "Make way for the shy young bride now! You don't want to crowd her, the poor girl. Here she is, all happy for her wedding, and you're hardly giving her room to breathe."

At this point she let herself be defeated. It was as if her brain were cracking with the horror of it: she almost no longer cared. The one consolation that remained with her was that at least she could kill herself. Not even Ferdy could prevent her doing that, and probably he would not care, once he had his hands on her money. She realized through the nightmare that they were now ascending the prison stairs. On either side she could see the cells where the inmates were often loaded with irons: one poor wretch, she saw, had his hands and neck fastened together by a metal clasp. The cells were like dungeons, and she seemed to remember something that Jamie had once told her of the Warden, Bambridge, who was so cruel that a Portuguese prisoner, on hearing that the Warden was visiting him, fainted dead away from terror, the blood gushing from his nose and mouth. And all these poor people had done was to fall in debt: it was very wrong of them, but surely such a venial crime did not deserve such punishment.

They were now walking along a kind of gallery, and the touts still crowded round them, explaining everything as if they were guides. "This," one said, "is the famous Lord Mayor's chapel, you will get married here cheaper than in any other part of the Fleet." But for saying this he received a blow across the face from a man who was dressed as a parson: Philadelphia perceived to her fright that this was the one apparently designated to marry her.

They came at last into a room that smelt of brandy and wine: it was small and dark yet plainly set for the wedding ceremony. And at the sight of this Philadelphia in her desperation summoned up a last shred of strength, managed to break away from Doll, whose attention had been distracted by one of the touts whisking at her petticoats, and fell with unconscious melodrama on her knees at the parson's feet. This was because she no longer had the power to stand upright, but so it was that Mr. Atherton, running with a speed that he had not exercised since his boyhood, found her: as Emma, running too, caught her in her arms, Philadelphia fainted.

Mr. Atherton had found that Emma's presence was providential: without it he might have found it difficult to gain an entry. The touts assumed that the pair of them wished to get married, and the fact that the bride looked so pale and desperate, with her hair half-down, meant nothing here: indeed, most of the women who came to the Liberties were marrying in some kind of desperation, either to avoid the law by changing their name or, like the poor heiress who had been abducted, brought here against their will. Mr. Atherton followed closely on Philadelphia's footsteps, and Emma too was appalled by the sights and sounds around her, the band of profligate clergymen who pressed against them, offering their services in every possible indecent manner, plying like porters for hire, prepared to perform the ceremony without license or question.

Ferdy had not immediately accompanied Doll and Philadelphia. He wished to refresh himself before the ceremony, and was at that moment in an adjoining brandy shop, swilling down three glasses with barely a pause between them. It was not a matter of conscience, for he had no more conscience in him than the ape he resembled. It was simply that he could do nothing without drink; besides, he was congratulating himself on what seemed to him a magnificent celebration. He had committed in his time most of the crimes in the calendar, but had never up till now abducted a young girl to marry her by force. He was delighted with himself. He thought he had been extremely clever, and Tom would not find out until it was too late, even if Emma informed him, which he now fancied she would not do: she would be far too frightened of revealing something that was partly her own fault. And because he had never loved anyone in his life, because he detested and despised the whole human race, he never really considered that Emma might feel such extravagant pity and remorse as to overcome any kind of fear.

As for Philadelphia, Ferdy was hardly thinking of her at all, though he was looking forward to the wedding night, especially as his new wife would be terrified and revolted. After that he would probably never see her again; he would have the fortune, and life would be remarkably agreeable, with Emma's free invitation to the social life that he had always wanted. Of course if the girl made too much fuss, he might have to kill her. This would be easy enough, for Ferdy, however unwelcome he might be in the *ton's* drawing rooms, had a free pass to half the dens and houses of ill fame in the capital: for money down there would be a hundred men to do the job.

At last he left the brandy shop, and lurched up the stairs again to the small chapel where the ceremony was to take place. He had paid his guinea for the license, certificate and crown stamp: he would have to pay rather more later on, but with Philadelphia's fortune he could well afford it.

He sauntered in, then in the doorway stopped, his eyes very bright, his mouth set in a wicked foolish grin. Doll, as soon as she saw him, burst into a screeching flood of speech, explaining that none of this was her fault. She ran up to him, and he knocked her down with such violence and precision that she lost consciousness and lay in an ungainly huddle on the floor. He looked up at Mr. Atherton. Emma had Philadelphia in her arms: being a strong, well-built girl, she was half-dragging her to the entrance, while the parson, a tawny fellow in a black coat and wig, so drunk that he could hardly stand, looked bemusedly round him, muttering, "I've been waiting for you, sir. I want my money. If you don't pay handsomely, I know them as will instruct you better in the future."

But Ferdy ignored him, only continued to stare at Mr. Atherton, who now stood only a couple of paces away. Ferdy recognized that this was retribution but, despite a savage disappointment, was delighted by the drama. Whatever he was, he was no coward: he enjoyed danger as others did wine, and he did not believe that Tom, however angry, could move as quickly as himself nor that he was as knowledgeable in the devious art of death. He had lost Philadelphia, which hardly mattered, and he had lost the fortune, which mattered a great deal, but Tom would not last long enough to be able to crow over him. And so he waited, until Mr. Atherton's words struck the smile from his lips.

"And all this for five hundred pounds," said Mr. Atherton.

For one of the rare times in his life Ferdy was utterly disconcerted. It was true that he would never touch the money any more than he would now touch Philadelphia. He had lost the game, yet that whole game had been played for what he had believed to be a vast sum of money, with revenge on Tom thrown in as make weight. And to learn that the fortune was

merely five hundred pounds! Five hundred pounds,
nothing, a mere pittance, a sum to be contemptuously
thrown on the tables when playing with people worth
no consideration—

The shock of it, the insult to his self-esteem, made
him completely lose his temper. Ferdy seldom lost
control of himself. It would often have been as much
as his life was worth, and there was scarcely anything
that mattered sufficiently to disturb him. He killed
with a smile, robbed with a song on his lips: he would
have raped Philadelphia without the slightest remorse.
But now he had been made a gull and a dolt, and the
rage consumed him. He raised his head, his lip snarl-
ing back, his eyes slitted with murder. He would have
given everything he possessed to kill the bitch who
had so entrapped him, and Emma with her—Emma,
still supporting Philadelphia in her arms, had stopped
to stare at him, only a few paces away, her free hand
fiddling with the clasp of her reticule. But even the
Fleet would hardly support a mass female killing, and
the parson was not so drunk that he might not report
on what had happened. There was only one person to
revenge himself on, and then it struck Ferdy that by
finishing Tom he would finish both the girls who
loved him: it would be a magnificent triple vengeance.

His hand moved, not to his pocket, but to the breast
of his coat.

Mr. Atherton, equally cold with anger, recognized
the gesture which he had seen before, but did not understand what it portended. However, he knew murder when he saw it, and he knew that Ferdy intended
to kill him. It was as if he looked upon his former
friend for the first time. It was to be the last, but he
did not know this. And his rage was so vast that he
was icily detached from it. He thought quite calmly

how strange it was that a human being could resemble a wild beast. They said that in foreign countries there were men who were half wolves, and Ferdy's countenance was that of a wolf and mad. He had walked beside this animal, gambled with him, jested with him, passed many a night in his company. He had always known him to be evil, but had hardly cared: now it seemed to him that the very sight of such a monster was enough to make a religious person cross himself and instantly walk away. His hand gripped his pistol, only Ferdy was before him and produced the long, slender knife from his coat before Mr. Atherton realized what was happening.

It was Ferdy's speciality, but the only people who knew about it were in no position to reveal his secret. Ferdy killed always with the knife, and had developed an extraordinary swiftness, throwing it with a deadly accuracy before his opponent had the slightest idea of the fate awaiting him. Only this time he was so concentrating on his enemy that he did not trouble even to glance at the two girls. He had never concerned himself with women as human beings: it never struck him that in an emergency they too could be dangerous, especially when someone they loved was involved. He did not see Emma drop her reticule, the pistol in her hand. The shot rang out just as the knife flew from his grasp. The bullet went into his chest and the knife, deflected, shot into the wall, so fiercely thrown that half of it was embedded in the wood.

Ferdy dropped to the floor. He was dead. He never knew what had happened. Philadelphia, still half unconscious, did not see, but Mr. Atherton, suddenly chalk-white, swung round to stare at Emma who regarded him with what seemed to him a detached, inhuman calm, and said in her husky voice, "I think we should go, Tom. Philadelphia should be instantly taken home and a doctor called." Then she gave a little sobbing gasp, and her own color dwindled. "Oh Tom, for Christ's sake, let us go."

To Mr. Atherton afterwards it was as if he were in some kind of sleepwalking nightmare. He was hardly aware of what he was doing. He remembered dimly that he picked Philadelphia up in his arms and carried her down the stairs, with Emma walking at his side, leaning a little against his shoulder. He did not notice the people around him. He was unaware of the complete silence. No one now jested about marriage, no one offered him a swift ceremony. The ceremony was over, and swift was the right word. The men here were all on the wrong side of the law, some of them were murderers, and most of them knew Ferdy: not one of them regretted his death. When Mr. Atherton had silently walked out into Fleet Market, two of the men who a few minutes back had been grinning and calling out picked up the body, stuffed it into some kind of tarpaulin, and disappeared with it through a back entrance that most of the Fleet's customers knew nothing about.

What was left of Ferdy disappeared with a splash into the River Fleet. There eventually he surfaced, floating down with the offal and dead rats and filthy debris that made the river stink so abominably in the summer months. When at last someone found him, entangled with the weeds, he was unrecognizable: simply one more unidentifiable corpse. The ducal family who had spawned him never knew what had happened, only when they heard nothing more from him, and he never turned up for his money, it dawned upon them that he was really gone for good. The sigh of relief that went up was enough to blow the ances-

tral roof off, and many toasts were drunk to celebrate
the happiest occasion that the family had known for
years. There was nobody to mourn him, nobody to
give a damn, and Doll, who was terrified of him and
knew well enough that if he had lived, he would have
made her pay for her stupidity, cheered her customers
for the rest of the year by retelling the story, much
embroidered and soon ornamented out of all recogni-
tion.

Chapter 12

⌒⌒⌒∿⌒∿⌒⌒⌒

Mr. Atherton and Emma drove home in complete silence. Philadelphia had now recovered from her swoon, but was too exhausted to speak: she lay in Mr. Atherton's arms, her eyes closed. The coachman thought privately that this was the oddest thing, but was too well-trained to make any comment: he was preparing to draw up at Number 23, when Emma at last spoke.

She said, "She must be taken to her own home."

Mr. Atherton, his nerves and temper sharpened to the point of hysteria, snapped, "Nonsense! She needs looking after."

"I will look after her," said Emma.

"You! Why should you imagine she—"

Philadelphia, still in Mr. Atherton's arms, raised her

head. They both turned to look at her, Mr. Atherton clasping her more tightly, Emma taking her hand.

She pushed Mr. Atherton's arms away, raised a hand to her wildly disheveled hair and said in a surprisingly strong voice, "I should be obliged if you would both stop talking about me as if I were not there. I know what I want to do, thank you. I want to go to my own home, I do not need a doctor, but I do very much need a good wash and a hot drink."

And having said this—received by Emma with a smile, and by Mr. Atherton with a scowl—she rose a little weakly to her feet and stepped out of the carriage on to the roadway.

Her face was very pale, and the marks of horror lay upon her countenance. But she would not let Mr. Atherton or the coachman—who had jumped down—help her, only paused, then with a sobbing sigh turned to survey the street. It was after all only eleven in the morning; a lifetime's events had happened to her, and it was only eleven in the morning. The odd numbers were stirring now. A couple of carriages had drawn up outside the front doors. The curtains were drawn back, goods were being delivered to the side doors, and one lady, seven doors down, was climbing into her carriage, for an early morning drive in the Park. There was a smell of hot chocolate and roasting meat: at Number 25 a footman appeared with a small dog and proceeded to trot the animal down the street. The even numbers were more animated. Steps were being scrubbed, windows cleaned, doors were open to let in the sharp autumn air.

It was all homely, familiar and comforting, and Philadelphia's eyes filled with tears. She said, as if to herself, "It was my own fault. Papa would have told me it was entirely my own fault."

Mr. Atherton, at her side, his hand extended lest she required support, exclaimed, "What can you possibly mean? How could this be your own fault?"

But Emma said nothing, only her eyes met Philadelphia's and, to Mr. Atherton's astonishment and irritation, the two girls smiled at each other like conspirators.

They all went into Number 22. Philadelphia exclaimed in horror at the disarray. She cried out, "Oh, I am so ashamed—What you must think of me. If you will only wait outside in the carriage for a wee while, I can set everything in order."

But here for once Emma and Mr. Atherton were completely in accord. They paid her no attention, only walked her into the parlor, then sat her down on the sofa, with her feet up and a cushion behind her. Mr. Atherton then produced a silver flask from his pocket and insisted on setting out glasses, which he took from the cupboard, pouring a large measure into each.

Philadelphia said a little weakly—it was true that she did not feel capable of housework, her legs were trembling, and there was a strange, cold emptiness at the pit of her stomach—"But that is some kind of spirit."

"That is brandy," said Mr. Atherton, "and I have just remarked that you have a large bottle of wine in your cupboard."

Philadelphia did not answer this, but a faint color came to her cheeks.

He went on, "Whether you keep wine in the house or not is entirely your business, but my business is to see that you instantly drink this brandy down, and without any further argument."

"Papa—" began Philadelphia, but Emma interrupted, saying, "Papa would entirely agree with Tom.

This is purely medicinal. You have suffered a most terrible shock and, if you do not drink your brandy, we shall have to call a doctor."

"Oh no—"

"Then do as you're told and drink it like a good girl."

Philadelphia said nothing more. She felt so exhausted that she no longer had the strength to argue. She raised her magnificent eyes briefly to Mr. Atherton, then accepted the glass that he put into her hand. She took a sip of it. It was very strong and made her cough, but as it flowed down her throat, a beautiful warmth engulfed her, and the weakness and exhaustion receded. With the second sip she felt even better, and when she finished the glass and Mr. Atherton refilled it, she made no further protest. She watched, feeling calm but a little remote, as Mr. Atherton picked up papa's portrait and set about knotting the cord, and she made no attempt to help when Emma fell to her knees on the floor and began to sweep some of the debris into her skirts. She only said at last, "I did not know brandy was so good." Then she added reflectively, "It is strange, but I am sure I have tasted it before."

Mr. Atherton had the grace to look rather self-conscious, and for a second Emma's eyes fixed sharply on his. But Philadelphia, innocently unaware of any sinister implication, went on, "Perhaps it was a flavoring in a cake or pudding. My sister uses alcohol, which is wrong of her as papa always forbade it, but then she is married and perhaps Henry likes it." She looked at Mr. Atherton and for the first time the dimples returned. "That bottle is hers. She brought it for mama. You will observe that it has never been opened." Then she sprang to her feet with quite her usual energy, and said, "I am so hungry, I cannot tell you. I must make something to eat."

Mr. Atherton said quickly, "I will have something sent over," but Philadelphia interrupted him, saying, "No. It will do me good." She turned to Emma. "Will you not come and help me?"

Emma had never been in a kitchen in her life, except occasionally to give orders, but she answered at once that she would, adding a little sadly, "I do not know how to cook. You will have to teach me, Philadelphia."

"You must call me Philly, and of course I will teach you. I am quite a good cook," said Philadelphia, "but in your world you have maids to do all the work for you, so I daresay you have never had occasion to try it. But it is useful all the same, because maids tend to leave you, and you would not want your husband to eat horrid, cold food. Men are so fond of their stomachs, they have to be fed like babies. We did have a girl to help us, she was called Lucy, but she was no use at all, and now I am quite glad to manage on my own. The kitchen," said Philadelphia who, what with the brandy, everything that had happened, and the relief of being home again, was positively babbling, "is over here, down the passage, and if, Miss—"

"Emma!"

"Emma. What a pretty name." She did not mention that she already knew it. "If you will come with me, Emma, it will make everything quicker, and then we can all eat something nice and hot. Can you really not cook at all?"

"I'm afraid not, Philly. I am a very ignorant girl."

"You are very beautiful," said Philadelphia, and with this the two young women set off down the corridor, their arms round each other, talking as if they had known each other all their lives. Mr. Atherton, who had now managed to put papa on the wall again, though without his glass protection, stared after them in a mixture of annoyance and bewilderment. He could hear them prattling in the kitchen. Indeed, they were giggling in the silliest fashion, and he could not understand it at all: he had never seen Emma behave in this way, and he had believed Philadelphia to be a shy girl. The whole thing was positively ridiculous. After all, the two of them were rivals, and in such circumstances most women hated each other. They should have been throwing out barbed remarks, hinting at unspeakable things, eyeing each other up and down with looks of jealous dislike, with himself playing the role of amused mediator. It had never entered his head that Emma and Philadelphia could even tolerate each other, and here they were gossiping away, leaving him, Tom Atherton, as the outsider.

When they returned, with a meat pasty, some buttered eggs and a plateful of vegetables, he could see that they were friends for life: he was still furious but too hungry to make any protest, and he had to be pleased that Philadelphia, after her shocking experience, had such a hearty appetite.

Emma said, "I put the pasty in the oven."

"Anyone could put a pasty in the oven," said Mr. Atherton sourly. "There is nothing clever about it."

"Ah, but she put it in the right place," said Philadelphia earnestly, "and many cooks forget to do that. Besides, she made the buttered eggs."

"Under your direction," said Emma.

"But next time you will know how to do it on your own," said Philadelphia.

It was really quite nauseating. Mr. Atherton could hardly believe his ears; besides, though they both stacked up his plate, they seemed so contented in each other's company that they hardly paid him any attention.

When, however, they had finished eating, Philadelphia became quiet, then presently she said, "I do not know how to thank you both. I shall never forget what you have done for me."

Emma said in a choked voice, "You do not have to thank me, Philly. It was largely my fault."

"That I do not believe. I could never believe it." Then Philadelphia said, turning towards Mr. Atherton, "I do not understand. Why did he do this to me? He didn't know me, not at all. I saw him once that first evening, and then when he called at your house, and Charlotte and I were with you. Was he really going to marry me? Why? He could not possibly love me."

"It was certainly nothing to do with love," said Mr. Atherton grimly. He was sitting in the easy chair that had once been papa's, and the two young women sat on the sofa before him. It could have been a setting for a family portrait, and the thought made him momentarily smile.

But the words he had just uttered echoed strangely in his head. *It was certainly nothing to do with love.* There they sat, side by side, their arms touching, and in a fashion he loved both of them, yet now he did not know if he loved either of them. They seemed to him—for he was utterly exhausted—almost without reality. Both had taken the opportunity, when out of the room, to tidy themselves, and both to him seemed strangers.

There was Emma whom he had loved passionately, whom he had slept with, quarreled with, laughed with—Emma, with her black hair and smooth, creamy face, the eyes a little larger than he remembered, the soft, plump body moving as gracefully as a cat's. Her dress was plain and unbecoming, there were great smudges under those eyes, and she seemed to have grown thinner and older. She had shot Ferdy down. She had murdered for him and saved his life. And he had never even known that Emma could handle a pistol. Most women could not, most women would probably blow their own heads off if they even tried. Emma. Emma, who had screamed at him like a whore, drunk herself into a stupor for him, who had once, long ago, threatened to kill any woman who set her sights on him.

And Philadelphia, his foolish little girl from the even numbers. She now was scrubbed and neat, she had changed her dress. She too was unusually pale, and sometimes her eyes moved sideways as if the terror still lurked in the shadows. Only her beauty remained intact: nothing could touch that, not Ferdy's filthy hands, his dirty designs, that appalling experience in the Fleet. Some women would have been driven out of their wits by such horror, but not Philadelphia, oh no, not Philadelphia. Philadelphia had climbed out of the carriage by herself, refused the safety of Mr. Atherton's home, and she had cooked and eaten a large dinner, apart from drinking two glasses of brandy without apparently turning a hair. I love you, said Mr. Atherton to himself then, No, I do not, you and I will always be strangers, you have little conception of my world and I none of yours. And now our worlds have collided in the filthiest place out of hell, and still you look untouched, still you do not fully realize what might have happened.

The light was dimming as the day closed. They were all encompassed in the small, shadowy room, with papa once again staring down at them. Mr. Atherton said, "Ferdy was a monster. The kindest thing would be to call him mad, but I do not believe he was mad. He was a natural outcast. His family disowned him."

Philadelphia remembered that family. It meant no more to her than a character in a novel. She vaguely connected it with battles and kings, and had once seen a picture of the ancestral castle, which was old and beautiful and set on the top of a hill. But then she thought of Ferdy, whose clothes were filthy, whose face was so coarse and cruel, and she shook her head in bewilderment. She asked, "What made him like that?"

"Oh," said Mr. Atherton, "who could say? Sometimes you have a litter of pups, and they are all white save one, and he is coalblack, and no one knows why. Ferdy was the odd one out. In the old days he would have been called a changeling. He was very wicked. He enjoyed hurting people. It did not matter to him who they were. He had to do evil. It was his only real pleasure in life."

Philadelphia said in a small voice, "Why do you speak of him in the past?"

Emma at her side stirred, and Mr. Atherton answered quickly, "We'll never see him again. He's gone, Philadelphia. He will never trouble you any more. What he did today was a hanging matter, and not even Ferdy would care to swing at Tyburn. His family are well rid of him. I daresay he has gone abroad. I pity the country that receives him."

Philadelphia raised her eyes to his, then looked down again. She did not comment. He suspected that she did not entirely believe him. But she would never find out, and this was something that Emma would surely never tell her. Philadelphia could endure a great deal, but he did not think she would excuse murder, even if the victim deserved his fate. She said after a long pause, "But why? I still do not understand. He said he was going to marry me in that terrible place. How could he do that? You cannot imagine I would ever have consented. And why should he want to? Why did he choose me, whom he did not even know?"

"In the Fleet Prison," said Mr. Atherton grimly, "you do not have to consent. There was a tale once of another girl, an heiress who was not very strong in the wits. She was abducted and married. Sometimes over a hundred couples are married in one day. There can be a marriage by proxy, and the certificates can be forged. Unfortunately, these marriages, however illegal, are still recognized. I can only pray that one day soon this will be made a criminal offense."

Philadelphia said faintly, "So I would have been married, whether I agreed or not?"

"I fear so." Then he saw that she had gone white again, and indeed, the prospect of marriage to Ferdy was enough to send any girl into a swoon. Emma at once put her arms round her, and Mr. Atherton nearly suggested another glass of brandy, then decided against it. She appeared to have a remarkable head for a girl unused to strong liquor, but if she became at all intoxicated she would certainly never forgive him.

However, she recovered quickly enough, saying, "But I still do not see why it was me he wanted to marry."

Mr. Atherton considered before replying. He found that he did not want Philadelphia to hear the whole story. He said at last, "There were a number of factors. Ferdy was a devious man, he bore grudges and he never forgave."

"But I never did anything to him!"

"No. But I did. And you have a fortune, ma'am."

"A fortune!" Philadelphia had indeed once believed it was a fortune, but since then had had time to consider it. She did not fully realize how absurd that money would seem to the odd numbers, but she knew now that it was nothing very much, it was not the kind of thing that would bring fortune-hunting gentlemen galloping after her. She said crossly, "It is five hundred pounds. Surely to someone like Ferdy that would not be very important."

"He would lose it at cards in five minutes. But he believed it to be much more. I think he heard your sister talking about it. He would believe that the word 'fortune' signified thousands."

And he hoped she would leave the matter there. This was pure surmise on his part: it was in fact largely true, but this he did not know.

Philadelphia only said, "Char always talks too much," and at this Emma giggled, and the two girls at once began gossiping again so that Mr. Atherton, in no mood for female rattling, rose to his feet.

He said, "Will you not change your mind, Philadelphia? There is a room for you, a comfortable bed, and my housekeeper would be delighted to look after you. Will you not come with me to Number 23?"

But Philadelphia shook her head, then looked appealingly at Emma. "This is my home," she said. "I am happy here, and I feel safe. Only—"

"I suggest," said Mr. Atherton a little ominously, "that you lock the door."

"Oh that, yes! It will never, never stay unlocked again. Only," said Philadelphia, "if, Emma, you would not mind staying for the one night. I know it is silly of me, and you say that Ferdy will never come near me again—"

"I can swear to that," said Mr. Atherton.

"—but I was so frightened. I have never been so frightened in my life."

"Of course I'll stay," said Emma. "Indeed, I always intended to. You would not have found it easy to get rid of me."

And so Mr. Atherton unbelievingly left them, apparently bosom friends, his jealous, passionate Emma and the beautiful, prim little miss who had all but supplanted her. They looked to him as if they were set for a most agreeable evening. Indeed, Philadelphia was already lighting the fire: it was autumn, the evening had grown cool, and she said it would be comforting. It was plain that they were going to talk their lives out with each other. And he had to be aware, like a myriad gentlemen before him, that he would doubtless be the number one item on the agenda: he resented this most fiercely, and there was nothing, absolutely nothing, that he could do about it. As he kissed Philadelphia's hand he was aware of a sardonic gleam in Emma's eye as if she knew perfectly well what he was thinking. He glowered at her but said nothing, and presently he was striding across the road to his own house, leaving Emma and Philadelphia kneeling on the floor by the fire.

Emma said, "Why did you say it was entirely your fault?"

"But I think you understood. You looked as if you understood," said Philadelphia. She held out her hands to the flames. She had not lit the lamp, and the two girls sat there in a small pool of light, the outer world remote. "I have done things I should not do, Emma."

Emma's dark eyes briefly widened, but she said calmly enough, "What is this you have done? It cannot be wicked."

"Oh no. I don't think it was wicked, though papa might have called it so."

"Your papa sounds a real old dragon!"

"He was the kindest man. He would never hurt anyone. But he believed we should all keep our proper stations."

"Oh, stuff!"

"In a way I think he was right, though I suppose you would think it old-fashioned. I walked out of my world, Emma. I cannot quite think how it happened, but I met your Mr. Atherton—"

"I do not think he is any longer mine."

"He is, you know. He could never be mine. I come from the even numbers and he comes from the odd."

"I do think," said Emma quite sharply, "that you talk the most terrible nonsense."

"Well," said Philadelphia, almost as she might have spoken to Tobias, "we will play a little game. You will tell me how you pass your day, and then I'll tell you about mine. Begin in the morning. What do you do?"

Emma considered the matter. "I do not get up early but then usually I am very late to bed. Louise, my maid, brings in my breakfast and the papers and letters. There are always quite a lot of letters. Most of them are invitations. Then she helps me dress and does my hair for me, and I come down about eleven. People call, we drink a little wine. Sometimes I go for a drive in the park with one of my beaux. We dine at three, and sometimes that lasts till five or six. I may call on friends. Then I change for the evening, I go to the playhouse, or perhaps, a ball. I go to bed at three or four in the morning."

She gave Philadelphia an amused look. "I daresay that is not the kind of life papa would approve of. It must sound very useless. But I like it, it is what I am used to. I see Tom, of course. At least I did until we quarreled. What do you do, Philly?"

"I am always up by seven, sometimes earlier. I clean the house. I do the shopping. When my mama was still alive, I attended to all her needs, and that took up half the day. I prepare meals. I do not see anyone, but then with an invalid it is impossible to have many friends, for one says one will go out and then one cannot. I read a great deal, and I keep a diary. I go to bed very early because it saves fire and light. You see how different our lives are. I could not lead your life, and you could not lead mine." She paused, then said, "When I tried to lead a different kind of life, you see what happened to me. It would never have done so if I had not been so thoughtless."

"That is a ridiculous thing to say. I imagine—I hope—one meets someone like Ferdy only once in a lifetime. Because you moved out of your world has nothing to do with this business of the Fleet. You happened to encounter a wicked lunatic. You cannot blame yourself for that. It might have happened anyway. He was a shocking man. I'm glad he—" She broke off.

"You speak of him in the past tense too," said Philadelphia wonderingly. "What really happened to him?"

"I shot him."

Philadelphia did not, as she expected, scream or wince away. Indeed, she showed no particular emotion. But then Emma was beginning to see that she seldom acted in the expected manner. She was silent for a while, then she said, "How could you do that? Oh, I know he was wicked, but to kill someone—I could not. I know I could not, whatever happened."

Emma said calmly, "He would have killed Tom."

"Oh no!"

"Certainly. I saw his hand move to his breast, and I knew he had some weapon there. I had a pistol in my bag. There was no time to hesitate. It was a knife. Tom would not have had a chance. And I daresay with Tom dead he would have murdered us as well. And do you know," said Emma, "I do not regret it at all. I am only thankful that my papa taught me how to shoot straight. He said that because I was a girl was no reason why I should not be able to defend myself. And I am very good, Philly. I believe I am better than my brother. Papa once said I would make a good duelist because I keep my head in an emergency and have a straight eye. You see, my dear friend, those of us who live among the odd numbers do very strange things of which your august papa would not approve at all. Are you very shocked at me? I daresay you are wishing you had not invited me to your home."

"He would really have killed Mr. Atherton?"

"Without the slightest scruple. He was a born killer. He would have murdered his own mother if he believed it would be of use to him."

"Then," said Philadelphia in her most didactic tone, "I would have shot him, myself."

Emma laughed and momentarily touched her hand. "We should go out as ladies of the road. I do not imagine Tom, or indeed any other gentleman, knows quite how bloodthirsty women can be."

"Sometimes," said Philadelphia, "I do not think the gentlemen know anything about us at all."

Emma asked, "Do you have a beau, Philly? You are such a prodigious pretty girl that I cannot believe there is not a legion of them fighting for your favors.

If you lived in my world, you would have all the mamas inviting you throughout the season, to marry off to one of their sons."

"I am betrothed," said Philadelphia. "At least I was until I broke it off. I think really it is not broken off at all. But he behaved badly to me, and I was angry and I gave him back his ring. I daresay he will be on the doorstep one day soon, apologizing to me and begging me to marry him again."

"And you will be very haughty and distant, and send him about his business. For a little while, of course."

"Of course. But only for a very little while. I love him very much, though you may not believe it. His name is Jamie, and we grew up together. I could be comfortable with him. I could never be comfortable with someone like your Mr. Atherton. I daresay I would offend him every minute of the day. I would not know how to address his fine friends—"

"I believe you would know how to address the King!"

Philadelphia unexpectedly giggled. "If one is young and not ill-looking, it perhaps would not matter. They say the King likes pretty women. But I do not dance, I have no fine clothes and, do you know, Emma, I believe your grand friends would bore me as much as I bore them. It would not do at all. Jamie and I know each other so well, but what is interesting is that now I am not sure if I know him at all."

"Does he think he knows you?"

"Oh, of course. All gentlemen do. They think we are simple and silly, without an idea in our little feather heads. I daresay he believes he can read me like a book."

Emma laughed then said presently, "I want to ask

you something, Philly. It is not anything I ever believed I could ask another woman. But I would like you to give me an honest reply."

"I always do," said Philadelphia. "I understand it is my greatest failing."

"Do you love Tom?"

"No."

"But you did. A little. At the beginning."

Philadelphia considered this, her face clear in the glow of the fire. Emma thought she was the most beautiful person she had ever seen, and wondered if she were really aware of her extraordinary loveliness. "No," said Philadelphia. "I think he enchanted me. But I did not really love him, any more than he loved me. I think I always knew in my heart that all he wanted to do was to seduce me. Like Pamela. I always thought he resembled her wicked master."

Emma said, a little helplessly, "You did not tell him this, did you?"

"I mentioned it, yes. He was very astonished."

"I imagine he was. But you did like him?"

"Of course. I liked him long before I met him. I will show you something, Emma."

Philadelphia rose to her feet, and produced the tiepin from the bowl on the mantelpiece. She said, "He must have dropped this in the street. I picked it up. I suppose that makes me a thief. But I used to watch him sometimes from the window, and I always admired him. I wanted to keep something of his. He is so very handsome."

"Yes," said Emma, and sighed.

"The tiepin somehow made me feel I knew him. But I do not want it any longer. I do not think Jamie would like it. Here it is, Emma. You can give it back to him."

"You can give it back to him yourself. But I think you must keep it as a memento. Tom will not mind. He will have forgotten all about it."

Philadelphia did not answer this. She looked down at the tiepin, lying across the palm of her hand. Then she slipped it into a drawer, and resumed her place by the fire.

Emma went on, "I think it would amuse and flatter him. Tell him about it."

"I do not think," said Philadelphia, "I will have the occasion."

"Why not? You surely do not imagine you will never see him again? You do not know Tom! He'll come, if only to find out what we have been saying about him."

"Do you know," said Philadelphia slowly, "I don't think he will. But if he does, it will be for the last time, for I shall say goodbye. I believe I was a little infatuated, for I have never met anyone like him. It was like a romantic novel. But these things do not work out in real life, and that I shall make plain to him."

"I wish," said Emma, "you were not quite so practical. I doubt anyone has ever said such a thing to Tom in his life. I do not think he will ever quite recover."

"You love him very much, don't you?" said Philadelphia.

"Oh, I love him so that I could die of it. I have never felt anything like it. He eats away my thoughts, my sleeping and my waking. I cannot really think of anyone else. I am like a heroine in one of your novels, Philly, I do truly believe that without him I shall pine away. I have a horrid conviction that there will never be anyone else. You see, I know that to you I must seem like a whore, but I have now come to the sad conclusion that I am entirely a respectable girl at heart. I would never believe that I could say such a thing, but I want my man, I want his children, and I do not give a rap for fine people and pretty gowns and all the things that make up my life." The dark eyes flickered up to Philadelphia's intent face. "And you, sweetheart, look such an eminently respectable girl."

Philadelphia exclaimed in genuine surprise and— Emma could have sworn to this—a barely subdued gratification, "Oh, do you really think I am—" She broke off, flushing a little. But her voice shook, and it was certainly not with anger.

"Well," said Emma, trying not to laugh, "I am not sure if your papa quite realized what he produced. Yet how strange it is, Philly. The world would brand me as a rake, and you as the prim little miss, and I believe it is entirely the other way round. But the world will never know. I only hope your Jamie knows how to keep you in order."

"He will think he does," said Philadelphia, "which is almost the same thing." She added, "I daresay Mr. Atherton thinks the same of you. You must marry him, Emma. I feel it in my bones that you are the only person for him."

"I only hope," said Emma a little bitterly, "that Tom's bones are equally prophetic." She stood up as she spoke, brushing down her skirts. "You should go to bed, Philly. I have no right to keep you up like this, after such a dreadful day. You need not be frightened. I will guard you. I have my pistol with me. And Ferdy will never trouble any of us again."

"Tomorrow," said Philadelphia, "I must see my sister, and offer her half my money. I do not know how I could have been so greedy. All this is simply a judgment on me." She added reflectively, "Of course Char does rub one up the wrong way."

Emma suppressed a smile at this, but only said, "I think you may find your sister needs you."

"Why? Has something happened to her? Oh, I—"

"She will tell you all about it. Calm yourself, Philly. She is in no danger. She called on you this morning. We met briefly. I think you will find her very pleased to see you. Will you tell her what happened?"

"Oh no. I will never tell anyone. I could not. It is beginning to seem like a bad dream to me." Philadelphia broke off, then said suddenly, "Did you ever see *A Midsummer Night's Dream?*"

"Of course. Several times. Why do you ask?"

"It is the only play I have ever seen. I told Mr. Atherton so. I think perhaps this is a little like the play. Were there not two sets of lovers who became confused by a potion and for a while loved the wrong person? Now the play is ended. You will go back to your Tom, and I to my Jamie."

"I hope," said Emma, "it proves quite as simple."

Then she let Philadelphia escort her to the room that had been mama's, the two girls kissed each other goodnight, and presently the house was dark and silent.

And Philadelphia slept, but Emma lay there wakeful for a long time, weeping a little for Tom, who should have been beside her and only sleeping when the dawn light came through the windows.

Chapter 13

In the morning, after breakfast which Emma helped Philadelphia to make—"I am becoming quite a good cook!"—the two girls prepared to leave: Philadelphia, pretending she was a lady's maid and foolishly calling her friend "madam," helped her with her hair. They then set off for Charlotte's in Emma's carriage.

They did not speak very much. Philadelphia was wondering what had happened to her sister, and thinking with an odd insistence of Jamie, while Emma sat silently beside her, studying the beautiful, clear-sculpted profile. She herself felt almost drained of emotion. In a few short hours she had quarreled with Tom, perhaps lost Tom, killed a man, made friends with her enemy, and she felt unmoored, swinging loose in a world she no longer understood, with not the faintest idea of what might be happening to her.

As the carriage drew into Chelsea Village, she spoke at last.

She said, "I would like to see you again, Philly. I have never cared much for my own sex, and mostly they resent and suspect me, but I think that you and I could be friends. May I call on you? You could come to see me too. You could take a closer look at the odd-number world. I daresay in the end you would not find it very different. What do you say?"

"No," said Philadelphia a little sadly. She turned her head and surveyed Emma with a grave intensity.

Emma, disconcerted, a little offended, said sharply, "Why not? That is not a very civil way to answer. Are we no longer friends that you speak to me so?"

"We will always be friends," said Philadelphia, "but I doubt we will ever meet again."

"I don't understand you. You must explain. This is ridiculous. Give me one good reason."

"Mr. Atherton would not like it."

Emma opened her mouth to protest angrily, then shut it again. She suspected that Philly, as always, was perfectly right. Tom would not like it at all. He had involved himself with both of them, he was vain like all men, and he would dislike very much the thought of two women, both of whom had seen him at a disadvantage, calling on each other and no doubt discussing him in the intimate detail peculiar to their sex.

Philadelphia went on, a certain strain in her voice, "And in the end, Emma, neither would you. You become cross when I talk of our different worlds, but they are different, and I am not so sure that we would be left with much to talk about. We will probably both be married. You would not want to listen to tales of Jamie and—and perhaps a baby, and I would not know what to say to your balls and routs and dinner parties. I think in the end," said Philadelphia, smiling, "it might come to your passing on your second-best gowns to me, giving me over-lavish presents that I would not be able to return, and perhaps introducing my Jamie to influential people who might give him better paid employment that would embarrass and humiliate him. You would never mean to be the lady bountiful, but I think in the end you would be compelled to patronize me. Then we would quarrel and be angry with each other, which would be a pity because I love you very much."

Emma said again in a helpless fashion, "I have never met anyone like you in my life."

"Well," said Philadelphia reasonably, "that is more or less what I am trying to say. I am only a country girl, you know. I was born in Inverness, I lived in a small house in a small lane, and my father was a strict and religious man. I know very little of the outside world, and what I saw of it yesterday does not make me want to know much more."

"Oh, that is absurd and unfair!"

"I daresay it is. I do not imagine your world really resembles that dreadful place. Though in a way it does. Money matters and marriage matters, and I think there are a lot of people in both our worlds who make a business out of it, just like the Fleet. But I still think that you and I, Emma, are now going to go our separate ways, and I cannot see how they can possibly meet." She smiled again, the smile that had fascinated Mr. Atherton, with the dimples in her cheeks. "I've often wondered, you know— Of course it was the only play I've ever seen, and I doubt I'll see many more, Jamie is no theater goer, and he is not much of a reader either, except for his classes—but I sometimes think that Hermia and Helena would not be seeing much more of each other, either."

"Now what do you mean by that?" demanded Emma, laughing despite herself.

"Well, they were fiery girls, were they not? Something about 'She was a vixen when she went to school.' And they both had a wee bout with each other's man, and I do not think that is so easily forgotten. I think Helena might be saying, 'You quite fancied Lysander yourself, my girl'—I've forgot the names, but it don't matter—and Hermia saying, 'Oh, I saw you making big eyes at my husband, it's not midsummer night, now, you know—' I know they were great friends at school, but I fancy they'd be seeing less and less of each other as the years went by. Don't you agree with me?"

"I think," said Emma, "Jamie is marrying a wise girl. And I daresay you'll be clever enough not to let him see it."

"This is where my sister lives—I think Mr. Atherton will be marrying a lovely girl, and I am not sure if he deserves you."

"Will you not come to my wedding? If there is a wedding—"

Philadelphia pursed her lips, "'Who,'" she said in a high-pitched Scots voice, "'is that funny, dowdy wee soul sitting there in the back, with not a word to throw at a dog, and that dreadful out of date gown? Why, Emma, you have the most peculiar friends. I suppose she is your maid, poor creature, and how out of place she looks—'"

"Be quiet, Philly, or I'll shake you. With a face like yours, you could never look dowdy, and all the men will be around you like flies." But Emma could not help smiling, despite herself, then she sighed, gave

Philadelphia a rueful, half-reproachful glance, and looked at Charlotte's house, which was small and un-fashionable and sadly in need of a lick of paint. She said firmly, "I am not accepting this, Philly. I'll be calling on you, whether you like it or not."

"I doubt it," said Philadelphia. The coachman opened the carriage door for her, and she stepped out. She looked up at Emma who leaned over to take her hand. "I'll not turn you away from the door, Emma. And I'll read about your wedding. I shall think of you. I might even send you a wee token of remembrance."

"A small potion to lay upon the eyes?"

"Oh, I don't think either of us needs a potion any-more. Goodbye, darling Emma."

"Goodbye, Philly." And Emma stooped down to kiss her: as she did so, she thought how strange it was that she should feel such affection for this young woman whom she had once wanted to kill, from hate and jeal-ousy.

She watched as Philadelphia, with one last wave, pulled at the bell. She could hear Charlotte's agitated voice as the door opened. Then she told James to drive her home. She did not at that moment want to see Tom, she did not want to see anyone. She felt drained of all emotion, exhausted to the point of tor-por: she would go to her bed and dream and doze the morning away.

Mr. Atherton, unaware that he was confirming Phila-delphia's prophecy, made no attempt next day to call at the house opposite. He was astonished not to see Emma, yet at the same time relieved. Every time he heard carriage wheels he was convinced that she would be ringing at the door, and once he even toyed with the idea of calling on her himself, not naturally from any particular desire to see her, but simply to ask if she were recovered from yesterday's experiences.

It had to be faced that Mr. Atherton felt he had made a complete fool of himself, and it seemed to him that Philadelphia was largely responsible. He knew deep within him that this was utterly unfair, but the thought of calling on her made him feel positively hostile. He felt he could not endure the sight of that beautiful, innocent face nor the sound of her soft Scots voice, nor that dreadful parlor with papa glowering down at the pair of them. He saw now, very clearly, that the two of them had nothing in common, and that what had seemed endearing, novel and even touching, would in a very short time become a dead bore. The sharp, witty little remarks, that had so entertained him, would grow tedious, the prim ways exasperating, and really, he could not tolerate a girl who not only did not drink wine, but would undoubtedly condemn him for doing so. It was true that she had downed her brandy like a man, but then she was so distraught that she could hardly have known what she was doing: she would certainly never be persuaded to indulge herself so again.

He knew as he thought all this that he was being unreasonable, unkind and indeed foolish. Philadelphia would always remain in his memory as the most beautiful creature he had ever seen, and she was highly intelligent in addition: no one could pretend that she was a simple, witless country girl. The point that really rankled was that it was entirely his fault that the poor wretch had been involved in such a horrifying experience. And, though he had admittedly rushed to her rescue, it was not he who had been her savior, but Emma. If Emma had not shot Ferdy down with such extraordinary accuracy—who the devil had taught her to shoot?—he, Tom Atherton, would probably by now be in some common grave or thrown into the River Fleet, while what would have happened to the two girls, he shuddered to think. But he really had not distinguished himself in any way, and he was ashamed too that he had abused Emma so viciously. All the poor girl had done was to drown her jealousy in drink—and Mr. Atherton had in his time drowned a great deal in a similar way.

Now completely exhausted after a bad night's sleep, he paced up and down his drawing room, hating himself and everybody in the whole, damned world. He saw in this black mood of self-condemnation that all he had really wanted was Philadelphia in bed with him and, though this thought still had its charms, he had never really been a seducer of young virgins. He could somehow imagine her sitting up after it was all over, wearing no doubt a calico nightgown, and saying in that didactic little voice of hers, "Why, really, Mr. Atherton, is this what it is all about? It seems to me very much over-estimated." Or something of the kind—He wondered vaguely if she would ever be familiar enough to call him Tom.

He was so raw, ashamed and mortified that he felt he could never see Philadelphia again. After all, God knew, he had done his duty by her and that quite appalling sister, who had proposed to fling her marriage problems at him. He had buried her mother, invited the family to his home and—and virtually buried Philadelphia too. He thought he would never forget that nightmare of a morning, and Ferdy, grinning in his mad way, standing there, his murderous hand moving to the breast of his coat. He heard again the filthy remarks hurled at them, smelled the drink and sweat and filth, saw poor Philadelphia half fainting in Emma's arms. And he groaned aloud, and poured himself out his third glass of wine. He must call on her, and he could not, he could not, and why did Emma not come, she must know she was forgiven, she would know how to comfort and reassure him, she had always understood his moods and known how to laugh him out of them.

Perhaps Emma had not forgiven him. Perhaps she would never forgive him.

And what the devil were those two girls talking about? Rattle, rattle, giggle, giggle—Christ, how he hated silly females, scandal mongering away, making fun of him, no doubt, calling him a coward, a seducer, a fickle, brutal creature who played his women one against the other.

Then Mr. Atherton at last returned to his senses, and for the first time that day managed to laugh at himself. It was true that he did not do this with much conviction, but still it was a step in the direction of sanity. He poured himself out a fourth glass of wine, vowed that he would call on both Emma and Philadelphia in the course of the day, slumped down on the nearest chair, and fell fast asleep.

Philadelphia listened to Charlotte's story for the seventh time. She found that her mind was sadly wandering, but of course it would do Char all the good in the world to get it out of her system: she always had to talk things out, even if it were to a complete stranger in the street. But she was still fatigued after yesterday's experiences, indeed, she felt rather worse than she had done yesterday, being both weak and depressed. She could not stop herself from wishing that furious, nervous voice would relent a little. She even wondered what would happen if she said, "Yesterday I was abducted and nearly married by force to the man who looks like Daftie Johnny, and Mr. Atherton's mistress shot the villain dead, and I was carried home and given quantities of brandy."

Charlotte would probably not even hear her. "It's been going on for years!" she cried. "And I trusted him, oh Philly, I trusted him, and how I loved that man. I've given him the best years of my life, waited on him hand and foot, sacrificed everything for him, and look how I've been repaid! Never trust men, Philly. You are so innocent that you trust everyone, but take it from me, pet, never trust men. I vow they are all the same. They make use of you, they pretend to love you, then suddenly they find someone else, and all you are is housekeeper and mother, someone to be discarded when they've had their will of you. And to think it's been going on for years, and I never knew—"

Philadelphia suspected that this last rankled with Charlotte most. Charlotte had always prided herself on her shrewdness and powers of observation: it must be dreadfully galling to find out that Henry had been consistently unfaithful for so many years.

The mistress appeared to be tucked away in a small house in Marylebone. She did not sound particularly young or handsome, and this was confirmed later on. The letters that Charlotte had frenziedly read were badly written, misspelled and obviously the product of a woman without the least education. They were however unmistakably loving and she knew from their cozily intimate tone that this was an affair of long standing. There was also a lock of hair—"blonde hair, Philly, and I swear it is dyed!"—and some disgusting keepsakes in the form of a pressed violet, a lace handkerchief and a couple of theater programs.

"I went round to see her," said Charlotte, and had the grace to blush as she spoke.

"Oh no, Char!"

"Of course. What else could you expect? Nobody deceives me and gets away with it. I went round immediately. The address was on a receipt for the rent. No wonder Henry is always short of money."

Philadelphia, though a little shocked, was curious enough to demand, "What was she like?"

"Terrible! Oh Philly, you cannot imagine—How Henry could! She is quite old and with no looks at all. She is fat and blowsy and vulgar, and her house is in the most shocking taste. No person of refinement could live there for an hour. All pink frills and—and cushions and hideous ornaments. She offered me a dish of tea. Can you believe it? Tea! Of course it was a deliberate insult. When I naturally refused, she suggested I might like a glass of gin. Philly! You're surely not finding this amusing—Oh, how could you? First my husband, and now my sister—I do not know why I am so cursed. I have been a good woman all my life, I have always done my duty, and now my own family turns against me. No doubt little Tobias will in due course do the same."

Philadelphia, ashamed of herself, put her arms round her sister and said, "Oh Char, I didn't mean to laugh, it was horrid of me, and of course it's all quite dreadful, but it was just the thought of her offering you gin. Gin! What did you say to her? I hope you sent her about her business."

Charlotte hesitated and flushed. This was the part of the story she would never tell anyone. She had indeed told the person that she must never see Henry again, and the person had laughed in a dreadful, common kind of way and said, "Well, you must discuss that with Henry, dear. It's his business, not yours. I don't fancy he'll give me up that easy. We suit each other very well, and you're not much use to him from all accounts, if you'll forgive the liberty. A man needs a nice bit of flesh and blood and something to warm his bed o'nights. From what he says I gather you'd freeze the toes off anyone. But you must do what you think best, dear. And now, if you'll forgive me, I got things to do, so—"

Charlotte had screamed at her. She did not mean to, but she had always been a screamer. It was all quite shockingly wrong. It should have been the vulgar little mistress who did the screaming, not the genteel, injured wife. However, it was Charlotte who screamed, and the person simply sat there with a self-satisfied grin on her face until Charlotte, sick and dizzy with her own emotion, suddenly wheeled round and ran from the house, to collapse into her carriage in floods of tears.

She told Philadelphia none of this. She said at last, "There was no point in talking to someone like that. I simply said I was disgusted, and that I should make sure she never saw Henry again. She was very set down. It is simply beyond my comprehension that Henry could even look at such a creature. Never trust men, Philly—"

Philadelphia, who did not believe one word of this, said quickly, "What did Henry have to say for himself?"

Charlotte flushed an ugly color. "He told me I had no right to spy on him. He said he was entitled to his own life, and it had never harmed me, he had always looked after me and Tobias. Of course I'm leaving him, Philly."

"Oh Char!"

"Of course. What do you expect? I have my pride.

Do you imagine I'd share my husband with another woman? Do you realize that all those times when I believed he was seeing to some consignment of tea, he was really staying with *her*? And that club he says he goes to in the evenings, to meet his business acquaintances—I don't suppose there is a club at all. He simply goes to that vulgar little house and—and—oh, it's like a nightmare to me. I just cannot believe it."

And the tears rained down again, as they had been doing off and on throughout the conversation.

Philadelphia waited until the worst of the storm was over. She put her arms tightly round Charlotte and made comforting noises. When it was at last done, and Charlotte was fumbling for the bottle of wine with which she had already liberally solaced herself, she said gravely, "Dear Char, you must not be so silly."

"What do you mean?" Charlotte's voice soared up into a shriek as she held a brimming glass to her lips. She had not offered any to Philadelphia, but then she knew her sister's aversion to drink.

"You cannot leave him," said Philadelphia. The words surprised herself. They seemed to emerge from their own volition.

Charlotte said in a tense voice, "You don't know what you're saying, Philly. You're just a child. How could I stay with him after this?"

"How could you leave him? You will have nothing to live on, and you will lose Tobias. Of course," said Philadelphia very quickly, "you will have half of mama's money, for I have been very selfish and I want you to have it. I don't need so much, and I shall speak to Mr. Bridges about it immediately. But it will hardly suffice you, for you are used to more luxury than I am—"

Charlotte said faintly, "We could live together."

Philadelphia shook her head. "Oh no, Char. You would not be happy with me. Besides, I am sure you really love Henry, and I daresay in his heart he really loves you. Of course I do not know about men as you do, but I believe they are often unfaithful, and it does not mean very much, it is the kind of thing that every sensible wife has to put up with."

Charlotte was staring at her, goggle-eyed, as if she could not believe her ears. She said at last, "Would you put up with it?"

"If I had to, and I loved my husband," said Philadelphia, "I probably would."

"I cannot imagine what papa would say if he heard you talking like this!"

"Well, Char, papa is dead."

"Philly!"

"And these are more modern times. You must stay with Henry. You must try to forgive him. After all, you are married and you have Tobias. You might have another baby. In the end that horrid woman is bound to lose, because really, she has nothing."

Charlotte said, "I think you are out of your mind. Is this what your Mr. Atherton has taught you?"

"I think perhaps it is," said Philadelphia.

She was driven home in Charlotte's carriage. She was as bewildered by herself as her sister had been. She thought how strange it was that two people could hold a conversation with scarcely one word of truth in it. Charlotte had not the least intention of leaving Henry. She did not love him any more than he loved her, but she needed a man, she needed her married status, and she enjoyed all the business of having a child, a pleasant home and the social entertaining involved. Henry would never be faithful to her, it was not in his nature. If it were not the vulgar little person in Marylebone, it would be another vulgar little person in Bloomsbury. In her heart, despite the screaming and the drinking—it was a pity she had taken so to the wine, but perhaps it did her good—Charlotte was enjoying the drama and, being always convinced that she was in the right, would never so much as consider that the situation might be partly her own fault. Henry would have a bad time of it for a while, and serve him right, but presently it would all blow over.

Until the next time.

I have become cynical, thought Philadelphia, and grew ashamed of herself, for it was only too true, papa would be horrified, and she had been brought up to believe that once people were married, they remained faithful for life. But she was still too tired to think coherently, and she drowsed off on the journey home, to wake up to find that Jamie was sitting on the top step of her house, with the air of one who had been there for some time.

Chapter 14

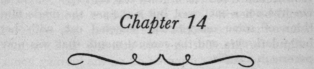

Jamie had been waiting for over an hour. He was both astonished and disappointed not to find Philadelphia in. It was unusual for her to go out, especially during the day, and he had taken it for granted that she would instantly open the door to him. He did not like to keep on knocking for fear it might disturb Mrs. Smith, but now that he had summoned up the courage to come, he felt he could not bear to go away again. So for a while he paced up and down the street, a tall, handsome young man who had grown rather thin, and whose face bore lines that had not been there at the last meeting.

At last he grew tired of this walking up and down, and there was still no sign of Philadelphia—where on earth could she be?—so for a time he leaned against the gate post, and watched as a carriage set down a handsome and plainly wealthy young woman at the house opposite. Jamie looked at her without any particular interest, for his mind was on other things, but he had to see from the brief glimpse he had of her face that she was very lovely. As she stepped on to the roadway, she turned her head and saw him. She seemed to hesitate, then to his amazement crossed the road and came up to him.

He hastily righted himself from his lounging position. He gazed at the thick, shining black hair and the beautiful magnolia complexion, which was so creamy that he had a sudden urge to run his finger across it. He was not a cat lover, but somehow she made him think of some magnificent, cosseted cat, with her huge dark eyes and the sensual mouth that was now parting in a smile.

She said, "Good afternoon, Jamie."

How could she possibly know his name? To the best of his knowledge he had never set eyes on her in his life: if he had done so he would certainly have remembered. That face was not of the kind one could easily forget. He flushed up foolishly, much to his chagrin, and stammered, "Ma'am—"

"You are Jamie, are you not?"

"Yes, ma'am."

"If you are looking for Philadelphia, she should not be long. She has been visiting her sister. She will doubtless be back any moment now."

Who in the name of God was she? She seemed to know all about him. He simply did not know what to say, and so he said nothing, the bright color that was always his shame, so thick upon his cheeks that he felt quite choked.

The lady eyed him up and down, always with this

little, secret, catlike smile, then she said, "I am pleased you are so handsome. I was not quite sure about you."

This was really too much. Jamie opened his mouth to answer her quite sharply, but before he could do so, she tapped his arm with her fan and said softly in a deep, husky voice:

> "*Jack shall have Jill;*
> *Nought shall go ill;*
> *The man shall have his mare again,*
> *And all shall be well.*"

And then, not giving him time to utter one word, she turned away from him, crossed the road again, and in a moment was pulling the bell at Number 23.

And Jamie, overcome with baffled bewilderment, sat down on the step, and it was there that Philadelphia found him, some twenty minutes later.

She stepped out of the carriage. Jamie recognized it as Charlotte's carriage. He did not know Charlotte very well, and what he knew of her, he disliked. He never understood how the two of them could be sisters. He was thankful to note that she was not accompanying Philly: she was at this moment the last person in the world he wanted to see. He stepped forward instantly to greet Philadelphia, and the two of them stood there, and surveyed each other, while the carriage turned and made its way back to Chelsea.

The street was deserted. It was five o'clock in the afternoon. Philadelphia was thinking, How he has changed, and Jamie was thinking much the same. She looked somehow older and less approachable, no more the little girl next-door, whose hair he had once pulled, who had been his friend and ally before she became his sweetheart. She seemed unusually pale, with dark shadows beneath her eyes, but she was even more beautiful than he remembered, and a vast and desperate longing for her overcame him, so agonizing that he could have forgotten his manhood and wept. After she heard what he had to say, she would probably never speak to him again, and he cursed himself for the stupidity that might lose him everything he so passionately wanted.

She said at last in a cool, brisk little voice, "Well, Jamie! I did not expect you. But we cannot stand here in the road, so you must come in with me."

She turned to unfasten the door, and he stood behind her, feeling remarkably sheepish: he screwed up his eyes as if he were one of his former pupils due for an unhappy interview with the headmaster. He followed her into the house. It seemed to him so dear and familiar that he wondered again at his folly in leaving it.

They came into the parlor, and Philadelphia lit the lamp.

Then she turned to face him, her hands linked behind her back. He longed to kiss her, but did not dare: he could not touch her until he had made his confession, and after that he might never have the chance to touch her again.

She said gently, "Will you not sit down? I did not expect you so soon, Jamie. I thought by now you would be in France or Italy with your lord."

He said in a gruff, wretched voice, "I have never been to France or Italy, Philly. I have never left this country."

She exclaimed in astonishment, "But you said—"

"Oh ay. I said. It was true then. I believed I was going. It was no lie I told you, Philly. But the day after we—we parted, I called on my lord as arranged, and found him greatly disturbed, indeed, he was in such a state that he could hardly speak. The whole trip was to be abandoned. It appeared that the night before he had lost a vast sum of money at the hazard table, and had nothing left to pay either his journey or my salary. He offered me a few shillings as, I suppose, some kind of compensation, but I did not wish to take it. And so I left him. I do not know what has become of him, and frankly, I do not care. I daresay he managed to borrow enough money to recoup his losses, and for all I know, he has now left on his Grand Tour. But not with me."

Philadelphia listened to all this in silence, and still did not say a word, though Jamie, expecting an angry question, paused.

Her silence did not make it any easier for him. He said at last, twisting his hands together, "I should have come straight back to you. But I could not. I do not suppose you will understand, but I could not."

She said, "I understand very well. I daresay I would have done the same."

He stared at her, astounded. He did not know how to answer this. At last he went on, "We had quarreled. I behaved abominably to you, I know it. And I had left my job, Philly, and there I was, with no work, precious little money, and the memory of the words that had passed between us. And I thought—oh, I was a fool, I see that now—but I thought that this perhaps was my one and only opportunity to see something of London and find out about its life. So I walked into Holborn, and there I have lived ever since, in one of the big warrens there, consorting with a type of person you have, thank God, never met and never will know anything about."

Philadelphia's gaze briefly lowered. She said nothing to this, but turned a little away. The lamplight was too soft for him to see her clearly, otherwise he might have noticed a faint flush on her cheek.

Jamie took this silence to denote horror and disapproval. But he had gone too far to stop now, and in a kind of frenzied anger spoke of the thing that had never been entirely out of his mind, and which would inevitably break his betrothal to Philly for good and all.

He said harshly, "There was a girl. I should not tell you this, Philly, but I could not marry you with it on my conscience. Even," he added, "if you still wish to marry me, which I cannot believe you do. I did not mean it, it signified nothing to me, but she invited me to her room, and I went. And—Oh, my darling, you could never understand in a hundred years, I would not wish you to do so, and there is no excuse I can offer, only I was alone and she was pretty, she seemed so kind." Then he said in a loud, defiant voice, "She was a prostitute. I believe she was not a bad lass, though I daresay you'd not believe that. She was after all very poor, and there is little for women to do in our world if they have neither money nor education. And I'll tell you this too, for nothing could make it worse. You and I, Philly, we live in such a small world, we always meet people of our own kind. I was sick of it, I had a sort of fancy to see the other side. We lived together for a wee while. It did not last very long. When I found out what she was, I became frightened. You see, I am a coward in everything, to you and to Polly, who meant me no harm and who couldn't understand why I left her. After that I did not know what to do. I had no money at all. I took all kinds of jobs. I swept the road, and for a time I worked in a tavern where I served a dubious kind of gentry. Highwaymen and their women, and the like. It was a terrible world. I hope I never see it again, yet Philly, I am glad I did see it, and it had a kind of adventure to it that I've never met before. They'll most of them end on the gallows, these friends of mine, and I could not lead their life, but it was time perhaps that I moved from folk like us, if only to find out how different people can be. And they were kind too—oh, I met such kindness. There were people who gave me half of their bread when they did not have enough for themselves, and others too who offered me a room for the night even when they knew I could not pay. I'll tell you something else, Philly, for I am after all making my confession, am I not? I nearly stayed. I was often afraid and sometimes disgusted, but I felt so alive—Oh, I cannot tell you, and how could someone so good and innocent understand? But I thought of you, and so here I am. If it had not been for you, I might well have stayed. And, though you will now despise me, I'll say this before I go. I am going back to my school. I went to see the headmaster, and he agreed to give me back my old job. I daresay it will mean less money for a while, but at least I have work. And I swear I'll be the better teacher for all this. I'll not be so quick to criticize, I'll not be so hard on the stupid pupils, and I do not believe I'll ever willingly beat them again, for I have seen so much violence that it sickened me. It is violence and poverty that breeds these people, it is not their fault that they behave as they do."

Jamie broke off. He had grown so impassioned with what he was saying that he had almost forgotten his rôle of penitent. He remembered it now only too well. He looked with utter desolation at Philadelphia, whose face was averted from him, and who stood there so still, leaning against the window sill.

He said, "It is goodbye, is it not? I cannot blame you. But before I go, I'll say this. I love you, Philly. I love you with all my heart. I have played you false, I have mistreated you, I do not deserve ever to see you again, but I do love you, I doubt if there'll be anyone to replace you."

Philadelphia spoke at last. Her voice was cool and calm. She said, "Well, Jamie, I think you would perhaps like a glass of wine."

If she had screamed vile abuse at him, or sworn or struck him, he could not have been more utterly taken aback. He could not believe he had heard correctly. A glass of wine! From Philly, who had been brought up to abjure all liquor, who had been taught by her papa that drinking was the surest way to damnation—He positively stuttered. He repeated, "A g-glass of wine?"

"I think," said Philadelphia, "it would do us both good. I believe I should enjoy it, myself."

And saying this, she moved quickly towards the cupboard where Charlotte's bottle still reposed, unopened, and took it out to set it on the table.

"Perhaps," she went on, "you will open it for me, Jamie, and I will fetch some glasses."

A few minutes later the wine was poured out, and she raised the glass to her lips with, for the first time, a slightly apprehensive expression on her face. Jamie, still incredulous, watched her. His eyes moved once and instinctively to papa's portrait. The glass seemed to be missing. The old man would surely go up in a puff of smoke. He did not touch his own wine; he could not take his eyes off Philadelphia.

She swallowed the first mouthful, then took a second. It did not seem to be as strong as brandy. She looked up at Jamie, smiling. "But it is very agreeable! I cannot believe that something so pleasant is really wicked. You are not drinking, Jamie. Have we changed places? Is it you now who do not approve of wine?"

Then he set his glass down with a bang that nearly broke it, ran across the room to Philadelphia with such speed that he sent a chair flying back, and caught her in his arms, crushing her against him, kissing her wildly on cheek and nose and mouth. He muttered, almost sobbing, "Oh Philly, I do love you, I don't know what I've done without you, you are the most wonderful girl, don't be angry with me any more, please marry me, marry me tomorrow—"

And Philadelphia, as if she had not done enough to astonish him, then burst into floods of tears. For a while they remained enlaced, she crying and Jamie patting her, stroking her, kissing her, behaving indeed with an abandon for which once he would certainly have been sent to the door.

At last she managed to release herself. After an interval, in which she blew her nose, mopped at her cheeks and struggled to rearrange her hair, they found themselves sitting side by side on the sofa, each with a glass of wine.

Then Philadelphia said in a choked voice, the smile and dimples at last in evidence, "Good evening, Jamie Sinclair. How do you do? I trust you are well."

And he answered, "Good evening, darling Philly. I have never felt better. I love you."

And for a while they sat in a companionable silence, sipping at their wine, their free hands tightly enlaced.

He exclaimed suddenly, "But your mama—she will be wondering what has happened. Do you think I should go up to see her? Perhaps she is so angry with me for the way I treated you that—" He broke off. He saw the expression on Philadelphia's face. He said in a muted, shocked voice, "Oh no! Oh, my poor little sweetheart. And I was not even here to comfort you. When did it happen?"

Philadelphia told him that mama had died peacefully in her sleep. She did not however say that it happened on the day that Jamie left her. This might have been partly due to a reluctance to upset him further, for in his own way he was a responsible young man, and it woud hit him hard to learn that he had added to her distress, but this was also due to something less praiseworthy. She had long ago decided that Jamie must never learn about Mr. Atherton. If he realized how lost and alone she had been when her mother died, he might begin to inquire how she had managed. If, however, he believed the death had occurred some time later, he would simply assume that Charlotte and Henry had rallied round as families should: he would never suspect that another gentleman, and a handsome one at that, had come so unexpectedly to her rescue.

After a while they talked again, and kissed again, and had another glass of wine. Then Jamie said, "Philly, let us get married as soon as possible. I have not much money, but there is this little house, and I feel I can no longer live without you. Will you marry me, sweetheart? I'll do my very best to make you a good husband. I daresay," said Jamie with a humility unusual in him, "I am not much of a catch, and I am sure you could do better. You are so beautiful that I am sure a wealthy gentleman would think himself fortunate to have you."

"And what would you do if he did?" asked Philadelphia.

"I'd break his damned head!"

Philadelphia found this entirely satisfactory, and if her fertile imagination played a few odd tricks with her at this moment, it was really not important, and Jamie would never know it. He might confide his misdeeds to Philadelphia, but she had not the least intention of confiding hers to him, and the little tiepin that Emma had insisted on her keeping would be consigned to the rubbish heap.

Emma told Mr. Atherton that Philadelphia would weave rings round her Jamie, and this was true: she was already weaving her rings as she would continue to do for the rest of her life. Jamie was so dazzled by her—she seemed to him immeasurably more beautiful than at their last meeting—that he could hardly drag himself away from her. It was late by the standards of the even numbers when he rose reluctantly to go. The church clock at the top of the street chimed ten o'clock.

"That is where we will be married," he said.

"We will have at least six children," said Philadelphia.

Then Jamie, as he was about to say good night, asked suddenly, "You were always the reader, Philly. There's a line of verse now. Something about 'Jack shall have Jill, nought shall go ill—' I do not remember it all. Do you know where it comes from?"

She answered, surprised, "Why, yes. It is from *A Midsummer Night's Dream.* It is the only play I ever saw. I did not know you read Shakespeare, Jamie."

He said vaguely, "Oh, I heard it somewhere. It is not important."

She kissed him again, very tenderly, then gently

pushed him towards the door, following him out on to the front steps, so as not to miss a moment of his company.

Emma knelt beside Mr. Atherton, her head pressed against him. They were completely reconciled. He said, his hand caressing her cheek and throat, "I do not know what possessed me. She is a beautiful little girl, but we have nothing in common, we would have ended by boring each other."

"I am not sure," murmured Emma, "if Philadelphia would bore you. But, as she is always saying, she comes from so different a world."

"She is perhaps a little stupid," said Mr. Atherton.

Emma did not think Philadelphia was stupid at all, but recognized this simply as an expression of injured masculine vanity, which was confirmed by his continuing, rather bitterly, "I think I have made a complete fool of myself."

"Oh," she said, "it is midsummer night after all."

He jerked his hand away. He exclaimed, "What nonsense is this? It is near the end of October."

"Never mind," said Emma, "never mind."

"I suppose I really must go over to see her. I do not want to. You know that. I cannot imagine what we would talk about. But I feel it would be uncivil not to see her at least once again. What do you think? Would you mind?"

Tom had never asked her if she minded before. Emma caught at his hand and pressed it to her lips. She said, "Of course not. But I do not think it would be wise. After all, her young man has returned. I met him on the doorstep."

"What is he like?" There was a faint acerbity in Mr. Atherton's voice: he was human after all.

"Oh, he is very handsome. But he is just a country boy." And Emma said again, "She will weave rings round him."

Mr. Atherton dismissed all thoughts of Philadelphia. He was to think of her again at less and less frequent intervals, and occasionally a dim regret would stir within him. She was after all so exceptionally lovely. But there was Emma, and he knew in some strange way, that Emma was part of him, he might quarrel with her, be unfaithful to her, but he could not do without her. He said a little drowsily, "Let's go to bed." Then he said, "Do you think we should marry?"

But this she would not answer, only kissed him. When at last she rose to go upstairs, he held on to her hand as if he could not endure even so brief a parting, his eyes following every line and movement of her silky, catlike body.

Before joining her, he opened the front door and stepped out for a moment to breathe in the cool, autumn air.

Philadelphia and Jamie saw him as they were saying their dozenth final good night. Mr. Atherton, on the other side of the street, bowed to her, and she made a faint inclination of her head.

"Who is that fellow?" demanded Jamie. "He seems to know you. He bowed."

"Oh," said Philadelphia, "he is one of the rich people who live in the odd numbers. I meet him occasionally when I am out. That is all." And she smiled as she said this, a small, secret smile. "That is all."

"It is strange," said Jamie, reluctant to go, trying to postpone the moment of separation, "how we are divided. This is only a street, after all, yet there is all the world between us. I cannot fathom how the odd and even numbers can be such miles apart. They all have so much money. I sometimes find it hard to believe that the rich are quite human. After all, they are cushioned and protected against everything. What do you think they are really like, Philly?"

"I think," said Philadelphia, "they fall in love, they fall out of love, they are happy and unhappy, they are born and they die. They are people, just like us."

"You have become quite a philosopher," said Jamie.

When at last he disappeared round the corner, Philadelphia moved towards the door. She saw Mr. Atherton was doing likewise. Only for a second he turned his head and looked steadily at her, with the narrow road between them. Philadelphia, her face calm and peaceful, returned his gaze.

It was the one moment of real love between them, a moment of warmth and affection and understanding. For that brief second of time the road narrowed so that odd and even numbers touched: they were enclosed in a leafy glade on midsummer night's eve.

They made no gesture. They did not speak one word. Then they turned away from each other into their own houses, odd and even numbers, 23 and 22.

The front doors shut behind them.

ABOUT THE AUTHOR

PAULA ALLARDYCE was born in London and has worked in a great variety of capacities in England and France. Her chief interests are, besides her writing, music and foreign travel. She is the author of ten previous books.